An
Act
of
God

Robert Y. Ellis

AN ACT OF GOD

iUniverse books may be ordered through booksellers or by contacting:

iUniverse
1663 Liberty Drive
Bloomington, IN 47403
www.iuniverse.com
1-800-Authors (1-800-288-4677)

ISBN: 978-1-5320-9272-5 (sc)
ISBN: 978-1-5320-9273-2 (e)

Library of Congress Control Number: 2020906760

Print information available on the last page.

iUniverse rev. date: 04/16/2020

Chapter 1

✝

I was standing on a putting green with a woman. She was in
her late thirties and had stark features, dark hair tied back in
a bun, and no makeup. Her eyes were blue. Her light gray long-
sleeved blouse was demurely buttoned to her neck but nevertheless
revealed a full figure. Her dark gray skirt reached well below her
knees. She wore black hose and practical black golf shoes. She was
bent over a golf ball, holding a putter. She took aim and sank her
putt. About a five footer.

I now stepped up to my ball and took careful aim. If I missed
this one, I would lose the game. I examined every possible contour
of the three feet between my ball and the hole. I couldn't possibly
miss. But I was nervous. I'd never played with a woman before,
much less a nun. And she had proven a very capable adversary.
Finally, I struck the ball ...

"Father," a voice intruded. "Father, how are you feeling?"

I opened my eyes. I was lying on a bed in what appeared to
be a hospital room. I blinked. I had been on a golf course with a
nun. Now I was here with a woman in white—a nurse?

"Are you feeling better?" she asked.

"Uh ... I don't know." I looked more closely at the woman.
Was she a nurse? I saw Father Clancy standing behind her, staring
at me with a concerned expression. "What's happening?"

"You've been given a sedative to help you recover from the shock," Father Clancy said.

"What shock?"

"It's why I brought you here, Iggy!" He turned to the nurse. "Why doesn't he remember?"

"It's the shock and the sedative. His head will clear. It'll come back to him."

"Iggy," said Father Clancy, "the police are here. They want to question you. Are you up to it?"

"The police? What for? What's happened?"

"I think we had better give him a few more minutes," said the nurse.

"All right. I'll tell the detective it's going to be a while."

I closed my eyes.

Chapter 2

✝

I didn't know how many minutes or hours went by after the nurse and Father Clancy tried to wake me. But I was now sitting in a wheelchair at a table in a small room. Across from me was a man I did not know. He wore a brown tweed jacket, a brown-and-blue striped necktie, and a beige shirt. These were the only signs of color in the room. The walls, ceiling, and even the floor were white. A cold white fluorescent light hummed above us.

"How are you feeling, Father?" the man asked.

"I believe I'm feeling fine, a bit fuzzy headed perhaps. Can you tell me what's going on? Why I'm here?"

"Of course, Father. I'm detective Martin Folger. I'm with the NYPD, and we're investigating the incident at the Van Cortland Park Golf Course."

"What incident?"

"Are you saying you don't remember what happened at Van Cortland this morning?"

"I don't believe so. But ..."

"But what, Father?"

Suddenly my consciousness was flooded: the nun on the golf green and then ... a blank ... and then my wandering into Father Clancy's office.

Iggy! You look a wreck. What's happened?" Father Clancy asked.

"You haven't heard?"

"Heard what? I've been stuck at this desk all day trying to sort out our finances. What is it? Don't tell me you've ruined yet another golf club. That's becoming an expensive game you play."

"Sister Mary was killed today. By lightning," I blurted out.

"Sister Mary! Killed? Where? How?"

"On the ninth hole. The putting green."

"What are you talking about? You're not making any sense. And you're all disheveled. I've never seen you looking like this. And what's that smell I'm getting?"

"I was with her, right next to her."

"Now hold on. You're saying you were with Sister Mary when she was struck by lightning? Where was this?

"Like I said, on the ninth hole at the Van Cortland Park Golf Course. The thing is, I don't know when it happened or how it happened. I must've been wandering around for hours. All I can remember is we were playing golf—"

"You and Sister Mary? Since when do you play golf with a nun?"

"Since I couldn't find anyone else to join me. Jimmy was all tied up and so was everyone else. Finally, Jimmy suggested Sister Mary to me. I told him I didn't see myself playing with a nun. I mean, how good a player could she be?"

"All right. All right. We're straying from the main point. What about the police and the medical staff? What do they say?"

"I don't know."

"What do you mean you don't know? You were there!"

"Right. When it happened. But I don't remember anything after that. Just that she was burnt to a crisp right before my eyes. I think I may have gotten a bit of a jolt as well. My clothes are singed. And I'm so confused. It wasn't until I walked into the rectory that I realized where I was and that I had to talk to you."

Father Clancy leaned back in his chair. "You'd better sit down," he said after what seemed an eternity. "Are you telling me that you walked off the golf course and left Sister Mary's body there without telling anyone? Was anyone else around? Do you know whether or not she's still there waiting to be discovered?"

"I don't know," I said. "There was no one else on the green when we were there. It was a quiet day. Not many people at all. I have to believe that somebody would have found her by now. But I can't say."

"This is terrible. We have to call the police."

"Right, I know we should … I should. It's just that …"

"If what you've told me is the truth, and I have no reason to doubt you, then it's no wonder you're confused, maybe in a state of shock. I'll call the police and then I'll take you to the emergency room at North Central." He was referring to the North Central Bronx Hospital not far from us off Mosholu Parkway. He picked up the phone with his left hand while looking through his address book for the number for the police. His right forefinger ran down the page and stopped at *police*. He punched in the number.

I leaned back in my chair, closed my eyes, and tried to remember, tried to understand. I hadn't told Father Clancy the whole truth. How could I? He'd never believe me. Nobody would. Hopefully the lightning strike would be seen for what it really was—an act of God. Pure and simple. Why complicate matters any further than that?

The phone beeped as Father Clancy returned it to its cradle. He looked at me. "Well, we had better get going," he said.

"What did they say?"

"You weren't listening? C'mon, Iggy. This is serious business."

"I know, Father. But my mind keeps wandering."

"All right. All the more reason to get you to the hospital. The police are meeting us there. They were aware of the incident. That's what they called it. An 'incident.' And their investigators are still at the scene—again their words. They know at least one other person was there when it happened, but they don't know who. So they want to interview you. I'm no lawyer, Iggy, but if I were you, I'd say as little as possible to them until you have a good understanding of where they're coming from, if you get my drift."

"Why? Do they think I've done something?"

"Let's just say the detective was very interested to learn of your presence at the so-called scene and wants very much to question you. So a word to the wise: don't say anything you don't have to until you know what they know. Let's go." He got up, came around his desk, gave me a hand, and pulled me out of the chair.

I felt like lead. He took me by the elbow and led me out of his office, down the stairs, and out of the rectory. He opened the door to the passenger side of his black Toyota Corolla. I got in, pulled the door closed, and fastened my seat belt. He walked around to the driver's side and got in.

"You do understand," he said as he fastened his seat belt. "I'm advising you to put yourself into the care of the doctors and not to say anything more than you absolutely must to the police. I have a dreadful feeling that there's more to this and they know it."

I remained silent. Did he suspect I had more to tell?

"You do get my drift?" he said.

"Yes, thanks," I said.

I looked at the detective.

"You look like you've seen a ghost, Father. Has it come back to you?" he asked.

"I believe it has. Though I'm still not certain what really happened. Could you tell me, please? What has happened at Van Cortland?"

"I can't say a lot to you, Father, until you are able to tell me everything you saw there. I don't want to give you information that might color what you have to say. I need to hear it all from you first. By the way, I hope you don't mind that I'm recording this." He nodded toward a tiny instrument lying next to his left hand. He was also taking notes on a white pad of paper.

My head was beginning to clear. "The thing is, Detective, I'm very confused about what happened this morning. I can tell you that I remember playing a game of golf at the Van Cortland Park Golf Course with Sister Mary, who teaches at St. Ann's Elementary School next door to our church. I remember being on a putting green and her sinking her putt. I remember I had to sink mine or I'd lose the game to her. I remember striking the ball and that's it. Nothing more will come to me. Except that ..."

"Except what?"

"Except that I think I had better ask for a lawyer. I want to get out of here and get some solid advice before I go any farther with any questions. I know I've done nothing wrong. But I can imagine what you and others might be thinking. So if you don't mind ..." I looked him squarely in the eye.

"What is it that we might be thinking, Father?"

"Sorry, I'm going to leave it at that. I'd like to leave now." I forgot that I was in a wheelchair, and it rolled out from under me as I pushed up on the arms to get up. I tottered a bit but caught myself on the edge of the table.

"Hold on, Father. Take it easy. I'll get Father Clancy and the nurse. We'll stop for now. But we'll want to see you for more questions ASAP. We have a dead woman on the ninth hole of Van Cortland and a ton of questions. So you get yourself an attorney and come see us real soon. Like tomorrow. Okay, Father?"

"Yes. I understand."

Chapter 3

✝

"So what did the detective ask you? Did he tell you anything?" Father Clancy asked as we drove out of the hospital parking lot. He turned left onto Mosholu, heading toward St. Ann's.

"Only that they have a dead woman—that's how he put it—on the ninth hole of Van Cortland and that he has a ton of questions—again, that's how he said it—and that he wants to see me for questioning tomorrow."

"What did you tell him?"

"Nothing he didn't already know. Mostly that I was confused and wanted out of the room until I could clear my head and get a lawyer."

"You told him you wanted a lawyer?"

"Yes. I'm not sure why. It just seemed the thing to say. You have to understand, Father. I've done nothing wrong. I know that in my heart. But if I'm so confused, then maybe there's more to this whole thing than I realize, and I feel I need to proceed carefully."

"I've been thinking the same thing. If this were a simple case of a lightning strike on a golf course, why would the police be wanting to question you? Hopefully only to help confirm that it was a simple act of God. But there seems to me to be an undertone of suspicion regarding your presence there. So, with your approval, I'd like to call an attorney for you. He's a man I know well and trust implicitly. Will that be all right with you?"

"I'd be very grateful to you if you would. I wouldn't have a clue who to call."

"All right," he said as he pulled into the parking lot next to the rectory. "Here's what I want you to do. You go to your quarters, get yourself cleaned up, lie down, and try to get some sleep. You need a real rest. I'll leave you alone for at least a couple of hours. Meantime, I'll call my friend and see if we can get together with him later this afternoon and then have him be with you when you talk with the detective tomorrow."

"Thanks, Father."

He looked at me with what I could only call a gentle smile. "Look, Iggy, you and I have known each other for a few years now. I know I'm your boss. But I'd like to think I'm also a friend. You're a good man. I've known that from the first day you arrived here. Whatever happened on that golf course cannot have been your fault. So I think if ever there was a time for us to lose some of the formality in our relationship, this would be it. Everybody I consider a friend calls me Jack, and I think it's time you did the same. Except, of course, when we are conducting official church business."

"Thank you for your trust." I said as I looked into his concerned eyes. "I'm not sure I can ever stop calling you Father. But I appreciate your confidence in me."

"Well, you think about it. Now go get some rest."

We got out of the car and climbed the six steps into the rectory. He turned left toward his office. I headed upstairs to my room. I had known Father Clancy's first name since I first met him. He had proven to be an excellent leader of his staff at the church. A very decent man, fair with us all, always willing to see both sides of an issue. I regarded him very highly, but he was also somewhat of a father figure to me. He was around the same age as my own father in Philadelphia. Maybe a little younger. I was thirty-three. Could I ever call him Jack?

I followed his advice and stripped out of my scorched clothing, took a shower, put on clean clothes, and stretched out on my bed.

Would I ever be able to truly rest?

Chapter 4

✝

"**W**ake up, Iggy." Someone was shaking me gently by my shoulder. I opened my eyes. Father Clancy peered down at me. "Wake up, lad. I have a visitor I want you to meet. He's downstairs in my office. Get up, pull yourself together, comb your hair, and come on down."

I sat on the edge of my bed and tried to clear my head. For a moment, I didn't know where I was.

Then suddenly, everything came rushing into my consciousness.

I looked at my clock. It was almost 4:00 p.m. We had gotten back from the hospital around 12:30. So I must have slept close to three hours.

I got up, went to the bathroom, splashed some cold water on my face, and combed my hair. Then I went to the closet, grabbed a black wool cardigan, and headed downstairs while I zipped it up the front.

I knocked on Father Clancy's open door and went in.

"Come in, Iggy. I'd like you to meet Jacob Rothschild. Jacob's a longtime and very close friend of mine, and he's an attorney of some repute. He's done me the favor of coming over here to meet you and listen to your story."

Mr. Rothschild rose from the seat I had occupied earlier,

13

turned to me, and smiled. He offered his hand, and I shook it rather limply. "Nice to meet you, Father," he said.

"Thank you, Mr. Rothschild," I replied.

"Why don't you pull up that chair over there against the wall and join us here?" Father Clancy said.

I fetched the chair and placed it in front of Father Clancy's desk at an angle to Mr. Rothschild's. We all sat down. Mr. Rothschild twisted his chair around so that he faced me more directly.

"Jack has given me what I believe could best be described as the bare bones of the events that occurred today at the golf course. At first blush, it sounds rather straightforward. I understand from Jack that you were very confused. Who wouldn't be under the circumstances? But according to Jack, the police seem to have expressed more than a passing interest in your presence. And you want to make certain you don't do or say anything to them that might, shall we say, complicate matters."

"Right," I said.

Father Clancy interrupted. "You know, it's occurred to me that you've had nothing to eat for a long time, Iggy. Why don't I go see if I can rustle something up for you? Maybe a ham and cheese and some coffee? Would that be good?"

My mouth started watering. "Yes, Father. That would be great."

"The fact that you're hungry's probably a good sign. Hopefully the shock of it all has worn off and you can be more coherent with Jacob. I'll leave you two alone and get the food. Would you like something, Jacob—coffee or tea?"

"Coffee would be good. With cream and sugar? Thanks."

"Yes. I'm well aware of your sweet tooth." Father Clancy left the room.

Mr. Rothschild leaned back in his chair. He appeared to be

about the same age as Father Clancy. But where Father Clancy was a tall, thin, almost skinny man with a full head of black hair graying slightly at the temples, Mr. Rothschild was considerably shorter and round. He had a round face and a round body. He wasn't grossly overweight, but he had narrow shoulders and a body that swelled from them to a wide waist and then narrowed again down to his feet. His hair was practically nonexistent, with only a small steel gray fringe around the edge and a shiny pate. His ears stuck out a bit. On his nose sat a pair of reading glasses, over which he looked at me. His piercing eyes, however, belied his physical appearance. They were dark brown, large, and very intelligent.

"Why don't you tell me what happened?" Mr. Rothschild said.

"I don't know where to begin."

"Start with the beginning of your day today. Assume I've learned nothing from Jack and just let me hear what you have to say."

I related to him everything that I had told Father Clancy and everything I could recall from the hospital right up to my waking up and coming down to the office.

Just as I was finishing, Father Clancy came back in with a tray full of food. He placed it in front of the two of us, and I reached for the sandwich and started eating hungrily.

"How are you two getting along?" Father Clancy asked.

"Fine," said Mr. Rothschild. "Father Costello has given me a pretty good description of what he recalls. I do, however, have a few questions for him. I wonder if you'd mind leaving us alone for a spell, Jack. Or perhaps we could go to another area. For us to have true attorney-client privilege, we do need to be alone."

"Yes, of course. I should have thought of that. You two stay right here. I have plenty to occupy me elsewhere. Give a shout when you're done." He left the room once more.

After Father Clancy left Mr. Rothschild closed the door, sat back down and said, "Now, why don't you tell me what's really bothering you, Father? So far what you've told me doesn't make me feel that you have much to worry about from the police. Though, we don't know what they've found at the scene, and we will want to find that out. But I suspect there's more. Am I right?"

"I'm not sure."

He raised his eyebrow and with a quizzical expression said, "You see, that kind of answer only confirms my suspicion. Look, you and I don't know each other. You have absolutely no reason to trust me nor I you, other than what we've each been told by Jack, or in your case, I suppose it's Father Clancy."

"He's told me to call him Jack. But I can't bring myself to."

"Perfectly understandable. Okay, to you he's Father Clancy. To me he's Jack."

He paused briefly then said, "I know you've heard of attorney-client privilege and that it's basically the same as clergy-parishioner privilege."

"Yes."

"But for the privilege to work properly, there needs to be an element of trust between the attorney and his or her client. So let me give you a little background regarding me and how I know Jack." He leaned back in his chair. "Did you know that Jack never went to parochial school?"

"No, I didn't know that." *What a surprise!* I thought.

"For whatever reason, his parents sent him to public school. In fact, PS 81 just down Riverdale Avenue from here."

"I had no idea. I assumed he went to Catholic school just like me."

"He also went to Dewitt Clinton High School here in the

Bronx instead of a Catholic school. I've often suspected his parents were concerned that Jack had always indicated that he wanted to go into the priesthood and they wanted to be certain he was making a well-educated decision.

He leaned forward. "But here's the point. He and I were classmates. From kindergarten all the way through our senior year of high school, we were together. We were also from the same neighborhood here in Riverdale and walked to school together every day. We became known as the Bobbsey Twins by our parents and teachers. In spite of the fact that I'm Jewish and my parents were very observant, as were Jack's parents very observant Catholics, we became close friends. It was only when we graduated from high school that we parted. I went to Harvard University and then to Harvard Law. Jack went right into seminary with the Jesuits in Weston, Massachusetts. And our friendship has never waned. Jack is an extremely intelligent and wise man. You have every reason to trust him in his judgment."

"I've always felt I was fortunate to be working under him."

"As well you should. I'll add that I am married and have two kids, neither of whom has continued in the faith. I'm somewhat lapsed in my faith, though I do go to temple fairly frequently for the sake of my wife and because we have a family plot in the Jewish cemetery that I'd like to maintain."

He leaned back in his chair again and said, "So that should be enough about me. Now why don't you give me your story. Start by telling me who you really are. Where you come from. Then, when you're ready, maybe you'll be able to tell me what hasn't been expressed yet about today's events?"

"You mean about my family and all that?"

"Yes." He smiled broadly. "Give me the works. Let me decide what's relevant or not."

"Okay. I guess I'll start with where I was raised, which was in Philadelphia. I was the last of fifteen children."

Mr. Rothschild's bushy eyebrows rose at least a half inch.

I began to relax as I thought about my family. "That's right, fifteen. We lived in a row house. My mother presented my father with yet another child almost annually. My oldest brother is seventeen years older than I am. I've always figured I got the name Ignatius because my parents had run out of good, recognizable names of saints after whom they named their boys. We had Joseph, John, Thomas, even Jude. On the other hand, Saint Ignatius founded the Jesuits. So maybe my parents had big plans for me.

"My father was a truck driver. He delivered mushrooms from the farms west of Philadelphia to the markets in the city. I bet you didn't know Pennsylvania is the number one producer of mushrooms in the United States."

"No. I had no idea," Mr. Rothschild said.

"Well, it is. My father told me often. Anyway, being the youngest male in an Irish Catholic home, there seemed to be nothing left for me but to become a priest. After all, every honorable Irish Catholic family with a brood of children was expected to have at least one priest in the family. I never gave it much thought. It was expected of me, and I was a dutiful son. Besides, it wasn't a bad life. If I took my vows as a priest seriously, I could expect to become a highly respected person in the community, and possibly, I could advance into the governance of the church in some way. God willing." I paused for a second to collect my thoughts. Mr. Rothschild looked at me with an expectant smile.

"Upon graduating from seminary," I continued, "I was assigned to assist Father Clancy here at St. Ann's. That's about it as far as background is concerned. I can't think of anyone else I should talk about except perhaps for Sister Mary. But until today, I had only met her in passing. She teaches or, rather, taught next door. I don't even know what class. So I had no chance to get to know anything about her, except that I learned quickly she was an excellent golfer."

"All right. Now let's see if you can let me know what is really bothering you," he said.

How did he know I had held something back? "This is really difficult for me," I said.

"Perhaps I can help you out. Do you mind if I call you Iggy? That seems to be what Jack calls you, and I assume your friends do too?"

"No, I don't mind. Except for in the confessional, everybody calls me Iggy."

"Okay. Now I think it's time I gave you a sense of where I'm coming from. I've been a defense attorney for quite a few years, and I have to tell you that the majority of the people I've defended, especially in the early years when I was a public defender, were guilty as sin. But I've also represented lots of innocent folks. And I've discovered that the innocent often feel some kind of guilt, some kind of dark secret that keeps them from coming clean with me. In the end, however, it always comes out. And it isn't until it does come out that we're able to mount an effective defense."

He looked at me with a serious but expectant expression and waited for me to respond.

Finally, I took a deep breath, exhaled, and said, "I guess I might as well get it off my chest, and I can't think of anyone else I could tell it to. Not even in the confessional."

I paused, took another deep breath. "It's like this. I've been worrying over what happened, trying to make sense of it. It's like my whole education for the priesthood has been brought into question, and I can't get my mind around it. So maybe by telling it to you, I'll get an answer."

He remained silent. Perhaps he didn't want to interrupt the

flow of my thinking. So I went on. "You know how when there's an earthquake or a tsunami or a volcano eruption we call it an act of God?"

"Yes," he said.

"Well, in this case it was a bolt of lightning."

"Yes, I know that."

"Yes. But what I'm saying is that we know that those earthquakes, tsunamis, and volcanoes are really the result of natural forces that have come into play. Some may argue that those forces were created by God, so ultimately, we have witnessed an act of God. But that's another story.

"What I'm trying to say is that something did happen on that golf course that I haven't told anyone. And that something really was an act of God. I mean, God actually said so. To me." I looked into his eyes. I couldn't believe that I had said out loud that God had spoken to me.

"Are you saying that you heard the voice of God literally speaking to you?" He was clearly attempting to keep any expression of disbelief off his face.

"Yes."

"What did you hear?"

"I heard God declare right out of the thundercloud from which the lightning had come that he had struck Sister Mary."

"In so many words?"

"Not in those exact words."

"Then in exactly what words?"

"You need the exact words?"

"Yes. Please."

I knew he wouldn't believe me, but I said, "*Damn, I missed again!* Those were his exact words." I looked into his eyes.

I fully expected him to quit the conversation right there and leave. Instead, he sat still and returned my stare. Finally, he said,

"Iggy, let me make certain I understand you. Are you telling me that the Lord God, Jehovah, after a bolt of lightning struck Sister Mary, spoke out of the cloud and said he had missed his target?"

"Yes." I could tell he was going along with me and not believing a word. Maybe he thought I had gone bonkers.

"So the logic of this assertion by God would seem to be that someone or something else was the intended target."

"Yes."

"And that target would be ...?"

"Me," I said very quietly.

"You!" he said. "Any particular reason?"

"For this to make any sense, I have to back up a bit and describe more of what happened. Do you want me to continue?"

"You can't stop now!" Mr. Rothschild said almost sharply.

"The thing is, I have a bit of a temper that sometimes comes out when I'm playing golf."

"Yes. Jack told me you've broken more than one golf club."

"It's true. I've wrapped a few around the occasional tree or bent one or two badly when striking the earth after a missed shot. But that's not what I'm referring to here."

"You didn't break a club today?"

"Actually, I'm pretty sure I did. But that's not the point."

"Then what is the point?" I had the feeling he was getting a bit impatient.

"I swore."

"You swore."

"Yes. More than once."

"More than once."

"Yes."

"Iggy, you're losing me."

"Sorry. It's hard to tell this sensibly." I took another deep breath and exhaled. "Okay, here goes. I couldn't find anyone to play golf with me, so I finally called Sister Mary. But you know this."

"Yes. Let's start at the golf course."

"Right. Okay." I paused, looked off into the distance, and then began. "I expected Sister Mary to be a terrible golfer, but it turned out that she was very good. Her drives were true and long, and she was a terror on the putting green. I'm not a bad golfer myself. But she was really giving me a run for my money. So we got to the first putting green, and we were neck and neck. She sank a long, complicated putt, and that put her dead even with me. I took aim for my five or six footer, and the ball slipped right around the edge of the cup and went on a couple of feet. I couldn't believe it, and without thinking, I said, 'Damn, I missed!'

"You'd have thought it was the end of the world for Sister Mary. She exclaimed, 'Father, I can't play golf with a man who swears, be he priest or not!' I responded that I wouldn't let it happen again, and she said okay but that she'd quit the game if I swore again. So we played on, and I managed to contain myself for a couple of holes. But on the fourth hole after I missed another crucial putt, I forgot and said, 'Damn, I missed again!'

"Well, you'd have thought that once again it was the end of the world. She stopped cold. Her eyes were as wide as saucers as they drilled into mine, and she declared in no uncertain terms that she'd have to leave the course. I remonstrated with her. She refused. I practically got on my knees until finally I convinced her that I would contain myself. She finally agreed to play on.

"And I did contain myself. I was quite proud of myself, actually. But then on the eighth hole, it happened again. Same situation, and when I missed my putt, I said, 'Damn, I missed again.' With that, Sister Mary started to gather her things together while saying she was leaving the course.

"I couldn't believe it. I mean, we were only planning to play nine holes and had only one more to play. She turned her back on me. I pleaded again. But no. So, in desperation, I said to her, 'Look, Sister Mary, I really mean it. I promise that it won't happen again. And if it does, may the good Lord strike me dead.' I was that anxious to finish the game.

"She stopped in her tracks. 'Well,' she said, 'if you put it that way … All right then. Let's play on. But God help you if you do swear again.' I didn't think she believed God would actually strike me dead, only that I was serious about wanting to behave, as it were.

"So here I was, frustrated as could be, trying to contain my frustration by not letting a single swear word come out. But as fate would have it, when we got to the ninth hole, we once again were neck and neck. She sank a relatively easy five footer, putting her in the lead by one stroke. I had only a two footer to sink. I couldn't believe how nervous I was as I lined up my putt. I did my best to take deep breaths and get my nerves under control. Nevertheless, I missed the putt, and I couldn't hold it in any longer. I banged my club on the ground while yelling rather loudly, 'Damn, I missed again!'

"And with that, on this clear day with not a cloud in the sky, a huge dark cloud formed, and a howling wind came up. Sister and I looked up. Then we looked at each other. We were maybe two club lengths apart. Her expression went from fear and puzzlement to a kind of 'I told you so.' It was almost as though she wagged her finger at me. And then the bolt of lightning came down. And it struck not me but Sister Mary! Dead! And then I heard the voice I told you about. Very loud and deep. It came right out of that cloud, 'Damn, I missed again.'"

I looked at Mr. Rothschild. Utter silence. He was clearly trying to contain himself. Finally, he said, "Uh. Iggy, I have to tell you that I've heard a lot of stories in my day. But I've never heard anything like this. I don't know whether to laugh or cry. I mean, you are very serious about this?"

"Yes. I'm serious. That's what happened. Now you know why I couldn't tell anyone. I can't believe it myself. I mean, I know it's what happened. But …"

Mr. Rothschild looked over my head, to my left, and then to my right. Finally, he looked into my eyes. "I think, Iggy, at least for now, it would be best if you didn't tell another soul this story."

"Not even Father Clancy?"

"Not even Father Clancy. He'll never believe it. He'll think you've gone daft. You can see that, can't you?"

"Yes. Like I said, I can't even believe it myself. I even wonder if maybe I have gone daft, as you say. Maybe the lightning caused it. Maybe the shock of it all."

"That's an interesting theory. I have to give this some thought." He paused for a few seconds. Then he said, "In the meantime, you need to know I arrived here maybe an hour before Jack woke you. During our discussion, the question came up: Where are Iggy's golf clubs? So we conducted a search. They were not anywhere to be found. Not in your room, not in the trunk of your car, not anywhere. Can you tell me where they are?"

"No. I forgot all about them. I would have thought I'd have brought them back. I usually leave them locked in the trunk of my car. You say you checked there?"

"Yes. You left your car unlocked, and there was nothing in the trunk in the way of any golf paraphernalia."

"Do you think my clubs were stolen?"

"Out of the trunk of your car in the rectory parking lot? I suppose it's possible. But I have to wonder if you left them on that ninth hole and if the police have them. Here's what's occurring to me. I suspect that the police have your clubs. I think you do need to have representation during any questioning that might take place. With your approval, I'd like to contact the police and find out what they have found and what their intentions are toward you, if they'll let me know. Then, if they still want you to come in for questioning, I'll schedule a time that is convenient for us, not them. Will that be all right with you?"

"Yes. At this point, I'm completely in your hands."

"Well, before you make that decision, let's see what's going on at the Fiftieth Precinct."

Chapter 5

✝

At 3:00 p.m. the next day, I was perfectly aware of where I was—in an interview room at the NYPD Fiftieth Precinct off Kingsbridge Road in the Bronx. It was amazingly similar to interview rooms depicted on *Law and Order*, even down to the large two-way mirror on the wall facing me. I had no idea who might be on the other side. The room was half paneled in dark wood up to a dado strip. Above, the walls were a pale green. We sat at a steel table with a Formica top. Across the table from me sat Detective Folger. He informed us that our interview was being videoed, presumably through the mirror.

Mr. Rothschild sat next to me. At his suggestion, I was dressed in my clerical garb. Detective Folger appeared to be wearing the same outfit as yesterday, except his tie was now solid brown. I couldn't help thinking that he must like beige shirts. He was around forty-five years old and reasonably fit, but a few jowls were beginning to show on his cheeks and he had a bit of a paunch.

"Thanks for coming in, Father Costello," he said. "I'll try to keep this as brief as possible."

"It's okay, Detective. Father Clancy told me to take as much time as we need to get this business sorted out." Mr. Rothschild had told me to sound as cooperative as possible but to stay away from the theological thing, as he put it.

"Okay then. I'm wondering if you remember more of what happened than you were able to tell me yesterday?"

"I don't believe I have much to add."

"You're sticking with the lightning story."

"Yes, of course. It's what happened."

"Hold on, Detective," Mr. Rothschild interrupted. "Do you have some other scenario in mind? Something else you need to tell us?"

On our way over here in his car, Mr. Rothschild had told me he had not been able to get any information from the police. Not even whether or not they had retrieved my golf clubs.

"No, Mr. Rothschild. So far we don't have some other scenario. But we do have some questions about what could be inconsistencies in Father Costello's rendition. I was hoping Father Costello might volunteer the information instead of me having to drag it out of him."

I started to remonstrate, but Mr. Rothschild put his hand on my arm. "Detective, let me assure you that Father Costello wants to be as forthcoming as he can. But neither he nor I have any idea what it is you're after. Why don't you enlighten us?"

"All right. I'll cut right to the chase. Father, where are your golf clubs?"

"I don't know. I think I must have left them at the course. I'm hoping you have found them."

"In fact we have."

"Oh good. They're not the most expensive in the world. But I wouldn't want to have to buy a whole new set. Can I have them back?"

"Not quite yet. Were they all in good order?"

"I believe so except that I may have ruined my putter."

"How's that?"

"I struck the ground with it after I missed my putt." Mr.

Rothschild also told me that he suspected the detectives had my clubs and would have found the broken one. Best to be forthcoming with that information.

"So you remember doing that?"

"Yes. A lot came back to me yesterday afternoon after I had a rest."

"Do you make a habit of smashing your putter after missing a shot?"

"Not a habit, Detective. I mean I have been known to wrap a golf club around a tree or into the ground after a missed shot. It's not a good trait, and I tried to keep myself from misbehaving in front of Sister Mary. But, in the end, I may have broken my putter."

"On the ground?"

"Yes."

"Not on Sister Mary's head." He said it like a statement, not a question.

It took me a second or two to realize what he had said. "Excuse me?"

"I asked if you were certain that you struck the ground and not Sister Mary's head."

"Okay, we're done here," Mr. Rothschild interrupted.

"I don't believe I'm hearing you correctly, Detective." I hardly heard Mr. Rothschild's protest.

"You heard him correctly, Father, and we're not answering any more questions until we know just what it is Detective Folger has up his sleeve. And, unless he's willing to tell us now, we're leaving."

"Okay. Here's our problem," Detective Folger said. "We have no definitive cause of death for Sister Mary. The Medical Examiner has yet to give us a report. Meantime, we've checked with every possible meteorologist in New York, all the TV channels, radio stations, and the US Meteorological Service, and none can show any evidence of any thunder and lightning cloud having shown up anywhere near the Van Cortland Park golf course, or indeed anywhere in the northeastern United States. The weather was, as you know, as clear and storm free as it could be. So we have to ask ourselves: Where did this lightning bolt come from?" He looked from Mr. Rothschild to me and back again with a stern expression on his face.

"To fill you in completely," he continued, "it does appear that Sister Mary was scorched in some manner. And the area around her body shows similar signs, as did your clothes yesterday, Father. But we have to ask ourselves: What caused the scorching? And there appears to be some evidence that Sister Mary was struck on the head. By what, we can't be certain. There were a number of rocks strewn about. At first we assumed one of them might have been tossed about by the storm and struck the victim. But with no evidence of a storm that day … Finally, we have your clubs, Father, and your broken putter. So you can see why we're scratching our heads."

"I've had a look at the scene as well," Mr. Rothschild said. "I couldn't help but notice you had yellow crime scene tape sealing off the entire green, making it impossible for golfers to play the hole. I also noticed that there were rocks strewn about. Strange on a putting green. That, it seems to me, should be clear evidence that a pretty sizable force, such as lightning, had to have been the cause."

"Yes," said Detective Folger. "However, how do you explain absolutely no meteorological evidence of a storm, no radar, no nothing? And to give you the complete picture, I'll add that there's absolutely nothing to have prevented someone from placing those rocks around the scene. There are thousands of rocks in the landscaping on the western side of the green, very near where we found Sister Mary's body."

Folger stared at me with a slightly accusatory yet questioning look. I had no response. This was too much. Were they constructing a case against me? I felt myself heading back into yesterday's state of mind.

"All right, Detective. I appreciate your candor. But I can see where you're heading, and it's not a pretty scenario. I have to ask: Are you thinking of accusing Father Costello of a crime?"

"Not now. The ME has yet to perform an autopsy, and forensics is examining the golf clubs and the putter. We'll be going back to the green to search once again for any possible evidence that would either confirm or deny the lightning scenario. If Father Costello were anybody else, we might be holding him for further questioning. We only suggest very strongly, Father, that you don't leave the area." He looked at me.

"I don't know what to say," I said. "I'm totally at a loss. No, I won't go anywhere. But I have to tell you, Detective, that I've done nothing wrong. I did not in any way harm Sister Mary. This was, in every sense of the word, an act of God."

"So are we finished?" Mr. Rothschild asked.

"For now, yes."

Chapter 6

✝

It was about a twenty minute drive back to St. Ann's. We rode in silence for perhaps five minutes until I couldn't hold it in. "I can't believe this is happening. They're actually thinking I may have killed Sister Mary in a fit of pique because I missed that putt! I can't believe it!"

"I'll not gloss things over, Iggy. I agree that Folger gave that impression. But let me assure you that, in my experience, the police do try to simply do their job. Collect the evidence, see where it points, and then make their conclusions. They don't accuse anyone lightly, especially not someone such as yourself. You have a completely spotless record, and you can be sure they've found that out. The one blemish might be your seeming lack of control at times on the golf course. But that's a very weak hook on which to hang an indictment."

"Yes. But how do you explain no evidence of a storm anywhere in the Northeast? I can see where they might start looking for other causes of death."

"Right. But there's plenty of evidence of something very violent having occurred on that green—all those rocks, the scorched grass, your singed clothing, and of course, Sister Mary's scorched body."

We continued to ride in silence for a few more minutes. Then he said, "Something's occurring to me. I have a close friend at Columbia University. He teaches physics and meteorology. I think I'll ask him if he'd be willing to have a look at the scene. No radar evidence of a storm having occurred is not at all conclusive. It just means the storm, which according to you was very brief, wasn't picked up. It wouldn't be the first time that ever happened."

"Well, I've been wondering if a storm literally created by God for the purpose of creating a single bolt of lightning would be detected?"

"Why wouldn't it?" Mr. Rothschild asked.

"Such a thing isn't your normal meteorological event. Physics didn't cause it. Maybe radar wouldn't be able to see it."

Utter silence from Mr. Rothschild. We arrived at St. Ann's, and he pulled over to the curb. "Let's not go there just yet, Iggy," he said and then turned his gaze in my direction. "What are you going to say to Father Clancy?"

"I don't know."

"Well, if I were you, I'd stay away from the theological thing. Only relate to him exactly what was said by Folger. He needs to know we have a serious situation on our hands and that you need legal representation. There's no question about that now." He paused. "Look, I can well imagine that you'd want to tell Jack what you told me. You'd have clergy-parishioner privilege, and Jack would never repeat your story to anyone. Nevertheless, I believe it would be prudent to see if we can't make the physical evidence do the job of clearing things up. If we can show that, despite no radar evidence, there was a lightning strike and that it killed Sister Mary, especially if the ME's report confirms the lightning, then we need look no further. It was an act of God, as you say. But in the eyes of the police, that will only mean what it always means. It was caused by a physical force beyond the control of any man."

"Okay. I'll do as you suggest. For now. But this thing is eating me up. I mean, I saw what I saw. I heard what I heard. I don't believe any amount of physical evidence will make me ever be able to get it out of my head."

"Well, let's not open that can of worms unless we absolutely have to."

"All right." I opened the door. "So what should I do now?"

"For now, report to Jack and then go about your normal routine. You're not guilty of anything. So try to let it go. In the meantime, let me look into this storm question. I have to get going on it quickly before the police finish and reopen that ninth hole. I have a feeling I'll get some good information from my Columbia friend. I'll let you know as soon as I have something."

"Thanks, Mr. Rothschild. I hope you're right." I closed the door and walked across the sidewalk, up the stairs, and into the church. I had always felt the church was unnecessarily dark inside, even a little depressing. The only light came in through rather narrow stained glass windows and from the candles. More modern churches allowed for much more light. But this church was built in the late nineteenth century when solid, dark structures seemed to be preferred. Right now, though, the cool, dark atmosphere felt good to me. It was very quiet. Only a few parishioners were scattered about the pews, praying. If they knew what I believed had happened to me, would they include me in their prayers?

I headed down the center aisle, turned right in front of the alter, and headed through the side exit and into the rectory. What was I going to say to Father Clancy?

Chapter 7

I found Father Clancy in the rectory kitchen. "I'm grabbing a bite to eat," he said. "So how did it go? I trust they're finished with you. Bishop Scanlan's after me to get our financials to him. So I have to get back to my desk. I'm glad you're here. Jimmy's performing his chaplain duties at the hospital, and I've been hoping you'd be able to hear confession today."

"I'm afraid they're not finished with me," I said. "But Mr. Rothschild suggested I leave things up to him for the moment and get back to my routine. So I probably should hear confession. I have to admit that being alone with God would do me some good. I've a lot to digest, and sitting in the confessional might be just the place for me. The occasional sinner interrupting my thoughts with their own problems might even be helpful."

"What do you mean they're not finished with you? Surely it's clear that Sister Mary was killed by lightning?"

"Actually, the police say it isn't all that clear."

"You'd better come to my office. Let's discuss this there. And I have something to show you."

We returned to his office. The chair I sat in yesterday had been moved back to its place against the far wall. Father Clancy placed his plate of food in front of him and sat down. He had papers all over his desk. It was clear that he was in the middle of a mess of financial figures.

"I hope you don't mind if I eat while we talk. I skipped lunch today. I should have thought: Do you want something?" he said.

"No thanks. I'm fine."

"All right. Before you tell me about your interview, have a look at this." He turned around and reached for a copy of the *New York Daily News* that was on the windowsill of the bay window behind his seat. "Look at page seven, bottom right."

I saw that it was this morning's paper. I turned to page seven. A headline read: *Nun Struck Dead on Ninth Hole.* I looked up at Father Clancy.

"Go ahead, read it."

I read.

> In a strange twist of fate, an act of God appears to have struck dead a devoted Roman Catholic Church servant on the ninth hole of the Van Cortland Park Golf Course yesterday morning.
>
> According to police, the body of Sister Mary Magdalene, fifth grade teacher at St. Ann's Roman Catholic School in Riverdale was apparently struck by lightning while she was playing golf with Father Ignatius Costello, priest at St. Ann's Church located next door to the school.
>
> There were no witnesses to the incident, according to police. The nun's body was found by other golfers as they approached the ninth hole. They had not noticed any lightning strike, they are reported to have said. And they saw no one else on the green. Father Costello reported his presence to the police after receiving medical

aid at North Central Bronx Hospital a few hours later.

The ninth hole has been closed off by police pending further examination of conditions on the green, which was very badly damaged, according to Detective Martin Folger of the Fiftieth Precinct in the Bronx. "We want to be absolutely certain of the cause of death," he said. He was unable to predict when the ninth hole would be reopened.

I looked at Father Clancy. "My God," I said. I had no idea it had made the papers.

"Apparently it only made the *News*. I get the *New York Times* and I found nothing there. Sister Helen showed it to me while you were at the Fiftieth. She, as you can imagine, is very upset. The whole school is in a state of mourning. Of course, it's summer vacation, so there are no students. But the staff ..."

"I must admit, I've been so consumed with my own worries that I hadn't given them much thought."

"Very understandable."

"But this is very worrying," I said, pointing to the newspaper. "It sort of confirms my concerns."

"Well, what did they have to say at your interview?"

Keeping Mr. Rothschild's admonition in mind, I kept to the bare essentials of Detective Folger's questions and my answers. Father Clancy asked no questions. He only chewed his sandwich and sipped his tea while I spoke.

When I stopped relating my story, he said, "There's no meteorological evidence of a lightning storm?"

"None whatsoever, according to the detective. And, according to the paper, no one else saw anything."

"And they have your clubs, including a broken putter."

"Yes."

He stuffed the rest of his sandwich into his mouth, swiveled his chair slightly off to his right, and stared into space. I said nothing. He made a last swallow and said, "What does Jacob think of all this?" He continued staring at the wall on his right.

"I don't know what he actually thinks about all this. I only know what he told me to do and what he's going to do."

"And that is?" He turned back in my direction and sipped his tea.

"He has a meteorologist friend at Columbia who he's going to ask to have a look at the scene. See if there's any physical evidence of a lightning strike. He also hopes the ME will confirm the lightning. In the meantime, he told me to do nothing other than to report to you and go about my normal routine. I should add that he also said I definitely do need to have legal representation until the matter is resolved. And that has me worried."

"Good advice. You can trust him implicitly. Why does it worry you?"

"How can I ever afford his fees?"

"Why don't you let me worry about that. Up till now Jacob's efforts have been purely exploratory. He told me that. So I doubt if any fees have been incurred. He'll let us know if and when that becomes an issue. He's a very decent man, Iggy. He won't take advantage. And if expenses do become an issue, the church, as you know, has legal council, and when hiring outside council, we have a budget for such expenses. I'll speak to the bishop if need be. But let's not worry about that now."

"Well, it has been a concern, but I'll leave it in your hands, if that's all right."

"Yes, of course it is. That's what I just said. Now I need to ask you something. And I don't want you to take this the wrong way.

I simply have to ask. Is there anything else you can tell me? I get the sense that we haven't seen the full picture yet."

Was he wondering if I had in some way harmed Sister Mary? Why else would he ask such a thing? I had told him everything I had learned from the police and that I had told them. On the other hand, I had not mentioned the theological thing per Mr. Rothschild's instructions. Is that what he was searching for? I wasn't sure what to do.

Finally I said, "I can't think of anything else to say. Mr. Rothschild hopes that physical evidence at the green and the ME examination of Sister Mary's body will demonstrate that a lightning bolt did strike Sister Mary. And he's hoping that will point them to the fact that this was an act of God. That's all I can say."

"All right. Let's trust this matter will soon be behind us. Meantime, I need to get back to this mess." He looked at his desk. "I'll appreciate it if you'll tend to the confessional. You really need to get to it. People probably are waiting."

"Right. Thanks, Father."

"Iggy. It's Jack."

"Right." *I'll never be able to call him Jack*, I thought as I left his office.

Chapter 8

✝

There I was, thirty-three years old, hearing the confessions of three women in their fifties and sixties whom I knew and who knew me. One right after the other. These, I knew, were good women, married and with lovely families. What could they possibly have to confess? And who was I, a young man in their eyes, to listen to their telling of their sins? But in the confessional, I became a sort of disembodied presence, an agent of God—we were taught and believed—who could give absolution. I heard their confessions of real or imagined sins, gave them absolution, and sent them off to do penance.

There were only the three. I waited quietly. No one else came into the box. *And what about my own sins?* I thought as I sat there. What had I done to bring on all this consternation on my part and on the part of everyone else concerned and, most especially, the death of a nun—a perfectly innocent victim?

What I had done was swear. And then I had invoked the wrath of God. And look what had happened: God had struck the wrong victim!

Was that why I was being threatened by the police? Was this God's way of somehow correcting things? Maybe punishing me? Was I going to end up in prison? Because I used the word *damn* ... more than once ... on that golf course ... in front of that nun ...

and in front of God? Or was this all a huge mistake? Maybe I dreamed the whole thing. Or maybe I did kill Sister Mary and my brain was making all this up.

Thoughts flew around in my head. I decided I had to calm down. Take stock of things.

If I had dreamed it, where might the reality have left off and the dream started? I decided to work backward. I knew I was sitting in this confessional. I knew that Father Clancy, or Jack—would I ever get used to that, or did I dream that too? Had he told me to call him Jack? Yes, he had. Okay, not part of the dream. Next, I knew that Jacob Rothschild had dropped me off here and told me to go see Father Clancy. I knew that he drove me here from the Fiftieth after I was interviewed rather sternly by Detective Folger. I knew all the stuff that he said to me and that I said to him. None of that was a dream. It happened.

How about yesterday? I knew that Jack brought me to the hospital. I knew that I was very fuzzy headed. So maybe that was where the dream started. But no, I was definitely in that hospital and was questioned by Folger. And I knew that earlier in the day I had played a game of golf with Sister Mary. There was no way any of this so far was a dream.

So it came down to the ninth hole. I knew that something horrible happened there. That Sister Mary was killed. By a lightning bolt, according to my memory. Did I dream that part? No, I did not dream it. Sister Mary was burnt. My clothes were scorched. There was that smell that Father Clancy noticed. So then, the question had to be if I dreamed the God part. Did I dream my promise to Sister Mary: *May God strike me dead?* If so, then I must have dreamed God's words: *Damn I missed again.*

But I knew I lost my temper several times on that course and that Sister Mary had kept threatening to quit the game. I knew that I promised her several times that I'd not swear again. And that I did swear again. Swearing happened to me all the time on the golf course. It was something I needed to correct. Perhaps this incident (what a word) would make me change my ways. Or maybe I'd just never play another game. Or maybe I was going to end up in prison and never have an opportunity to play anyway.

My God! I thought. *What am I going to do? Did you speak? Did you say those words? Did I dream it?* It made no sense that our almighty perfect God would be capable of making a mistake, much less declaring it. But—

The door to the confessional opened. The woman spoke for some time before I pulled myself together. I gave her the absolution she needed without understanding anything she had said.

I was the one who desperately needed absolution. Would I ever get it?

Chapter 9

✟

I had always thought of Fieldston, just south of Riverdale, as a rather posh neighborhood, though I'd had little reason to visit the area until now. I was not disappointed. Jacob Rothschild lived at the dead-end of Indian Road just a few blocks east of the Henry Hudson Parkway. He maintained his office in his home, having closed his office in Manhattan.

"I'm in a position these days to pick and choose the cases I want to handle," he had explained to me, "and I don't need a fancy downtown office anymore."

Soon after I had finished hearing confessions the previous afternoon, Mr. Rothschild had phoned me on my mobile and suggested we meet at his home the next morning. Father Clancy had given him my number when he tried to reach me at the rectory.

Now, as I pulled into his circular driveway, I saw that Fieldston was indeed a rather posh area. Mr. Rothschild's solid white brick home and the others in his neighborhood were very well settled into their properties, with well-tended gardens and tall mature oaks, maples, and a few birches. In spite of the fact that I was only a few blocks from the Henry Hudson Parkway and we were in New York City, there were hardly any of the normal city sounds. I was conscious only of a slight breeze blowing through the trees and a number of birds singing. Back at St. Ann's, only a few miles away, all these sounds were drowned out by the sound of traffic on Riverdale Avenue.

I parked my car in front of the steps leading to the front door and got out. As I started to climb the stairs, Mr. Rothschild opened the front door.

"Glad you could come here," he said. "I felt it would be better if we met in a nonclerical and nonthreatening atmosphere. Come on into my office and have a seat."

He led me into a moderately sized foyer, past a staircase, and into a long room that overlooked a large patio and garden beyond a wide set of sliding doors. His desk was located about halfway between the entrance to the room and the sliding doors. The desk extended out from a wall filled with law books, and his padded office chair faced the sliding doors. A sitting area was arranged between the desk and the patio. An oriental rug covered most of the hardwood floor. He directed me to sit in a small easy chair that faced the view. He sat in a duplicate chair half facing me and the view. The atmosphere had a much-needed calming effect on me as I settled into my seat.

"I can imagine you must be wondering what, if anything, I've learned since we met yesterday. So let me get straight to it," he said.

"Thanks," I said. "I have to admit I didn't get much sleep last night."

"I can imagine. Let's see if we can put your mind at rest. First of all, I was able to reach my friend at Columbia, and we were able to view the scene while the police still had it taped off. Second, he made some very interesting observations, one of which was that there definitely was a lightning strike and that it was quite unusual. Did you know that there are thousands of lightning strikes each day around the world and that there's a whole variety of types of lightning?"

"No," I said.

"Well, it's true. And surprisingly, with all the technological advances we've had in recent decades, scientists still don't know for sure what causes many types of strikes. I won't bore you with all that Professor Ingersoll told me. But he said temperatures at lightning strikes can reach as high as 54,000 degrees Fahrenheit. That's as hot as the surface of the sun. I never knew that. And they can, of course, cause huge damage. And they often don't strike as a single bolt. Frequently, it's a series of strikes that occur. It's only because they come in such rapid succession that we think we're seeing a single strike. But here's the thing. Those series of strikes normally happen one right after the other but follow the same channel as the first. They wouldn't normally bounce all over the surface where they are striking. That sort of strike has been known to happen. But it's rare. And that's what he says happened at the ninth hole."

He looked at me. My face must have expressed little emotion. I wasn't really taking it all in. But then he said, "It's as if the lightning was looking for its target. That's what Harry said."

"Excuse me?"

"You heard me right. And I had not said a word to Harry about your experience. That was entirely his conclusion. He actually seemed a bit mystified by the evidence."

"Mystified?"

"Yes. He said he had heard of strikes of this kind but never seen one. He also said there was no question that it was a lightning strike of great force overall and that because of the way the lightning had bounced around, it was no wonder that there were so many rocks strewn all over the place. And it would not be at all surprising if anyone near the spot were struck by a rock, to say nothing of the lightning."

"So what do we do now?" I asked.

"Well, the police have finished their investigation at the golf course and have removed the yellow tape. So they must have reached some conclusions. They haven't phoned you, have they?"

"No."

"That's probably a good sign. If they thought you were in some way implicated in Sister Mary's death, I would think they would be asking you to come back down to the Fiftieth. Or even coming to you. On the other hand, they may have some scenario up their sleeve that we can't imagine and could be waiting until they have all their evidence in order before proceeding. I'm not saying that's the case. It's just that you never really know with these guys. So what I suggest is that you let me follow up with Folger and try to get some answers. One thing that would be very interesting to know is what the ME has concluded. I have to believe an autopsy has been performed by now."

"Is there anything I should do?" I was feeling numb. Never in my wildest imagination had I thought I would be hearing my name, medical examiner and autopsy together.

"I think it would be best if you simply went about your normal daily routine. I know you are troubled and anxious and wish you could put all this behind you. Hopefully that will happen very soon. Meantime, just behave as if you have nothing to fear. You have done nothing wrong."

"But I have."

"What do you mean?"

"What happened on the golf course ... what caused the lightning and death of Sister Mary."

There was a long pause. I could see Mr. Rothschild struggling over what to say. "Look, Iggy, I understand that from your point of view, and with your theological training and you living your life in strict concordance with that training, it could seem to you that you in some way caused Sister Mary's death. But from an outsider's point of view, I have to tell you that your experience on that course, which you believe may have caused her death, was nothing more than coincidence. She was struck by lightning. Lightning happens all the time in all kinds of places and under some of the most unusual sets of circumstances. There's so much of it going one that physicists have been unable to fully grasp what causes it in many cases. So if I were you, I'd drop the scenario you keep playing in your head and get on with your daily business."

A lot easier said than done, I thought. "I wish I could. But it keeps eating away at me."

"Perhaps you should get some counseling. The church offers counseling for its priests. Anything you said in that kind of setting would be completely confidential. Right?"

"Yes. It probably would."

"Well then …?"

"My problem is that I feel I have sinned. And there's no getting around it."

Mr. Rothschild looked at me with what seemed to be an almost fatherly expression.

"Look, I'm a Jew. I simply do not have the same outlook that you have. I'm not suggesting that your feelings are not legitimate, only that I am not able to view them from your perspective. I can objectively, of course. But not from the depth of my being the way you must be experiencing it. But, Iggy, thousands of golfers every day get frustrated, swear, and break their clubs. The sport is famous for it. And as far as your invoking the wrath of God with your promise to Sister Mary is concerned, you never actually took it seriously. And the strike was, in the last analysis, a coincidence. So I can't see the problem."

"Sister Mary believed it."

"Do you really think she did?"

"Absolutely. That's why she played on."

"I don't know. I mean, how many times a day do you suppose people suggest the good Lord should strike them dead if they don't keep a promise—whatever the promise. I'll bet it's thousands of times a day. I simply feel you're taking on a completely unnecessary sense of guilt."

"Yes. But how many of those thousands of people are priests making promises to nuns? I wager none. I'm sorry. I can't get rid of the fact that I said what I said and did what I did."

"Are you telling me there's more to this—that you've done something more than you told me?"

"Not physically. No. What I did was invoke the wrath of God. But God struck Sister Mary by mistake. And I'm now having to pay penance for my sin. That's what I'm telling you."

"The sin being swearing one last time? Or invoking God's wrath?"

"I'm not certain. Perhaps both."

"All right, Iggy. This is way beyond my purview. I'm a lawyer, not a theologian. As far as the legalities are concerned, I see my job to be making sure the facts speak to what really happened on that course and to do my best to make certain the police see that you have absolutely nothing to answer for in the matter of the death of Sister Mary. Beyond that, I think you really do need to get some help with regard to this sense of guilt you are carrying."

"What I need is absolution."

"By absolution you mean forgiveness?"

"That's a frequent use of the word. But I need release. I need to somehow know that I did not cause Sister Mary's death with my actions. And I've been thinking I should follow the normal route for a Catholic and go to the confessional."

"Where? Certainly not at St. Ann's."

"No. I'd want to go to a priest in some parish far removed from this neighborhood, where they'd have no idea who I was. I thought I might drive over to Brooklyn or maybe New Jersey."

We had been talking with each other while staring out the glass doors at his patio and garden, almost as though we were both thinking out loud.

Mr. Rothschild stayed silent for a spell. Then he said, "It might be a good idea. But I'd suggest you first be certain that whatever is said will never be repeated. We simply do not want to complicate matters. We don't want to have this theological problem of yours interfere with what otherwise, hopefully, will be a very simple conclusion to this matter. I'd suggest you do some research and find yourself the right man or priest for the job—somebody intelligent and with a good sense of reality. Jack would be the perfect man. I know him to be a perfectly rational and very intelligent man. But I've never had any discussions of a theological nature with him. And I have to believe that, even if you went to him in the confessional, your story might color your relationship with him from then on."

"I know what you mean. But even though logic tells me to confess to a complete stranger, I keep thinking I want to spill the beans to him. I mean, he's my boss, and I feel he has a right to know. And, as he has made clear, he has become a good friend and confidant."

"Let's think about this a bit. You've made a good point—I mean, about his being your boss. If for some reason matters aren't cleared up with dispatch, you'll certainly want Jack on your side all the way. Spilling the beans to him, as you put it, at a later time might not be a good thing. He might wonder why you hadn't trusted him in the first place. That could color your relationship worse than his knowing what's going on in your head. And he is a very level-headed guy. I know that for a fact."

"So ..." I paused briefly "... you're thinking I should confess to Father Clancy?"

"In the last analysis, Iggy, this has to be your decision. I'm a lawyer, and a Jewish one at that. I can advise you with confidence on legal matters. And you know my position on your telling anyone about what you believe happened on that golf course. I'd rather you left it alone. I haven't even begun to think about how your story might be received by the police or, God forbid, in the courtroom. And I certainly have no understanding of how your story might be received in the confessional by whomever might hear your confession, be it Jack or anyone else. If I were in your shoes, I'd stay silent. But I'm not in your shoes. You are a Roman Catholic priest. You've had a good deal of theological instruction, and I'm sure you've heard some interesting confessions. So you, I believe, have to make this decision on your own. I know this is eating at your gut. And I'll accept whatever you decide to do. Hopefully, if you do confess, your story will never see the light of day."

I stared out the glass doors without actually seeing anything. It was very quiet. "I feel so confused," I finally said.

We fell silent.

Then Mr. Rothschild said, "Here's what comes to me. Let me get some answers from the police. We need to know what the ME has concluded and what else may have been found on the golf course. Let's assume that whatever has been discovered has cleared up this matter. That will leave you with no legal problem and only your theological issue. Why don't you go back to St. Ann's and get back into your routine? Leave the legal questions to me. Clear your head of them as best you can. Perhaps if you can do that you'll be able to better decide whether or not you need to visit the confessional. Does that make sense?"

"In the abstract, yes, it makes sense. All right. I'll give it a try."

"Keep me posted, Iggy. If you hear anything from Folger or if anything else comes to mind that might have any bearing, no matter how insignificant, let me know. Okay?"

I rose from my chair. "Yes. I'll let you know. And thanks. I really mean that."

He rose and turned toward me. We shook hands, and he followed me to the front door.

Chapter 10

✝

On the following Tuesday, my day off, I drove to a church in Morristown, New Jersey—over the George Washington Bridge, out Interstate 80 to 287, and then on a short drive to the exit that took me to my destination. I figured there was a good chance they hadn't heard about the death of Sister Mary out here. The church was dark red brick with a high steeple and set in a lovely area with tall trees. I felt myself relax a bit when I saw it.

I was dressed in casual clothes. I didn't see the need to have anybody wondering why a strange priest was entering the confessional, and I did not reveal that I was a priest to the priest who heard my confession. I figured my being a priest was irrelevant to the dilemma I felt I was in. The question, as I saw it, was whether any person—priest or not—could receive absolution from the events that took place at that ninth hole.

Several minutes went by as I told my story. The priest remained silent, but I could hear him fidgeting in his seat. When I finished, he declared, "Young man, I don't know who you are or why you have come to this place to confess. I have only one word of advice for you. You need to get down on your knees and pray to the Lord in heaven that he forgive you for telling such lies." With that, he left the confessional, almost slamming his door behind him.

I was stunned! I could not imagine any priest hearing any

confession and behaving that way. I waited a few seconds before quickly leaving the church, hoping that the priest was gone and that no one else might witness my exit. As far as I could tell, no one took any notice as I got in my car and drove off. My car had a clergy license plate on the back. It occurred to me that if anyone was watching, they'd know they had just seen a priest leaving their parking lot.

I drove a couple blocks and found a place to pull over. "Now what?" I asked myself. I felt totally at a loss. I sat there and stared out the windshield, seeing nothing. Finally, I heard myself saying, "There's nothing for it. You've no choice. You have to tell Father Clancy. He'll at least listen to you."

I had hoped that I would be feeling a sense of relief on my drive back home. But I made the forty-five minute drive back to St. Ann's with a greater sense of trepidation than I'd had on my way to Morristown. What would Father Clancy's reaction be?

I went straight to Father Clancy's office when I got back, filled with unease but also a sense of resolve after my experience in Morristown. There was no one else in the church to whom I could tell this story. He was sitting at his desk but had swiveled around in his seat and seemed to be staring out the window, contemplating I knew not what.

As I entered, he swiveled his chair back, and I said, "I'm wondering if you'd be willing to hear my confession. You're the only priest I can think of to go to."

"I've been wondering when you'd let me know what's really been bothering you," he said. "I've realized for some time, as I think you know, that something went on out on that golf course that you've not been able to tell me about. But I hoped you'd tell me when you were ready."

He suggested that I close the door to his office. I agreed that his office would constitute a proper confessional. Hopefully, we'd be a bit more comfortable and I would have an easier time of it. I now understood what Mr. Rothschild had meant when he said Father Clancy was a very sensible man. Why hadn't I gone to him from the start?

He looked at me with the expression of expectancy one might see in one's father who was waiting for his son to finally tell the truth.

"I don't know where to begin," I said.

"Why don't you begin by telling me why you suddenly came into my office on your day off? What brought you here?"

I had hoped not to have to tell him about my excursion to New Jersey. I somehow felt that I had been disloyal. "This is hard for me," I said. "I've been in a terribly confused state of mind. I felt a great need for absolution, and I hoped that by confessing to a complete stranger, I might find it. So I drove over to a church in New Jersey where I figured nobody would know me. But it was a disaster."

"Why? What happened?"

"He told me to get down on my knees and pray to the Lord in heaven for forgiveness for telling such lies."

"Lies! What did you tell him?"

"What I haven't told you. What I haven't told anyone except Mr. Rothschild. And what he told me not to tell anyone. Not even you."

"All right, Father Costello, I think it's time you filled me in. Consider yourself in the confessional and just let it all out. You know that when a priest hears a confession, one of his jobs is to be as nonjudgmental as possible. I can't imagine what it is you're about to tell me. But I have to say that that New Jersey priest's behavior sounds very incorrect, to say the least. So let's hear it."

"It's like this. I believe that I caused that lightning to strike Sister Mary."

A startled look passed across Father Clancy's face, but he quickly resumed a noncommittal mask. After thinking over my declaration, he said, "I can well understand that such a concern would cause a tremendous sense of guilt. We both know that lightning is caused by nature, not by man. So I presume you're going to tell me why you feel this way."

"Actually, in this case the lightning was not caused by nature. It literally was an act of God. He told me so."

"Who told you so?"

"God. God told me."

"God told you that he had struck Sister Mary with lightning." It was a statement, not a question. "When did God tell you this?"

"On the golf course. At the ninth hole. Immediately after she was struck. Right out of the cloud from which the lightning came."

"You're telling me that God said to you audibly, 'I struck Sister Mary with that lightning.'"

"Not in those exact words. But yes."

"I'm beginning to understand why your New Jersey priest might have felt a bit incredulous. Can you please tell me the exact circumstances that led you to your telling this story?"

I described to him the entire series of events that had led up to the disaster on the ninth hole—my swearing, Sister Mary's protestations, my final invocation of God's wrath should I swear again, and God's declaration.

"God told you that he had missed again. Those were his words?" Father Clancy asked.

"Yes. In a loud, booming voice right out of the cloud."

Father Clancy looked away from me. He remained silent for

a spell and then asked, "You said that you've told this to Jacob? What was his reaction?"

"He told me that I should not tell anyone else because they'd think I was daft. That was his word. He also hopes that the physical evidence will prove that I had nothing to do with Sister Mary's death and that any sense of guilt I might feel because of this will not be an issue for the police, only something for me to resolve in my own thinking. He also told me that, if I had to confess, you would be a good person to talk to. He was only concerned that if I did tell you, it might color our relationship adversely, presumably because you'd doubt my sanity."

Father Clancy continued staring at the wall as he said, "I have to confess, no pun intended, that I've never heard such a story. But it's not for me, as your priest, to judge what I have heard. You are here confessing and seeking absolution. I'll not attempt to judge the possible or impossible veracity of what you have told me. I'll not suggest a bunch of Hail Marys. Rather, I want you to go to your quarters, close the door behind you, get down on your knees, as your New Jersey priest suggested, and pray. But you don't need to pray for forgiveness. Let's assume, for the sake of this confession, that what you've told me is pure fiction, a figment of your imagination. But it is so real to you that it has you troubled. Or, on the other hand, let's assume that what you've told me actually did happen in some form or other that is incomprehensible to me or others. In either case, you need to get on your knees and pray for divine guidance.

"Let me add this. You're a very troubled lad right now. And it's true that this information has me troubled as well. It's something I have to ponder. But this doesn't change the fact that you are a good man. The very fact that you are troubled over this is proof of that fact. So rest assured that you've not lost my support. Go and do as I've told you. Hopefully you'll get your absolution."

Chapter 11

✝

I prayed long and hard that afternoon. But the next morning, I had to conclude that my prayers had not been heard. Mr. Rothschild telephoned and had me come back to his office.

"Bad news, I'm afraid," he said as he held the front door for me and I entered the foyer. As we walked to his office, he added, "The medical examiner has declared that it is not clear that Sister Mary was killed by lightning. Or, rather, that lightning was the sole cause of her death. She says she was struck on the head. It's not clear that the lightning struck her first. She wonders if something struck and killed her before the lightning struck."

Despite knowing what his answer would be, I had to ask, "What struck her on the head?"

"They are inclined to believe it was your putter. Though they have no forensic evidence to that effect other than that your bent-in-half putter was lying on the ground near her body."

"I can't believe this is happening," I said. "I did not strike that woman. I am absolutely certain of that. You have to believe me."

"I do believe you. Look, the news is not all bad. They have confirmed that an incredibly powerful force, possibly lightning, struck. When I suggested a rock might have struck her, they hemmed and hawed somewhat but said they had not found any specific rock that might have struck her. So at the moment, any evidence they claim they have is very thin and purely circumstantial. They have nothing to directly connect you to her death other than the fact that you were there and at least peripherally struck by lightning as well."

We were now sitting in the same two chairs we had occupied during my first visit. I remained silent for some time. Finally, I said, "You said 'they.' Who is they? Folger? Somebody else?"

"Folger and a Bronx assistant DA, name of Waterman. Works out of the Bronx County Court House."

"You met with them?"

"I did. Yesterday, late afternoon. That's why I asked you to come over this morning."

Out of the blue, I said, "I confessed to Father Clancy yesterday. Told him the whole story."

"What was his reaction?"

"He said my portrayal of the events may be a figment of my imagination or the events may have occurred even though the idea is incomprehensible to him. And that, no matter what, I had his full support." Then I added, "I also confessed to a priest in a church in New Jersey, before I went to Father Clancy."

"Why confess twice to two different priests?"

"Because the first thought I was nuts or a liar and told me so. He left the confessional and practically slammed the door behind him."

"Do you think he knew who you were?"

"No. I was dressed casually and I never told him."

"There's no chance Jack would repeat your story without your permission?"

"None. It was a confession."

"Do you think he believed you?"

"I know he believes that I believe it. I think he has great doubt about the event."

"Well, let's keep this to ourselves. What I haven't told you is that you are going to have to appear in court."

"What? Why?"

"You're to be arraigned on a charge of second-degree murder." He said it very matter-of-factly. As though it were a simple matter.

"I'm being charged with murder? But why are they doing this to me? They have to know it's all a mistake. Literally. An accident. An act of God! Why do they want to charge me?"

"To be honest, I don't know. It seems like an incredible rush to judgment on their part. Unless they have something else they haven't told me, their evidence is very thin. But here's the good part of this: An arraignment is only that. It's not a trial. I'm quite certain you'll be released on your own recognizance. And once you've been charged, the DA will have to reveal to us everything they have. It's called discovery, and they are required by law to show us everything. I've asked them not to make a big spectacle of this and to allow me to bring you in rather than them coming to your church and arresting you. They agreed. What I'd like to do is tell them that we'll be coming in this afternoon. I know the judge who will be presiding then. He's a good man and will listen to what we have to say regarding his releasing you."

"My God. I can't believe I'm hearing all this," I said. Then I thought, *It's my punishment. I swear it is.* Suddenly I felt a sense of relief. Indeed, this was my punishment. *So I must do whatever I must. Go through whatever God has planned for me. Perhaps this is the answer to my prayers.*

I said quietly to Mr. Rothschild, "All right. So what must I do?"

"Go home," he said. "Change into your clerical garb. I'll telephone the assistant DA and tell him we're coming in, and then I'll pick you up in about a half hour."

I only nodded. Then I got out of my chair. He rose as well and led me to his front door. "You'll be all right, Iggy. I've talked with the DA. I'm pretty certain he won't object to your being released. And once you've been arraigned, we can get to the bottom of this business and find out what's really bothering them."

Again I nodded and then left.

I hardly remembered the short drive back to St. Ann's. I only remembered thinking that I was involved in a terrible mess. It was of my making but also of God's. *I should not be here,* I thought. *I should be dead. Sister Mary should be alive and well, maybe even a bit chastised over what she had wrought with her adamant refusal to hear the word* damn.

But her death also was an accident. Even worse, a mistake. Made by God. Our Lord Jesus taught us to love one another. Even the sinners. That's the God I knew. But the Old Testament God of wrath appeared to be at work here. Was it the same God? What was I thinking? Could the God who created the world and everything in it, the God we all believed to be perfect, infallible, have made a mistake and missed his target?

Chapter 12

✝

I had first visited the Bronx County Court House early after my arrival at Saint Ann's for the purpose of obtaining a New York State driver's license. I had my Pennsylvania license, so it was mostly a formality. I had to take a brief verbal examination administered by a very friendly Department of Motor Vehicles officer. Then I stood in line until a rather dour but courteous woman gave me a temporary license. A few weeks later, my permanent license arrived in the mail.

Today was rather different. When obtaining my license, I had not taken notice of the court house building's massive architecture. I had entered a side entrance to reach the Department of Motor Vehicles area, which was removed from the court facilities. Now Mr. Rothschild escorted me through the main entrance of the building and into a very ornate marble interior with huge arches and vaulted elevator lobbies with bronze doors. The building had been erected, Mr. Rothschild told me, in the 1930s, during the Great Depression. I didn't know if the intent of the architecture was to intimidate prospective defendants, but if it was, it worked on me.

Mr. Rothschild ushered me onto an elevator, and we ascended several floors. The doors opened onto a small reception area. We approached the receptionist, and Mr. Rothschild greeted her.

"Hello, Judy. We're here to see Mr. Waterman."

"He's expecting you," she said as she picked up her phone. She dialed an extension and announced our arrival. "Go right on in," she said. She gave me a slight once-over, undoubtedly noticing my clerical outfit, but her expression remained neutral.

I guessed this was routine for her. For me it was nerve-racking. My heart must have been beating at twice its normal rate. I began to wonder if I was going to have a heart attack right on the spot. Mr. Rothschild took me by the elbow and led me through a network of halls and offices until we arrived at a door with a nameplate that read Assistant District Attorney Daniel Waterman. Above the nameplate was a window. Mr. Waterman saw us approaching, rose from his chair, came around his desk, and opened the door.

"Hello, Jacob," he said.

"Hello, Dan," Mr. Rothschild replied. "I'd like to introduce to you Father Ignatius Costello."

Mr. Waterman surprised me by reaching out to shake my hand. "Hello, Father. Thanks for coming in."

He was in his fifties, I guessed, with dark salt-and-pepper hair and a rather handsome chiseled face. He looked at me over reading glasses, which he wore near the end of his nose.

"You're welcome," I replied. This man was about to have me arraigned on a charge of murder, and here we were exchanging pleasantries as though we were in a restaurant. I couldn't believe it. It was as though I was in the middle of some kind of farcical comedy.

"I've given your concern about publicity over the arraignment some thought, Jacob," Mr. Waterman said as he turned to Mr. Rothschild. "I've decided to have Helen bring Father Costello down and do the honors. If I were to do it, a lot of eyebrows might be raised."

"That makes sense," Mr. Rothschild said.

"I've also instructed the officer who will be bringing you to the courtroom to not handcuff you," Mr. Waterman said to me. "Normally, defendants in this kind of case are handcuffed. But Mr. Rothschild has assured me that will not be necessary in your case. I trust that he is correct?"

"Yes, sir. Thank you."

"All right." He picked up his phone and dialed someone. "We're ready." That was all he said. Soon a uniformed policeman entered the office with a young woman. "This is officer Bates. He'll be escorting you to the courtroom. And this is Ms. Wainwright, who will be handling the prosecution side of the arraignment."

Officer Bates was a rather large man. He was very muscular with arms that seemed to nearly burst his dark blue uniform shirt. His blond hair was cropped short. His clean-shaven face and dark eyes remained blank as he looked at me. No smile. No greeting. He just stood there with his right hand resting on his pistol.

Ms. Wainwright was quite tall, almost my height, and very slender. She had bright blue eyes and dark hair down to the shoulders of her tailored business suit. She smiled at me and also extended her hand.

"Hello, Father," she said. "I'll be handling the prosecution side of your case. I believe you understand that this is an arraignment during which I will represent the State of New York and present the charges against you."

"Yes, I understand," I said as I held her hand ever so briefly. "Mr. Rothschild has explained everything to me. But I also want you to understand that I completely and categorically deny that I have done anything wrong. I am totally nonplussed that you would think that I had anything to do with Sister Mary's death."

"Right," said Mr. Rothschild. "Let's leave it at that." He spoke rather sternly to me. He had instructed me to say nothing, but I hadn't been able to help myself. I was feeling overwhelmed by the entire process. He grabbed my arm rather firmly and said to Ms. Wainwright, "Let's get this over with, shall we?"

Ms. Wainwright led the way out of Mr. Waterman's office. Mr. Rothschild and I followed her. Officer Bates followed behind us. We took a different route this time, down a hall that led to another elevator that was much less elegant than the one we had ridden up. After we entered the elevator, Bates took up his position at the rear, ever vigilant with his hand on his pistol.

Does he really expect me to misbehave? I kept asking myself. I took no note of how many floors we descended, only that we soon exited the elevator into a room lined with chairs filled with men and women. Many were handcuffed to the arms of their chairs. Two uniformed officers stood on either side of a door over which a sign read Courtroom 4.

Ms. Wainwright ushered me to a chair near the door. "Have a seat," she said. She left through the courtroom door. Officer Bates positioned himself to our left, hand still on his pistol.

Mr. Rothschild sat to my left. "How are you doing?" he asked.

"I'm completely numb."

"Well, I have every expectation that this arraignment will be over soon."

I didn't respond. My gaze traveled around the room. Almost everyone was staring at me. How many times had they seen a priest awaiting arraignment? Or did they think I might be a chaplain? I had visited prisons from time to time in that capacity. They couldn't possibly suspect that I was here on a charge of second-degree murder. Could they?

Suddenly the door opened and another uniformed officer announced, "Ignatius Costello."

I almost jumped out of my skin. Mr. Rothschild took my

elbow, and we both rose. He led me into the courtroom and to a table behind which he indicated we should stand.

The officer who had called my name announced to the entire courtroom, "Docket number D8682. State of New York versus Ignatius Costello on the charge of second-degree murder."

"Okay, Ms. Wainwright, what's this all about?" the judge asked. He sat behind a raised rostrum that was paneled in dark wood. A small nameplate resting on his desk identified him as Justice Harold Cohen.

"Your Honor, the defendant is charged with second-degree murder in the death of Sister Mary Magdalene on the Van Cortland Park Golf Course."

"Is this the case of the nun who was struck by lightning?"

"Yes, Your Honor, but there's quite a bit more to the case."

"All right, Mr. Rothschild. How does the defendant plead?" The judge looked at me.

"Not guilty!" I practically shouted.

"Not guilty it is," Judge Cohen said. "What about bail?" he asked Ms. Wainwright.

"Your Honor, we recognize that Father Costello is not a hardened criminal. Nevertheless, we must ask for bail since this is a case of second-degree murder."

"How much did you have in mind?"

"We're willing to leave that up to you."

"That's very nice of you," Judge Cohen said almost sarcastically. "Mr. Rothschild, what do you have to say?"

"Your Honor, so far we have been unable to ascertain any credible evidence as to why the prosecution is wasting your time and ours on this matter. If they have anything, it is completely circumstantial and definitely not conclusive. Add to that the fact that Father Costello has absolutely no criminal record whatsoever, not even a parking ticket. He's a hard-working Roman Catholic priest who takes his duties seriously. It is inconceivable to me that the prosecution is taking this route, and it is inconceivable to me that Father Costello has been caught up in this mess."

"That's all very nice, Jacob. But as you know, you really need to save those remarks for your closing at trial. What do you have to say about bail?"

"I say let the man go on his personal recognizance."

"On a charge of second-degree murder?"

"Your Honor, this truly is an incredibly flimsy case. Add to that the fact of Father Costello's absolutely clean record. He's not a flight risk. He wants this matter cleared up and expects to attend to every call for his appearance to that end. I can personally vouch for his reliability. His church is behind him 100 percent. As a priest, he has taken a vow of poverty. He has absolutely no resources beyond what he needs for basic necessities. Forcing him to post bail means putting him behind bars for the duration of this mess. That makes no sense, with all due respect to Ms. Wainwright."

"Well, since Ms. Wainwright has left it up to me as to an appropriate amount of bail, I'll waive any bail and release Father Costello on his own recognizance. However, I'll want him to surrender his passport, and he needs to understand that he must not leave this jurisdiction. If he does, he'll be remanded. Do I make myself clear, Father Costello?"

"Yes, sir. Only, I have no passport. I've never traveled outside of the United States."

"No passport?"

"No, Your Honor."

"Can we verify that, Ms. Wainwright?"

"I'm sure we can. But it could take a few days. The wheels of bureaucracy turn rather slowly at the State Department."

"Your Honor, if I may," said Mr. Rothschild. "Would it help

if we agreed to bail of $1,000 to be refunded once the passport question has been cleared up?"

"You're suggesting Father Costello post $1,000 bail for the few days it may take to verify his lack of a passport? That seems a bit unusual."

"Yes, sir. It is. But this also is an extremely unusual case."

I leaned over to Mr. Rothschild and whispered, "I don't have $1,000, and there's no way I can raise it."

"I know," he whispered back. "Don't worry. It can be raised. Let me handle this."

I stayed silent.

"I'll tell you what," Judge Cohen said. "I'm going to wave any need for bail at this time. You've convinced me, Jacob. But let it be understood that the conditions I noted must be adhered to. Is that clear?" He looked at me.

"Yes, sir. Thank you. I'll abide by every condition."

"You do that. Next case!"

Chapter 13

✝

"While you were in court, I was at a meeting with the archbishop," Father Clancy greeted me at the entrance to the rectory. "You need to come into my office," he added and turned in that direction.

I followed.

"Close the door behind you and sit down." He pointed to the chair in front of his desk, walked around to his own, and sat.

I had just been arraigned on a charge of second-degree murder, and now it appeared that the archbishop was involved?

Father Clancy had what I could only describe as a concerned expression on his face. "Before I fill you in on my visit downtown, please let me know what went on in court."

I nearly shouted, "I have been arraigned on a charge of second-degree murder!" I was feeling utterly incredulous and overwhelmed. What more punishment did God have in store for me?

"What did Jacob have to say?"

"He had told me this was going to happen and to try not to worry. He said now that I have been arraigned, the police have to show us everything they have. He told me to go back to my duties and let the process unfold. But how can I not worry? I'm beginning to feel like an Old Testament Job! I have to say, I don't see how I can stop worrying!"

"I can't even begin to know how you must be feeling," Father Clancy said. "But he is right. You have to trust that, in the end, the process will reveal the truth to us all. Now let me tell you about my trip to the archdiocese. Archbishop Mellon saw the *Daily News* article. He is concerned, of course, over what implications your situation might have for the church. He mentioned to me that with all the sex scandals we have had, the last thing we need is a priest murdering a nun over a missed putt on the golf course. That's basically how he put it."

"But I did not murder her! Doesn't he know that?"

"All he knew was what he read in the paper. I assured him that I believed in your complete innocence. He asked me how I knew that."

"Did you tell him what I told you?"

"I did not. For one thing, that was told to me in confession. For another, I feel if your explanation ever comes out, a whole can of worms will be opened. The holy church could never endorse such a story."

I didn't like that he called my explanation a story. But I asked, "Well then, what did you tell him?"

"Basically that I knew you well, that it was inconceivable to me that you had done anything wrong, that Jacob—who he knows—was handling it, and that ultimately, the evidence will prevail in your favor."

"Was he satisfied?"

"Let's just say he trusted that I would make certain that no smear would come upon the church as a result of your predicament."

"My predicament."

"Yes. That's how he put it."

"That doesn't sound very reassuring."

"Well, at least for now it's in our hands and he is not going to interfere, though he did instruct me to keep him posted."

"I suppose I should tell Mr. Rothschild."

"Yes. You probably should. Though the archbishop's interest is strictly a church matter at this point. I don't see how it could have any bearing on your legal situation."

"A church matter!" I exclaimed rather stridently.

"Look, Iggy. I cannot begin to imagine the turmoil you must be experiencing. It is literally an unbelievable turn of events that has come upon you. I understand that. But I suggest you leave any interest the archbishop may have in this entirely up to me. Let me handle any inquiries he may make. In fact, I suggest that you try to leave everything up to the experts. Let Jacob guide you going forward. And I will see that the church hierarchy stays out of it as best I can. The only thing they are aware of at the moment is the *Daily News* article. Let's just leave it there for now. Meantime, I do have one suggestion. It's entirely up to you to decide, but I have been thinking you might want to see a counselor, perhaps a psychologist or psychiatrist?"

Oh boy! I stayed silent for a spell, staring at Father Clancy with what must have been a dumfounded expression on my face, trying to process everything. Having to engage a lawyer, go to court, and be arraigned for murder wasn't enough. Now I should see a psychiatrist! I was beginning to feel more and more like Old Testament Job. What more Job-like trials could God have in store for me?

"See a psychiatrist?"

"Some kind of professional counselor who could help you get a sense of rest or release from everything."

"I can't imagine it. I mean, it couldn't be a priest or any

Catholic. Could it? I would have to tell them everything, including about the misaimed lightning!"

"An interesting way to put it ... And, yes, I would imagine that you would have to tell such a person everything, including your description of what happened on the ninth hole."

My description! So he really thought "my description" was, in the last analysis, daft. But I knew what happened! I was there. I swore, a dark cloud suddenly appeared, lightning struck, and I heard that thunderous voice.

"Do you have anyone in mind?" I asked.

"There are plenty of resources of this kind within the church, and I know several of them. But I agree that you probably should seek assistance from someone not particularly versed in the faith, if you get my drift, someone who can be completely objective, including regarding matters of religion, so that they can look at your situation with a completely open mind."

"But who would I go to? I don't know anybody in or out of the church."

"And I don't have an answer for you either ... You know? It's just coming to me. Why not ask Jacob? He might know just the person you should talk to."

Chapter 14

✝

D r. June Noble lived down the street from St. Ann's in a high-rise just off Riverdale Avenue on Hawthorne Lane. According to Jacob, she had had training in Jungian psychology.

We were exposed to Jung's concepts in seminary. After being born and living most of his life in Switzerland, Carl Jung had died in the middle of the twentieth century.

I had not thought much about Jung and his theories since leaving seminary, but Mr. Rothschild suggested I see Ms. Noble because he thought a Jungian psychologist might be receptive to my current mental turmoil. While she was not a Roman Catholic or, for all he knew, a member of any church, he thought she might be sympathetic to, even interested in, my story.

Mr. Rothschild told me that he had explained to her that I was a priest and that he had suggested I consult with her regarding a predicament I was in. He had not told her anything else. He suggested that I wear my uniform, as he put it.

She greeted me at the door, shook my hand, and led me out of an entrance foyer, through a living room, past a dining room and kitchen on the right, and into an office on the left, directly opposite the kitchen. This office had probably been intended to be a bedroom. It had a single fairly large window that looked out onto a courtyard that was surrounded by similar buildings. We were on the fourth floor. Her furnishings were somewhat spartan and very contemporary. The paintings on the walls were mostly abstract and somewhat of a mystery to me.

Ms. Noble was rather petite, not topping much more than five feet, and very slender with black hair done up in a bun, deep brown eyes, and a slight tan. She was probably in her mid thirties, though I was never very good at guessing people's age. She wore dark brown slacks and a light green blouse buttoned to the top. I couldn't help but think that she was very cute.

"Welcome to my humble abode," she said. "Have a seat." She pointed to a chair opposite her desk, which she sat behind. I had wondered if there might be a couch upon which I would recline. But there was no couch in the office.

"Mr. Rothschild has explained to me that you are having to deal with a rather amazing dilemma. But before we get to that, I think it would be helpful if you could tell me a bit about yourself in general."

"You mean my background, family?"

"Yes."

I filled her in on everything I had told Mr. Rothschild when we first met. She, too, raised her eyebrows considerably when I told her that I was the youngest of fifteen children. I explained how I had come to be a priest and how good an experience it had proven to be until the last several days.

"So the reason you are here," she said, "involves an experience that took place recently, within the last few days."

"Yes," I replied.

"Can you describe it to me?"

"I honestly don't know. I mean, that's why I am here, but it is so weird and confusing that I don't know how to go about telling it." Then I noticed a copy of the *New York Times* sitting on her desk. "Do you read the *Daily News*?" I asked.

"No, not very often."

"Did you by any chance see an article in it about a nun who was killed by lightning on the Van Cortland Park Golf Course a week ago? And a priest who was injured?"

"Sorry. No ... I didn't."

"Well, I am that priest. And I have been arraigned for murdering that nun! Which I did not do!"

"When you say 'arraigned,' you mean in a court of law?"

"Yes. At the Bronx County Courthouse."

"And is Mr. Rothschild representing you? Is that why he called me?"

"Yes. But he didn't call because I have been arraigned. He called because of the reason I am not guilty."

"And the reason would be ...?"

"I am going to come straight out with it. I've been holding it in for so long. It's something I can't say in court. Both Mr. Rothschild and my superior, Father Clancy, have said I mustn't repeat it to anyone. But that's why I am here, I guess."

"All right then. Let me have it."

"You're going to think I'm crazy. Literally."

"Why don't you let me be the judge of that?"

I suddenly bolted out of my chair. She pushed her chair back, perhaps concerned that I might do something wrong. But I turned around and started pacing back and forth.

"This is so hard," I said. "I can't sit still." I started breathing heavily, as if trying to catch my breath.

"Ignatius, are you all right? Try to relax. Here, take a sip of water."

There was a carafe and two glasses on her desk. She poured some water into one and handed it to me. I stopped pacing and took a sip. It helped a bit.

"I cannot imagine what you are trying to relate to me, Ignatius—can I call you that?"

"Most friends call me Iggy. You might as well call me that. Only my mother calls me Ignatius." I was speaking to the entrance to her office.

"All right then, Iggy. I am beginning to wonder if it was wise for you to come here. Let me assure you that if you are unable to relate to me what has you so concerned, it is perfectly fine. Not everyone can endure counseling. Just say the word and I assure you that there will be no hard feelings. And you can leave."

I stopped pacing and stood with my back to her. I had no idea how long the silence lasted. Finally, I said, "No. I have no place else to go." I turned, looked into her face, went to the chair, and sat down.

"Surely you have resources within the church to whom you can turn."

"Not in this case."

"Can you tell me why not?"

After a long pause, I said in a near whisper, "Because what happened on the ninth hole of the Van Cortland Park Golf Course violates the most important truth of all Judeo-Christian, and even Muslim, dogma."

She studied my face for some time. Then she gently asked, "Can you tell me what the most important truth of all Judeo-Christian and Muslim dogma is?"

"That the Lord God Almighty is perfect, infallible."

Once again she remained silent. Her expression was one of interest, as though she was truly curious and would be nonjudgmental. I had the impression that she wanted me to understand that no matter what I may have experienced, it would be okay in her eyes. Her interested, even sympathetic, eyes made me feel I was glad I had come to her.

"Well," she finally said, "while we may believe that God is perfect, we certainly know that this planet of ours and all the residents on it can at times be anything but. And now you seem to be suggesting to me that your experience demonstrated to you that God is not perfect. Do I understand you correctly?"

"Yes. That was my experience on the golf course."

"On the other hand, your experience might ultimately indicate some other explanation entirely. So why don't you tell me about it and then let us both consider what explanation there might be."

"I first have to say that the people I have told this to have said I should not repeat it to anyone else for fear that they will think I have gone daft or, in one case, that I am a sinner not even worthy of receiving absolution."

"Who have you told?"

"Only Mr. Rothschild and my boss, Father Clancy. And a priest in New Jersey, where I went to confess. He's the one who practically yelled at me that I should get down on my knees and pray to the Lord for forgiveness for telling such lies. Those were his words."

"How did Mr. Rothschild and Father Clancy react to your explanation?"

"Mr. Rothschild told me not to tell anyone else. He said it would only raise questions we would rather not deal with at this time. Father Clancy said he believed that I believed my story but that others probably would say I was daft."

"Father Clancy sounds like a level-headed man. But we do need to deal with your personal concerns, not a lawyer's or Father Clancy's. So I suggest you fill me in."

"Okay. It's like this: I enjoy the game of golf and am pretty good at it. So last Saturday, I had the day off. I couldn't find anyone to play a round with me until one of my friends suggested I ask one of the nuns who teaches at the school next to St. Ann's. I had never met the woman and was reluctant to ask a nun to play golf with me. I mean, how good could she be? But it turned out that she was very good at the game." I paused.

"And?" Ms. Noble said.

"And I had a hard time keeping up with her." I went on to describe everything I had told Mr. Rothschild, Father Clancy, and that New Jersey priest, ending with a description of the clouds gathering, the lightning striking and killing Sister Mary, and God saying out of the cloud, "Damn, I missed again!"

"You actually heard those words." It was a statement not a question.

"Yes."

"There's no doubt in your mind that you heard God declaring that he had 'missed again?'"

"I know it sounds like I've lost my mind, and I sometimes wonder if I have. But that really happened."

"I have to confess to you that I have never heard anything like this before. But no matter how incredulous it may seem at the moment, I have to ask, did you see the lightning strike?"

"Not really. But there's no doubt lightning struck. It killed Sister Mary, and I was also scorched to some extent. My clothes were a mess. You could even smell the burnt fabric."

"What did you do after the strike?

"This is where it gets foggy. I really don't know what I did. I only know that I somehow got to my car and drove back to St. Ann's. The next time I was at all aware of anything was when I woke up in the hospital."

"How did you get to the hospital?"

"Father Clancy drove me there. And that's where the police questioned me."

"The police!"

"Yes." I reviewed with her everything that had happened,

including meeting Mr. Rothschild, the article in the *New York Daily News*, the archbishop's getting involved, and my being arraigned on a charge of second-degree murder thanks to Sister Mary having been hit on the head and my bent putter lying on the green.

By now, her large brown eyes were as round as saucers. She didn't say a word, just stared at me. I could only stare back and wonder what was going to happen next. Would she throw me out? Or …?

Chapter 15

✝

D r. Noble turned her chair toward the wall on her left. Her elbows were propped on arms of the chair, and her hands were clasped just below her chin. Her eyes were nearly closed. Absolute silence fell over the room.

After what felt like hours, she turned back in my direction. "I have been in my practice for a while, Iggy, and I can confidently tell you that this is one of the most troubling situations I have ever heard. While I have had a fair amount of experience delving into people's problems and usually coming to understand what they must be going through mentally, in your case I can only imagine what you must be going through.

"What is occurring to me, though, is that you have two separate yet connected issues that we need to sort out. One, of course, is the religious conundrum. The second is how your perception of what happened on that golf course can be understood in a fashion that would satisfy the authorities. The latter, of course, is mainly what Mr. Rothschild will help you with. But I would like to see if you and I can in some manner sort out your religious experience because, that is what I believe you have had. Whether or not it is anything that could ever be explained satisfactorily to others remains to be seen. Does this make sense to you?"

"Yes."

"All right then. First, I think I should explain to you where I am coming from. I believe you know that I was trained as a Jungian psychotherapist."

"Yes, Mr. Rothschild told me. That was why he thought you might be able to help me."

"Then that suggests to me that he is not totally unconvinced of the possibility of your explanation of what happened on that golf course, no matter how it may defy scientific theories. And no matter how unwise he might think it would be to tell it to the authorities."

I nodded at her.

She continued, "Carl Jung died in 1961, as you probably know, and psychiatry has come a long way since then, to say nothing of knowledge of how the brain functions. Today psychiatrists tend to solve mental issues with a pill after diagnosing a person's issues rather than through psychoanalysis. And in many instances, this has shown progress in the area of mental disease. Nevertheless, Jung identified certain issues in the human experience that appear to be scientifically inexplicable. Are you aware of these issues?"

I was beginning to relax. "Only in very general terms. We studied Jung in seminary. But I didn't take it all in. I do recall that he was said to have had a sort of mystical side to him."

"I have to wonder if he would have called it mystical. But he certainly did identify numerous human experiences that defied any physical explanation."

"Such as?"

"Such as, for one, what he called synchronicity. Are you aware of what that is?"

"I know the term but don't really remember what it is."

"Well, it involves experiences we humans have that appear to be amazing coincidences but that Jung believed were the evidence of the functioning of a higher power."

"God," I said.

"He didn't call it God. You might, but he called it an acausal connecting principle. Would you like me to describe to you an actual experience?"

"Yes, please." This was getting interesting. Maybe my experience, as horrible as it was, wasn't beyond the realm of possibility.

"All right. This is an actual experience had by a hospital nurse. She was at home and running a bit late for work at the hospital. She dashed out her door and into her newly purchased car. It wouldn't start. In the few weeks she'd had this car, she had never had this problem. She tried several more times. No good. She called AAA. They said it would be forty-five minutes before they got to her. She was getting very frustrated. She tried her car again. No luck. She was about to call the hospital when her phone rang. It was her brother. There was a serious family problem that needed her attention. The situation was resolved, and she hung up. She tried her car again, and it started. And it never failed her again."

"So I guess the suggestion is that something kept her car from starting until her brother was able to reach her?"

"That would be the suggestion."

"Your acausal connecting principle."

"Not mine. Jung's."

"What does acausal mean, anyway?"

"In Jung's synchronicity, it means the existence of a principle—or one might call it a power—that operates outside of normal scientific cause-and-effect rules. Some describe it as universal. And some say that during the latter part of the twentieth century, after Jung's death, certain inexplicable discoveries in quantum physics suggest the universe is conscious. And that his synchronicity points in that direction."

"Conscious! In other words, God?"

"It's only theory, Iggy. And not supported by many strictly empirical, down-to-earth scientists, which is most of the scientific community. If they can't see clear physical cause-and-effect evidence, it can't be correct."

"I've never thought of myself as a particularly deep thinker," I said, "but this gives me some sense of wonderment. You're making me look at my situation with some sense of … I don't know what. Maybe hope? But then I have to ask the obvious question."

"What's that?"

"Assuming this principle, or power, exists, does it ever make mistakes? And if it does make mistakes, does it ever say so? Verbally? To us?"

She thought for a moment or two and then said, "I did not mean, with this description, to confirm or deny the truth or falsity of these theories. Only to give you a sense of the existence of the possibility that something beyond what we can see with our five physical senses may be real. With that understanding, you might be able to put your concerns about your own possible 'daftness,' as you put it, to rest."

She continued, "As to the question of mistakes, I can only say that we humans constantly make note of so-called acts of God such as tornadoes in one breath and in another thank God for being spared while our neighbor was not. Something went wrong there.

"And regarding verbal communication, I am sure that you, in your practice as a Roman Catholic priest—and I know many thousands of others—have literally 'heard' answers to their prayers and declared that to be the case. What the source of that 'voice' might be is, of course, open to question. But in your case, being who you are and considering your faith, I can only think of one answer."

She looked across her desk with a slight smile on her face. Her expression suggested compassion.

"You're not daft, Iggy. Something very real happened out on that golf course. Generally speaking, I suggest to my patients that until they get a complete and satisfactory answer to their issues, whatever those may be, they should stay silent and not try to reason with others about it. That will only get other minds working and confusing the issue. You know the expression, 'Be still and know that I am God?'"

"Yes. From Psalms."

"Well, I suggest you follow that course going forward. Take Mr. Rothschild's instruction and Father Clancy's advice, but stay silent until you find your peace."

Chapter 16

✝

When I returned to St. Ann's, I went directly to Father Clancy's office to report to him on my session with Dr. Noble. He agreed that her advice was good.

But then the next day the press got hold of the story. It was on all the major TV channels and in all the papers, including the *New York Post* and *New York Times*. The *Times* played it very straight, but the *New York Post*, as usual, played it to the hilt.

No matter how you looked at it, it was spectacular news. A priest had been accused of murdering a nun on the ninth hole of the Van Cortland Park Golf Course because he had missed his putt.

How was I going to be still? I was frantic with panic. Father Clancy could do nothing to calm me down. The archbishop called him back downtown. It was time for the church to batten down the hatches and pull in its horns, he told Father Clancy. He was refusing to answer any questions from the press, other than releasing a statement that said the church had no knowledge of the facts of the case and was leaving it up to the authorities to properly resolve any question regarding what may or may not have happened on that golf course.

To make things worse, the press knew my name and that I was a priest at St. Ann's. They were parked all over Riverdale Avenue trying to get a glimpse of me. When Father Clancy returned from downtown, he told me to stay indoors.

"Do not, under any circumstances, go outdoors without Jacob's instruction," he said.

He told me that the archbishop was leaving it in our hands as to how to proceed. He had complete faith in Jacob's capabilities.

To make matters even worse, our parishioners were wondering what to do. We had somewhat of a siege mentality. Finally, after conferring on the phone with Mr. Rothschild, Father Clancy stepped onto the front steps of the church and addressed the several reporters who were milling around. He informed them that he would answer no questions but that they should know that he and the church knew that I was innocent and that the reporters should turn their attention to the Bronx County Courthouse. He asked them to please be considerate of our parishioners and allow us to conduct our affairs. He turned his back on all the questions shouted at him and returned inside, closing the door, which was normally kept open, behind him.

He then came upstairs and found me sitting on the edge of my bed, staring into space. I was almost catatonic.

"Iggy. I can only imagine that any words I might have for you at this moment would seem hollow. But I ask you to have faith in the process. And to take Dr. Noble's advice to heart. Try to indeed be silent and trust in God. You are innocent of these charges, and the truth will ultimately come out."

"But I am not innocent," I said.

"What do you mean?" He was taken aback.

"I didn't kill Sister Mary directly, but I did indirectly cause her death," I said. I continued to stare into space. Then, speaking almost in a whisper, I added, "And I feel like Job in the Bible. But not like God is testing me. No … this is my punishment."

Father Clancy was silent for a while. Then he said, "But we

know that the book of Job is a fable. An allegory. Not an actual historical story. We do not believe in a vengeful God. Rather the loving, forgiving God of our Lord Jesus."

"Yes, I know. But—"

He interrupted me, "Furthermore, Iggy, Jacob assures me that the evidence that has been shown to him by the detectives is incredibly slim and based on their assumption that you, in some inexplicable way that they thus far have not been able to demonstrate, contrived the situation to cover your tracks."

"But that's my point. Of course they can't demonstrate it. It was caused by God. The lightning wasn't your normal so-called act of God. It was literally an act of God."

Father Clancy stayed quiet. Then he gently sat down next to me on the bed, which creaked with his additional weight. He leaned his elbows on his knees and stared ahead at the same wall I was looking at.

"All right. I now have to say something to you. I understand that you had a dreadful experience on that golf course and that you have a picture in your head of what happened. I am not going to attempt to disabuse you of that picture. It is undoubtedly embedded in your consciousness so deeply that there is no removing it with a few words coming from me. It might even be impossible to remove even with the help of an experienced counselor like Dr. Noble.

"And I'll go so far as to say that it might have actually happened. Despite my misgivings and that of the church, who am I or we to say? But, Iggy, you have to let it go. At least for now. Get this overriding sense of guilt that you are expressing out of your head. Let the facts demonstrated by the evidence do their job. Don't fight it. Then, once you have been exonerated, perhaps you can come to grips with your explanation. But don't let it get in the way of Jacob doing his job. Can you do that?"

I continued staring into the distance.

"What do you say, Iggy? Can you set this sense of guilt aside? At least for the duration of this ordeal that you are facing?"

"I don't know. I can try. But I don't even see how I can continue being a priest. I am so overcome."

"Okay. I do believe it would be good for you if you could perform your normal duties here. But I can well understand your reluctance to try, considering the mental stress you are feeling. It's late in the day now. Why don't you try to get some rest? Come on down at dinnertime and have a meal. I'll fill everyone else in, ask people not to burden you with a bunch of questions and to trust that we know what we are doing, and inform them of the need to stay silent while we await the logic of events.

"Then let's see what tomorrow brings. For all we know, Jacob may call with the news that the authorities have figured out that they have it wrong and are dropping the charges."

I did manage to get back into the swing of things at the church as the days went by with no notice from the authorities.

Everyone tried to make it seem as though nothing was amiss. The staff were very kind, and the parishioners acted as normally as they could, though I did hear a few whispers, especially during the first few days after the press had shown up. They were no longer out front. Other more interesting stories were getting their attention.

Then about two weeks later, Mr. Rothschild phoned.

The police did not drop the charges. A date for the trial had been set: two weeks hence.

Chapter 17

My trial was convened in courtroom 8 at the Bronx County Courthouse. This courtroom was quite a bit larger than the one in which I had been arraigned. Mr. Rothschild and I sat at a table on the left side of the courtroom, facing the dais upon which Judge Marion Johnson sat. We were positioned in front of a railing that separated us from where the public sat. Many members of the press were in attendance, but fortunately no cameras were allowed. Father Clancy sat just behind us. He had told me that he would be there but that Jimmy and the rest of the staff had to remain at St. Ann's for obvious reasons. To our right, Mr. Waterman sat along with two assistants.

Judge Johnson asked Mr. Waterman if he was ready.

"We are, Your Honor," he responded.

After a brief statement to the jury, Mr. Waterman called his first witness, Detective Folger, to the witness chair. Folger described the "scene" found by the police upon their arrival at the ninth hole and how they had found the scorched body of Sister Mary.

"What else?" asked Mr. Waterman.

"They found a bent golf club, a putter, near her body."

"Anything else?"

"Yes. The area around the body had been disturbed. A number of rocks were strewn about on the green."

"What did you surmise from what you found?"

"Initially we thought Sister Mary must have been stuck by lightning. But later evidence caused us to inquire further."

"Evidence such as …?"

"We discovered that the putter was not Sister Mary's. Hers was in her golf bag and undamaged. So we figured someone else must have been playing with her and that the bent putter belonged to that person. Also, later investigation told us that there had been no storm in the area at the time of her death. In fact, it had been clear and cloudless all day."

"How did you find that out?"

"We checked with various meteorological sources we have. No radar or even satellites had shown any kind of storm."

"All right then. Please describe how you proceeded once you had secured the ninth hole."

"We learned that a priest had turned himself in at the hospital and that he was semiconscious and his clothing was scorched."

Suddenly, Mr. Rothschild stood and called out, "Objection! There is no evidence," he said, "that the defendant turned himself in. There was and has been no confession on his part, and Detective Folger is fully aware of that fact."

The judge sustained Mr. Rothschild's objection and told the jury to ignore that phraseology.

"How did you find out that the defendant was in the hospital?" Mr. Waterman asked.

"We had been phoned by the defendant's superior that he was being brought to the hospital and a patrolman who was aware of the incident at Van Cortland was in the hospital and saw the defendant being brought in."

"By the defendant, you mean Father Costello."

"Yes."

"Please explain further, Detective?"

"When I arrived at the hospital, he was still under the influence of a sedative and was unable to tell me anything. But I did see that his clothing was scorched, and I could even detect an odor of something burnt. I was unable to question him. So we made arrangements for me to meet with him as soon as he was able."

The questioning went on like this for some time as Folger described everything that transpired after that.

Mr. Rothschild started his cross examination of Folger: "How do you explain the scorched clothing on Father Costello that you observed in the hospital?"

"I have no explanation other than to say that we surmised some kind of process involving heat had occurred on that green."

"Have you determined what that process might have been?"

"No. Not for certain. A number of scenarios have occurred to us. But we can't prove anything conclusively."

"What sort of scenario might have occurred to you?"

"Well, it had to be some kind of attempt made to cover up the fact that the nun had been struck on the head with the bent putter."

"So you all are going with the theory that Sister Mary was struck on the head by the bent putter that belonged to the defendant. Do I have that right?"

"Yes."

"And he struck her on the head because?"

"He had missed his putt."

I began to wonder if Mr. Rothschild was defending me or prosecuting me. But he had told me that I needed to trust him and that he knew what he was doing in his questioning.

"You are saying that in a fit of pique, after missing a putt in a game of golf, the defendant struck his opponent, a nun, on the head."

"Yes, that is the reason for the charge against him."

"Please tell us what proof you have of this theory."

"We found his bent putter next to Sister Mary, and she was struck on the head with a wound that could have been caused by the putter."

"Could have been."

"Yes."

"But no conclusive proof. No blood on the putter? No other possible cause of the wound?"

"No."

"Aren't you being a little disingenuous here, Detective?"

"Objection!" shouted Mr. Waterman. "The witness is merely stating what he knows."

"Why don't you rephrase, Counsel?" said the judge.

"All right, Detective. Let me put it more directly. Weren't there a number of rocks scattered about the green by some, to you, inexplicable force, many of which had sharp edges that could also explain the wound on her head?"

"Yes, theoretically. But there was no forensic evidence to indicate that."

"What forensic evidence would prove it?"

"There was no trace of blood on any of the rocks we examined."

"Ah," said Mr. Rothschild, "no blood on any of the rocks you examined. Did you examine all the rocks?"

"All that were on the green, yes."

"But there were others all around the green as well. Isn't that correct?"

"Well, yes."

"Did you examine them as well?"

"No, only those in the vicinity of the scene."

"Hmm. Interesting. How about the putter?"

"What about it"

"Did you examine it as well?"

"Yes, of course."

"And how much blood did you find on it?"

"Uh. None."

"Thank you, Detective. That will be all for now." Mr. Rothschild returned to our table and sat down.

Next Mr. Waterman had the medical examiner come to the stand. She was middle-aged, I guessed, maybe in her fifties. She couldn't have been much more than five feet tall and was rather plump. Her name was Harriet Dunham, and she was dressed in a flowery frock that belied her profession. Mr. Waterman had her describe her credentials and then asked her to review her findings.

"I found that Sister Mary had been struck on the head with a rather narrow instrument that could have been a golf putter. I also found that her entire body had been severely scorched by a very hot source, which I assumed at the time was lightning."

"Did you also examine the bent putter?" Mr. Waterman asked.

"Yes."

"And?"

"Its shank at the point of the bend fit the width of the wound."

"Did you visit the scene?"

"Yes. I was called there first."

"What did you see there?"

"I saw Sister Mary's body and that the green had been severely damaged, even burned, and that there were a number of rocks strewn about the green, which would not normally be found on a golf course green."

"Did you examine any of those rocks?"

"Yes, a few."

"And?"

"I found one or two that might match the wound on the body. But I have to say this was an afterthought. Seeing the putter next to the body made it the obvious cause of the wound, to me."

"What do you mean by 'afterthought'?"

"Well, as I said, the putter seemed very likely to me. It was only after the police told me that the question of whether a rock might have caused the wound was brought up that I took the possibility more seriously."

"Did you then examine the rocks more closely?"

"Detective Folger brought a few to me at the lab, and I did examine them. A couple came close to being possible causes of the wound."

"Came close? Not as close as the putter?"

"Well, that's hard to say."

"Hard to say? What do you mean? Are you suggesting the putter was more likely to have been the cause of the wound?"

"I haven't thought about it that way. I examined several rocks and the putter and found that if only one of them had been brought to me for examination, then each of them individually could have been the cause."

"So as far as you are concerned, the putter could easily have been the instrument of death."

"Yes. Along with the rocks, of course."

It seemed to me that Ms. Dunham was being very careful.

"Hmm. Interesting," said Mr. Waterman. "Did you examine the putter and the rocks for any evidence of blood?"

"Yes. I found no such evidence on either the putter or the rocks."

"How would you explain no trace of blood on the putter or, for that matter, the rocks if one of them had hit the victim? Isn't it very difficult, in fact almost impossible, to remove traces of human blood?"

"Yes. But assuming one of them was indeed the cause of death, then my only conclusion has to be that whatever the source of heat was, which was very intense, would possibly have destroyed any residue of blood."

"Thank you, Ms. Dunham."

Mr. Rothschild approached her with a smile. "Hello, Ms. Dunham."

"Hello, Mr. Rothschild." She responded with a smile. They clearly knew each other.

"I have only one question for you. When you examined the wound and the putter and found that the shank of the putter fit the width of the wound, do you mean that you were able to place the shank into the wound?"

"Yes."

"We have the putter here, as you know." He went over to the prosecution's table and picked up my putter. "As you can see, Ms. Dunham, this putter is rather severely bent at an angle."

"Yes, I know."

"What I am wondering is does this angle match the curvature of the wound?"

"I'm not sure what you mean."

"Well, I would think that if a person struck a putter such as this one over the head of a victim, the shank might well bend, of course. But wouldn't that bend conform to the shape of the victim's head?"

Ms. Dunham was silent for a second or two before answering. "That's an interesting question," she said. "I'm not certain that would have to be the case. I'm not an engineer and could not say with certainty how the shank would bend."

"Can you tell me if the detectives have examined that possibility, perhaps by experimenting with another putter?"

"No, I can't. I don't know."

"Thank you, Ms. Dunham."

Mr. Rothschild had explained to me that he already knew no experiment had been made thanks to discovery, but he wanted to bring it out in front of the jury.

Mr. Waterman called a few policemen who had witnessed the proceedings on the ninth hole, all of whom confirmed what Detective Folger had testified.

Now it was Mr. Rothschild's turn, but it was getting late in the day, so Judge Johnson asked him if we could put his presentation off until the next morning. He agreed. I was so concerned with what I had heard so far that, even with Mr. Rothschild's questioning, I felt doomed. What would tomorrow bring?

Chapter 18

✝

Father Clancy drove me back to St. Ann's. He remained rather silent. I wasn't sure what he was thinking. Hopefully, he was still on my side. He suggested that I get a bite to eat and try to get a good night's sleep. I had no appetite, so I nibbled on a few morsels and went to my room. I spent most of the night staring at the ceiling.

At eight o'clock the next morning, the bailiff called the courtroom to order. Judge Johnson came in, went to her dais, and asked Mr. Rothschild to proceed.

He addressed the jury, briefly explaining that the prosecution's evidence was entirely circumstantial. There had been no direct evidence produced that showed anyone's guilt, let alone mine, in the death of Sister Mary. He then said he would be calling several witnesses who would demonstrate without a doubt that the death of Sister Mary was caused by an act of God and not by any human intervention.

I knew he was correct about an act of God, but I was also pretty sure he would not have me testify to that effect.

"I call Dr. Harold Ingersoll to the stand."

There was a bit of a stir as Dr. Ingersoll, who I had not met but knew about, proceeded down the aisle and through the gate at the railing and took a seat in the witness box. The bailiff swore him in.

Mr. Rothschild greeted him. "Hello, Dr. Ingersoll. Can you please describe to us your credentials?"

"Yes, sure," he said. He was a tall man with gray hair falling slightly over his ears but balding on top. He was slender and had rather penetrating blue eyes. Very distinguished, even professorial looking. "I am a physicist and meteorologist and teach both at Columbia University. I have a PhD in both subjects."

"How long have you been studying and teaching physics and meteorology?"

"Well, I started in physics while in college about thirty years ago. Became interested in meteorology while in grad school. So it has been quite a while. I have been teaching, first at UCLA until about ten years ago and at Columbia since then. I am also a visiting lecturer at a number of institutions, and I consult with the United States Meteorological Service fairly frequently."

"Thank you. To what extent are you familiar with the case being tried in this courtroom?"

"I'm not particularly familiar with the case as it has been presented here. But I am familiar with the situation that occurred at Van Cortland Park."

"In what way?"

"You asked me to have a look at the scene, which I did."

"When was this, and what did you observe?"

"It was the day after the incident. The police still were there. The green was in absolute shambles. Much of the ground had been scorched. There was one spot that was dreadful, and you told me it was where the victim had been found. Also, there were all kinds of rocks scattered all over the green."

"Did you come to any conclusion as to what might have caused this?"

"Yes. My immediate conclusion was that there had been a particularly violent lightning strike."

"Do you consider yourself an expert regarding lightning?"

"Well, I have done a lot of research on the subject."

"Which you would say makes your conclusion very reliable?"

"I am not one to toot my own horn, so to speak, but yes, I am quite knowledgeable on the subject."

"You said it was a particularly violent strike. What did you mean by that?"

"I don't know if you are aware of it or not, but there are many thousands of lightning strikes a day on this globe of ours. It's a constant phenomenon going on all the time. There is no way one can examine all the strikes that take place, but I have studied quite a few, and I have never seen one that manifested in quite this way. Most of the time, lightning strikes in one spot. But every now and then, several strikes take place all at what seems to be the same time. Our senses are too slow to distinguish the space between strikes. In this case, I'd say the lightning struck many times on the green, almost as though it was searching for its target. Hence a lot of destruction."

My head popped up at that. Was Mr. Rothschild going to bring in the "religious thing" after all?

"And a lot of heat?"

"A tremendous amount of heat. Lightning can produce upwards of 54,000 degrees Fahrenheit of heat. Hotter than the surface of the sun."

"Surface of the sun!"

"Yes. Of course, it only lasts for a split second. But still, it can cause a lot of destruction, especially where, as in this case, it seems to have struck a wide area."

Suddenly Mr. Waterman stood. "Your Honor," he said, "this is certainly fascinating information. But could we please get to the point?"

"I'm getting there, Your Honor," Mr. Rothschild said.

"All right, Mr. Rothschild. But let's move it along."

"I assume you understand that the defendant, Father Costello, has been charged with the murder of the victim on the ninth hole and that the prosecution's theory is that he hit her over the head with his putter."

"Yes."

"The putter was examined by the forensics people and, while its shaft sort of fit the wound on her head, there was no evidence of blood on it. They also found a few rocks that could have just as easily caused the wound but found no blood on them either. Would you be able to explain how, if one of these items was indeed the cause of the wound, no blood was found?"

Dr. Ingersoll paused. He looked like he was seriously pondering the question.

Then he said, "This is the physicist in me speaking now. When you start speaking of temperatures replicating the sun's temperatures, you have an entirely different set of circumstances than we normally observe on earth. In essence, you have an extremely brief switch over from our normal physical rules to, forgive the word, a quantum world in which molecules and atoms and their subatomic particles get drastically rearranged. Fortunately, these events last only mini seconds, so for the most part, our normal everyday physics continue to prevail. But …"

"Then what are you suggesting regarding the lack of blood?"

"I am suggesting that it is not surprising. Whatever blood there may have been is no longer blood. Its atomic and molecular structure has been altered and is no longer identifiable as blood."

"Would the same process have altered the rocks as well as the putter?"

"I would imagine so."

Mr. Rothschild went over to the prosecution table and picked up my putter. "Would you be able to detect anything on this that might indicate such a molecular change?" He handed it to Dr. Ingersoll.

"I assume this is the putter in question?"

"Yes."

He took my putter from Mr. Rothschild and studied it, turning it this way and that, examining it very closely.

"To the casual observer, there is nothing here that would indicate anything was amiss other than that it is bent. But if you look here, you can see that there is a slight discoloration of the metal that, if you put it under a microscope, would probably show that the alloy has been changed to a similar but different alloy."

He was pointing to a slightly darker strip along the shank that I suspected no one had noticed before.

"What about the rocks, Dr. Ingersoll? Would the same be true for them?"

"Do you have them here?"

"Unfortunately no."

"Then I can only conjecture. But yes, most probably some of the rocks would have been altered in the same manner. Probably undetectable to the naked eye."

"All right. Now, Dr. Ingersoll, I have one more question for you. The prosecution has tried to assert that there was no storm at the time in question. No radar saw one, and there was no satellite evidence to that effect. They have suggested that some other inexplicable force created in some way by the defendant caused the destruction on that green. As a rather renowned physicist, can you comment on that?"

"I can only say that in my considered opinion, lightning was the cause. To speculate that some other force was created by a person, such as the defendant, is beyond my ability to credit. I can't imagine how even I would be able to do such a thing. It would require a great deal of knowledge about explosives or whatever and a great deal of time to put together. As I understand it, no such time could have been pondered by the defendant. As to the question regarding no radar or satellite evidence, that is not at all surprising. As I said earlier, there are literally thousands of lightning strikes every day. There is no way radar can see them all."

"Not even here in New York where we have pretty extensive radar coverage, not only by the weather service but also many television outlets?"

"Not even here. Radar installations can only cover so much territory, and they have to be pointed in the proper direction to pick up an anomaly. It is not at all amazing that this particular strike was not registered."

"But how about satellite coverage?"

"There, too, we have the same issues. Satellite coverage has made weather prediction amazingly better than it used to be in our earlier days. But even stationary satellites don't always see everything. As I understand it, this particular strike happened completely out of the blue, as they say, and was very brief. Easily missed."

"Thank you, Dr. Ingersoll. I have no further questions."

"Mr. Waterman?" Judge Johnson asked.

"I have only one question," Mr. Waterman said as he rose from his chair. "Are you asking the jury to actually believe that with today's technology, a lightning strike as theorized by the defense might not have been recorded in some manner by some radar or satellite imagery?"

"No, I am not asking them to believe that. I am saying that it is a fact that not all weather events, including lightning strikes, get recorded. Not even here in New York. It's not a matter of belief, sir. It is a matter of scientific fact."

"Ah! So if the scientists say it's so, it must be so," said Mr. Waterman as he headed back to his chair.

"Objection!" Mr. Rothschild declared as he rose from his chair.

"Sustained," said Judge Johnson. "Save such comments for your closing argument, Mr. Waterman. The jury will disregard the prosecution's last comment."

Mr. Rothschild then called Father Clancy to the stand as a character witness for me. Then he called my friend and fellow priest, Jimmy, who also extolled my virtues. They looked at me as they testified and smiled. It was comforting.

Finally, he called a close friend of mine who was no longer a Roman Catholic. In fact, he had often told me that he was an atheist, but we had known each other for as long as I could remember. We had gone to grammar school together in Philadelphia, participated in many school programs, gone to shows together, and most importantly, often played golf. He had moved to New York recently.

"Your name please?" Mr. Rothschild asked.

"Paul Cassady."

"Do you know Father Costello?"

"Yes. Very well. We are close friends."

"Tell us about your relationship with Father Costello."

"We've known each other since our grammar school days in Philadelphia. We were classmates. Somehow we became friends, and I would say that today Iggy is perhaps my best friend. I was recently transferred to New York."

"By Iggy you mean Father Ignatius Costello. Just to be clear."

"Yes. Of course."

"And what is your line of work?"

"I am a CPA with one of the largest accountancy firms in the US."

"And you two play golf a lot together?"

"Yes."

"Were you surprised to learn he played golf on the day in question?"

"No. Not at all. He had asked me to join him, but I couldn't. I had a huge report I had to finish."

"Please tell us what kind of a golfer Father Costello is."

"He's been playing the game for a long time, and he is very good."

"How about yourself? Are you as good as the defendant or better?"

"I wouldn't want to try to answer that question. I mean, he really is good, and we usually are very close in our scoring, if that's what you're referring to."

"Does he ever lose to you?"

"Yeah. Sure. And I to him."

"How does he behave when he loses?"

"How does he behave? I don't understand your question. I mean, how does anyone behave when they lose at golf. They express a certain kind of frustration, I suppose, then shake hands and go have a pint or two. Is that what you mean?"

"All right, I am going to come to the point. Has Father Costello ever damaged one of his golf clubs after losing a game to you?"

"Oh that! Oh yeah, he's done that once or twice. He's always mad as hell after because he has to buy another one, and they're not cheap, you know."

"Yes, I know. So how does he damage his club? Does he strike something or ..." Mr. Rothschild sort of shrugged.

"Well, it's not as though he does it routinely. I mean, he did wrap a club around a tree once that I saw. Another time he struck the ground with his putter. It was on the green. Left a huge divot. We had to repair it as best we could."

Mr. Rothschild went over to the prosecution's table and picked up my club.

"Does this look familiar, Mr. Cassady?" he asked.

"Jesus!" Paul exclaimed. "Oops, sorry." He covered his mouth and looked at the judge.

"It's all right," said Mr. Rothschild. "Does this look familiar?"

"Well, yeah, it's a putter and pretty badly bent."

"Does it look like Father Costello's?"

"I suppose so. Could be his. What did he do with it? Hit the ground?"

"That is what we are attempting to determine, Mr. Cassady. The prosecution is asserting that Father Costello struck a nun over the head with it on the ninth hole of Van Cortland Park Golf Course."

"Jesus!" He looked at me. His eyes were as wide as saucers. "I can't believe it. No, it's not possible. Iggy never hit anyone. Ever. He's a really nice guy. And he's a priest, for Christ's sake. He'd never do anything like that. Yeah, he gets upset with himself when he screws up on the course. But that's just it. He gets upset with himself. Not me or anyone else we might be playing with. And so every now and then, he hits the ground or a tree. But a person? A nun? Never."

I could see Judge Johnson about to react to Paul's swearing, but then as he continued, she stopped. I even saw a bit of a smile on her face.

"Thank you, Mr. Cassady." He turned to Judge Johnson.

"Mr. Waterman?" She looked in the prosecutor's direction.

"Just one question," he said, as he stood up from his chair. "Just to be clear, you say that you have seen the defendant damage a golf club more than once in frustration over losing a game."

"Yeah. Or over a bad stroke. But never did he ever, ever hit any person."

"So you say," said Mr. Waterman.

"Objection!" Mr. Rothschild shouted.

"Withdrawn," said Mr. Waterman.

"The jury will disregard that last statement by the prosecution," Judge Johnson said.

"The defense rests," said Mr. Rothschild.

"All right," Judge Johnson said. "Let's take a break for lunch and then we will hear closing arguments."

Chapter 19

✝

Father Clancy, Mr. Rothschild, Jimmy, Paul, and I went to a small cafe near the courthouse for lunch. It was rather like an old-fashioned diner with very plain tables and chairs and not-so-polite waitresses scurrying about, taking and bringing orders. It was one of Mr. Rothschild's favorite "eateries," as he put it.

Everyone except me ate large platters of various styles of hamburgers, hot dogs, and French fries. While it all looked devilishly fattening and delicious, I was unable to swallow much of anything.

"So how's it going?" Jimmy asked Mr. Rothschild.

"It's never easy to tell," Mr. Rothschild responded. "I have to say that I am still mystified as to why this case has gone this far. As you have seen, all the so-called evidence the prosecution has presented is purely circumstantial. They have not been able to present one iota of direct evidence. They haven't even been able to show conclusively that the putter was what struck Sister Mary. In fact, I would argue that we have demonstrated that it was not the cause of her wound."

He paused while he sipped his coffee then continued, "There's also the question of when Sister Mary was struck on the head. Was it before the lightning struck, in which case we would be looking at Iggy? Or, as we have argued, was it by a rock immediately after the lightning struck? The coroner couldn't say, thanks to the immense heat."

"Yeah, but how do you explain that there was lightning that caused a rock to hit her when there's no indication that there was any kind of storm that day?" Jimmy asked.

"I believe Dr. Ingersoll made it very clear that the absence of any radar or even satellite sightings does not mean that there could not have been a lightning strike. Thousands of these things happen every day, and many are not recorded simply because the radar was pointing in a different direction at the instant of impact or the satellite wasn't pointing in the correct direction. And he also showed that, while some satellites are stationary and thus always covering the same area on the earth, there are still instances when they don't see everything.

"Also, I don't see how anyone could think that a single person could possibly have produced the destruction that occurred on that green in the short time that might have been available to Iggy. It's inconceivable to me, and I trust the jury will see that."

"Can I ask why you didn't put Iggy on the stand?" Jimmy asked.

"Yes. It's a fair question. I won't go into all the reasons, but one is very important: At his arraignment, Iggy declared in no uncertain terms that he was not guilty. That statement of his carries over to this trial. There is no reason to put him on the stand here other than to have him declare his innocence again. I see no need for him to do that.

He had been addressing all of us. Now he looked directly at me. "The jury well understands that Iggy has declared his innocence. Why repeat it? And I will present that argument in my closing.

"In any case, the prosecution has to present a case that makes the defendant guilty beyond a reasonable doubt. And I don't believe they have come even close to that requirement."

"So will that be your argument in your closing statement to the jury?" Father Clancy asked.

"Yes. I have had it prepared for some time. You may not hear the same presentation in the order we have discussed it here, but yes, that will be my argument."

Strangely, at least to me, the defense went first when giving closing arguments and the prosecution got the last word.

Mr. Rothschild presented his argument in what seemed to me very convincing words. I got the sense that the jury listened to him closely and seemed sympathetic.

But then Mr. Waterman presented his closing argument.

He first looked at me, and then he said to the jury, "The defendant, Father Ignatius Costello, has certainly been described as a very nice guy, hasn't he?" He looked questioningly at the jury, and several jury members nodded in agreement. "And I don't doubt that he is ... most of the time. However, while he is a Roman Catholic priest, he also is a human being. We humans all have flaws of one kind or another. I do. So do you, even if you would rather not admit it.

"So what is the defendant's flaw about which we are concerned? It is his temper on the golf course. Tempers on the golf course are well known and usually seen as amusing in hindsight. But there is nothing amusing about what happened on the ninth hole of the Van Cortland Park Golf Course!" he exclaimed very sternly.

"So what did happen on that ninth hole? First, I am going to address the question of whether or not there was a lightning strike on that location and whether or not said lightning might have been the cause of Sister Mary's death."

He strode back and forth in front of the jury.

"It has been our premise that no evidence can be produced to prove that lightning did strike the scene other than the damage to the green and the burnt body of Sister Mary and even some scorching that occurred to the defendant. We further have intimated that the defendant in some manner caused a violent explosion to cover up his crime and, in the process, also—perhaps accidentally—caused his own scorching.

"We admit that we have not been able to produce any evidence of some kind of chemical or other mechanism having been used for the purpose described. And we can understand that a certain amount of doubt may be attached to that premise. So for the sake of argument, let us assume that lightning did indeed cause the damage to the green, the burning of the victim's body, and a certain amount of scorching to the defendant. Two very important questions remain. Did the defendant strike Sister Mary on the head, and did that strike cause her death? That is the only issue here. Whether or not there was lightning is of no concern if the defendant did indeed, in a fit of rage, strike Sister Mary on the head *before the lightning struck*." Waterman practically shouted those last words. "If he did strike her on the head before the lightning struck and that was the cause of her death, then the defendant is guilty of second-degree murder, no matter what happened after that fact.

"Now, the defense has argued somewhat convincingly that if there was lightning, then it would have eliminated all forensic evidence such as blood residue on the weapon. Let's accept that notion. Then we are left with a bent putter, which the medical examiner has declared clearly fit the opening of the wound to Sister Mary's head. Some rocks were produced that might also have fit the wound. But we have no evidence that a rock struck her.

"What we do have is a defendant who was on that green. We have a bent putter lying on the green near the victim's body. We have proof that the putter belongs to the defendant. While in theory all of this is circumstantial evidence, it nevertheless points to only one conclusion. That the defendant, Ignatius Costello, struck Sister Mary on the head and killed her.

Chapter 20

✝

Judge Johnson now charged the jury, which meant, according to Mr. Rothschild, that she explained the law as it applied to my case. She emphasized that for the jurors to deliver a guilty verdict, the prosecution must have convinced them *beyond a reasonable doubt* that I had killed Sister Mary. I even got the sense that she was so clear on that because, perhaps, she was not thoroughly convinced. On the other hand, I was grasping at any hopeful sign by this time.

She sent the jury off to deliberate in some room. I had no idea where.

"Now what?" I asked Mr. Rothschild.

"Now we wait. This can be the most painful part of a trial, waiting for the jury to decide your future. But in my experience, they, amazingly, usually get it right. Twelve individuals sit around a table, look at all the evidence that has been presented, study transcripts of everything that has been said, and somehow sort it out."

"So are they going to find me not guilty?"

"I would hope so. But there is no guarantee. If they do find you not guilty, then we're done and you are free to go on with your life. If not …? Then we will appeal their decision. But I am trusting it won't come to that."

"How long will it take?"

"No way of knowing. If they come out soon, then it probably means they were convinced of your guilt or lack of guilt from the beginning. But that's no help to you, is it? If they deliberate for a long time, then it may mean none of them were thoroughly convinced one way or the other and so they had to be convinced. Those are questions nobody has ever been able to solve: How long will it take for a jury to make up their collective mind, and what does a quick or lengthy decision mean?" He patted me on the back.

"Let's wait for an hour or so." He continued. "Then, if there has been no decision, I imagine Judge Johnson will send us home and we will trust that the jury figures things out by tomorrow morning. Meantime, let's step out into the hall and stretch our legs. The bailiff will let us know if the jury comes back."

I found I couldn't sit still on a bench in the hall while we waited, so I got up and walked back and forth. A number of other people went about their business around us, oblivious to my situation. Soon Father Clancy found me and tried to offer some hopeful words, but I didn't really hear what he said. Something about asking God to help the jury see the truth of the matter.

Then the bailiff came out.

"The jury is still deliberating," he said. "Judge Johnson has told them to continue with their deliberations but that we are adjourned."

"So what do we do now?" I asked.

"We go home," Mr. Rothschild said. "Chances are Judge Johnson will relieve them of their duties fairly soon, and if they haven't come to any conclusions, she'll excuse them for tonight and have them return to deliberate further starting tomorrow. Once they come to a decision, we will be called back to hear the verdict."

I had been through a lot of sleepless nights during this process, but this night was the worst. I just plain got no sleep. I couldn't help but wonder if Mr. Rothschild had been correct in not letting me bring up the "religious thing." After all, it was what happened. I still was convinced of that even though others had suggested it was a figment of my imagination brought on by the lightning. That was a reasonable explanation, I knew. But still ...

Ms. Noble's advice was no help. *Be still and know that I am God.* Really? God had made a mistake. He had missed his target, and so he had found this way to punish me. That was all I could think.

At ten o'clock the next morning, my phone rang.

"The jury has reached a verdict," Mr. Rothschild said. "We are reconvening in one hour. I'll pick you up in twenty minutes."

The courtroom was packed. I sat behind the defense table, looking, I was sure, almost ill I was so stressed. What was about to happen to me?

The jury filed in. They were all for the most part stone-faced, which I found distressing. They didn't look at me. But they also didn't look at the prosecution table. Just straight ahead.

"Has the jury reached a verdict?" Judge Johnson asked them.

"We have, Your Honor," said one juror, presumably the foreman.

"Will the defendant please rise?" Judge Johnson said.

Mr. Rothschild and I stood. I wasn't sure I would be able to stay up for long. I was feeling so plain scared.

Judge Johnson turned back to the jury and asked, "On the sole count of murder in the second degree, how do you find?"

"We find the defendant, Ignatius Costello, not guilty."

Chapter 21

✝

I collapsed back onto my chair and burst into tears. I couldn't help myself. Mr. Rothschild sat back down and patted me on the back.

"The court thanks the jury for your service," Judge Johnson said. Then she turned to me and said, "You are free to go, Father Costello."

I looked up at her and, through my tears, saw a gentle smile on her face. It appeared to me that perhaps she was relieved too.

Father Clancy, Jimmy, Paul, Mr. Rothschild, and I stood. My friends clapped me on the back over the railing. Then we traipsed down the aisle, out of the courtroom, down the long hall into the daylight, down the stairs, and over to Mr. Rothschild's favorite eatery. I ate a huge bacon cheeseburger with all the trimmings and a pile of French fries. It was the first real meal I'd had for a long time.

Father Clancy drove Jimmy and me back to St. Ann's. When we arrived, he turned to me. "I can only imagine how exhausted you must be. I suggest you take the rest of the day off. Have yourself a good sleep, and we'll see you in the morning."

I went to my room, took off my shoes, lay down, and didn't remember anything else until I woke up around seven o'clock the next morning, though I must have wakened and changed into my pajamas at some point.

I showered, dressed, and started down the stairs to get some breakfast and then see Father Clancy. Suddenly, I stopped in the middle of the stairs. "I am free! I don't have to worry about that ninth hole anymore. I can't believe it," I whispered to myself.

"But am I free?" I asked myself as I munched on my Cheerios. "Do I no longer need to be concerned over what happened on that ninth hole?"

I finished my breakfast, washed my dishes, and headed toward Father Clancy's office with a slight sense of trepidation.

"Well! You look like you've had a good rest," he said as I entered his office. "How are you doing? Up to returning to your normal self, I trust?"

"I can't believe it's over," I said. "I never imagined in my whole life that I would ever have to go through the last few weeks."

"Nor I. So what say you? Can I count on you to return to our normal routine?"

"Yes, sure. But can I ask you a question?"

"Of course."

"I can't help but wonder, am I truly finished with what happened on that golf course?"

"You are referring to the lightning, I presume, not the jury's finding."

"Yes. I can't get it out of my mind. And it's really troubling to me."

"By troubling, do you mean the fact that your story is still in your head or that you still believe it happened?"

"Both, I guess. I mean, it definitely is still in my head, as you put it. And I can't deny that I believe, deep down, that it happened."

"Meaning that God missed and you were the intended target?"

"Yes."

"I have to say, Iggy, I'm not surprised."

"You're not?"

"No. Not at all. You've been through an incredible experience, forgetting the lightning for the moment. All the emotional stress you've been through can't possibly be dropped by any human being with the snap of the fingers. And I am grateful that you brought it up rather than me having to drag it out of you. So I'd like to suggest something to you.

"I believe you can return to your routine here right away. I also have complete faith that you will find yourself able to return to your normal self with time. But it may take quite a while for you to overcome your misgivings. So I'm thinking that you might want to seek some counseling. And given the, shall we call it, religious quandary you are having to deal with, I wonder if, in this case, it might be wise for you to seek assistance from someone within the church."

"The church? But you said that the church would not tolerate such an explanation about the lightning. That everyone would think I was daft."

"Yes, I did. But I don't see your issue now as being one of dealing with a legal explanation. If that had been brought out in the courtroom, there would have been quite an uproar. But that's behind us now. So I have to ask: Would you agree that ultimately it is your faith that we are dealing with now?"

I leaned back in my chair and thought for a moment or two. "I hadn't thought of it that way. Rather, I have been thinking of my sanity, truth be told. But now that you put it ... It's true that the one basic truth I have always been taught has been brought into question."

"And that is?"

"That God is infallible. He does not, cannot, make mistakes or miss his target."

"Exactly."

"But wouldn't it be easier and just as helpful if I were to seek your counsel? You know that I trust you implicitly."

"Thank you for that, Iggy. But I believe you need counsel from someone who doesn't know you. Someone who can be completely objective. Also, I wouldn't want to risk having our relationship spoiled by whatever the outcome might be."

"The outcome?"

"Yes. A person seeking counseling needs to know that they can walk away from whatever happens in session without being concerned about their future relationship with that person."

"Humph. I hadn't thought of that … Do you have anyone in mind?"

"As a matter of fact, I do. His name is Father Lawrence Sedgwick. I have checked around and found that he is a very intelligent, very resourceful, and very decent fellow. His job is to counsel priests who have a need. He works for the archbishop. Would you like me to give him a ring and set up an appointment for you?"

"Does he report to the archbishop?"

"Yes. But he is very discrete. He would never betray a confidence."

Chapter 22

✝

I could have driven downtown to the offices of the archbishop, but the traffic and trying to park could be horrendous, so I took the subway.

I got on the elevated IRT at Broadway and 242nd Street, not far from St. Ann's. It went underground at Dykeman Street to Columbus Circle. I got off, transferred to the D train over to Fifth Avenue, and strolled to St. Patrick's Cathedral, which stood between Fiftieth and Fifty-First Streets on Fifth Avenue.

It was a lovely day, and I had left St. Ann's early to allow me time to visit the cathedral. It was an incredible edifice representing the true faith of the Roman Catholic Church in grand style.

After a quiet spell in the cathedral, I walked over to the archdiocesan offices a few blocks away. As I entered the Terence Cardinal Cooke Catholic Center on First Avenue and Fifty-Fifth Street, a sense of trepidation began to intrude. I was, after all, about to have my experience at the Van Cortland Park Golf Course reviewed all over again by a complete stranger who worked for the archbishop! I had been assured that he had a degree in psychology and was, as Father Clancy had said, a "decent fellow." But still, was I ready to enter what had now become my nightmare all over again?

The center was a large, busy place with areas devoted to adult faith formation, healthcare ministry, family life, instructional television, youth ministry, and the safe environment program, to name a few. A pleasant receptionist gave me directions to Father Sedgwick's office, which was in a suite of offices not delineated in any of the listings in the directory. His was located in a private space.

As I came off the elevator, I found a listing that included Father Sedgwick's office and pointed me in the right direction. I came to a door labeled with his name and knocked.

"Come on in," a pleasant, cheerful voice called. "You must be Father Costello," Father Sedgwick said as I entered. He got up from his rather cluttered desk.

"I am," I said as he came around and shook my hand.

"Have a seat." He returned to his chair.

I was surprised to find that Father Sedgwick was quite young; he couldn't have been much older than I am. He was taller and slender, with a full head of blond hair, blue eyes, and a sort of a Robert Redford look about him. Very handsome. I could imagine women saying, "What a waste," as I knew they often did when viewing some of the younger Roman Catholic clergymen.

Some priests, including me, went right into the priesthood after seminary. Others got postgraduate degrees. Sedgwick had apparently continued his studies in psychology. I wondered if he'd had any pastoral experience. I asked myself how this guy could have any experience that would qualify him to be here at the archdiocese, performing what must be some serious counseling of priests given all the scandals that had hit the church in recent years, mostly of a sexual nature.

I guess I'll soon find out, I thought as I sat in the only other chair in the rather small room. Aside from the standard crucifix hanging above his desk, there was no ornamentation of any kind on the walls or on his desk. It was a rather barren-looking space.

"So Father Clancy tells me you have a rather unusual issue you are having to deal with."

"That's putting it very mildly."

"Care to enlighten me?"

"Did he tell you anything at all?"

"No. Just that you have a really 'sticky wicket,' as he put it. Which, he added, was possibly giving you reason to question your faith. Does that sound right?"

"It wasn't until he and I chatted about it that the faith issue came out, at his suggestion. Rather, I have been wondering about my sanity. I've told only a very few people about it."

"Well, the fact that you are sitting here and telling me this suggests to me that you have not lost your sanity. Otherwise, it's quite unlikely that you would be attempting to have a conversation about it. So how about you let me hear what has you so concerned?"

"Okay. Here goes. Did you read in the newspapers or see on TV the news about the death of a nun at the Van Cortland Park Golf Course?"

"Yes, I did. A very strange set of circumstances. She was struck by lightning? And there was a priest with her at the time. Oh my! That would have been you. His name was Costello, right?"

"Yes."

"You were playing golf with her. And I believe it was on the ninth hole that she was struck and killed, and you were singed as well."

"That's right."

"To such an extent that you required hospitalization?"

"Yes, briefly."

"It must have been a horrible experience for you."

"It was. Still is. But not so much for the reasons you are probably thinking."

"What do you mean?"

"I still have a hard time relating what actually happened on that ninth hole. I've only told it to a few people who were very kind and told me other people hearing it would think I was daft, but they refrained from telling me directly that I was daft. So now I guess it's your turn."

Leaning way back in his chair, Father Sedgwick maintained an interested facial expression as I described everything that had led up to Sister Mary and me being on that ninth hole. But when I told him that I had heard God say, "Damn, I missed again," he nearly fell out of his chair.

He quickly recovered his composure, but there was stunned silence for what seemed like an eternity. Finally, he said, "I can well understand that you are troubled, even questioning your own sanity. I would be questioning my sanity if I had ever had such an experience and heard such a thing."

"But of course, you never have."

"No, never anything like it. And I have to confess to you that I am rather at a loss as to what to say. Most of my priestly clients have a kind of standard operating procedure type of issue. And then there are those who have been involved in some of the scandals we know about within the church. But this! This is without question way out of the purview with which I am familiar."

"But you are a priest. You've been to seminary just like me. You have the same religious training and understanding. And then you have your psychological studies. So I would hope that, long term, you would find it in your purview. That you could help me see through this."

"Sounds like you are counseling me rather than the other way around. Don't get me wrong. You've made a good point. I agree with you. And once again, your analysis of our situation tells me you need not concern yourself over your sanity. There's no question that the event that you have described can be logically analyzed and solved. I've yet to meet a problem that was, in the end, unsolvable. Would you mind telling me a little about yourself—where you come from, your family, that kind of thing?"

I described to him everything I had told Dr. Noble and Mr. Rothschild. Father Sedgwick's eyebrows arched considerably when I told him about my fourteen siblings.

"You are one of fifteen kids!"

"Yes. There was hardly any time that my mother wasn't great with child, as they say."

"That must have been rather hard on her, to say nothing of your father, who had to support such a family."

"You know, I've often wondered about that. But I have to tell you, I don't remember a time when there was anything but joy in our household. I mean, sure, my parents argued from time to time. And we kids all had our battles. But really, we were a happy lot."

"So what brought you into the priesthood? Were any of your brothers or sisters so inclined?"

"No, I'm the only one. The rest of my brothers and sisters are lawyers, nurses, schoolteachers, businesspeople. I don't know how my parents did it, but we all went to college, even graduate school. I, of course, went into the seminary."

"You're making it sound kind of nice, sort of all-American, if you know what I mean."

"Yeah. I do. It was. Still is. We're a very close family. I visit my folks in Philly whenever I can, and we all get together, including various spouses and children, whenever we can. As I think about it, I'm very fortunate in that respect."

"How are things at St. Ann's?"

"I suppose you mean how do I get along with everyone?"

"Yes. Or perhaps, how does everyone else get along with you?"

"As far as I can tell, we all get along very well. One of my best friends is Father James Conan. I call him Jimmy. He calls me Iggy. So does everyone else on the staff. My name's actually Ignatius. My boss is Father John Clancy. A super nice man. Very intelligent. A wonderful man to work for. He's said that he has a high regard for me. And I believe him. He's been wonderful during this whole golf business."

"Okay. So now here we are, reasonably relaxed. Any chance you can tell me what you believe really happened on that ninth hole?"

"What honestly and truly happened is that I swore, 'Damn, I missed again'; a dark cloud came out of nowhere; a bolt of lightning roared down out of that cloud and struck Sister Mary dead; and a voice came out of that cloud and said loud, deep throated, and clear, 'Damn, I missed again.' That's not what I believe happened. It's what I know happened."

He leaned back in his chair rather precariously and looked at me with a slightly scholarly expression on his face. It was as though I were a subject of great interest, rather like a bug under a microscope.

"Would you be willing to consider the possibility that things didn't happen quite as you have related?"

"I'm not sure I understand what you are saying. But yes, I am willing to listen to a different narrative if one can be suggested."

"Well, this is going to require a lot of thought on both our parts. But let me ask you one more question. Are you able to perform your normal duties at St. Ann's? Hearing confessions, hospital visits, all of it?"

"I think so."

"You only think so?"

"Yes. I mean, I go about my routine, including everything you described and more, and I seem to be getting along fine with the staff and with our parishioners. But, especially in the confessional when I'm listening to individuals seeking absolution, I often find myself wondering if I will ever find my absolution. The question is always there. Always nagging at me. How can I give comfort to these people when I myself am so troubled?"

"When you say troubled, in what way do you mean?"

"I mean what happened on that golf course has challenged my faith to the core." There! I had said it. To this priest who worked for the archbishop.

"How do you mean?"

"How can our all-powerful, all-knowing God have made a mistake? That's what I mean."

"Hmm. Interesting question."

Suddenly, his cell phone rang, sounding like an old-fashioned telephone. He lunged forward in his chair, which catapulted him into a standing position and enabled him to reach for the cell phone in his pocket.

"Hello? All right, Jane. Tell him I'll get right back to him. I'm with a client at the moment, but I'll be able to get to him very soon. Thanks." He pushed the little red off button and looked at me. "I'm afraid I do have to pay attention to this one. In any case, what has been occurring to me is that I know I need some time to think about things. So can we take a break for a while now? Give it a couple of days? I'll call you as soon as I can find another opening. Shouldn't take that long. And meantime, perhaps you could give some thought to my suggestion."

"You mean about another narrative?" I asked.

"Yes. I'm not sure I would call it a narrative. But yes, the possibility of some other logical explanation might come to us. Don't get me wrong. I understand completely your question. And

I'd like some time to think about it. So can we leave it at that for now?"

"Of course. I'm fine with taking a break for a while. Maybe something will come to me. And I'll await your call, right?"

"Yes," he said.

As I headed back to St. Ann's, I couldn't stop asking myself if I would ever be able to come up with a different "narrative?"

Chapter 23

✟

Three days later, Father Sedgwick showed up at St. Ann's. It was a bit of a shock seeing him coming down the aisle toward me. I had just finished my tour in the confessional. Father Clancy had asked me to see him, and I was heading toward his office.

"I hope I'm not intruding," Father Sedgwick said with a big smile as we shook hands.

"Not at all. But what a surprise to see you here. Father Clancy wants to see me, and I was just heading there. Why don't you come along and meet him?"

"I've already chatted with him. Why don't you see him and I'll just sit in this pew until you are done?"

I went to Father Clancy's office. He needed me to say Mass out of our normal schedule. It was no problem for me.

"So what brings you here?" I asked Father Sedgwick when I returned and sat down next to him in the pew.

"I've been giving your situation a lot of thought, and I decided I'd like to see where you work, get a sense of your surroundings."

"So did you discuss my situation with Father Clancy?"

"Yes. He confirmed what you told me, including his complete faith in your truthfulness and reliability. Sometimes a priest's superior can pose a problem for him, which contributes to whatever issue he might be having. But I can see that's not the case here."

"I'm glad of that."

We were practically whispering, as there were a few parishioners scattered about the pews.

"Is there someplace we can have a private chat?" he asked.

"We could go to my room, but that's pretty cramped. Any place else another person could come in unexpectedly. There's a nice little luncheonette and coffee shop about a half block from here on Riverdale Avenue. We could go there."

"I don't want to intrude on your schedule here at the church. Will that be okay with Father Clancy?"

"Yes. He told me to do whatever I needed. I'm basically free for the next couple of hours. I'll go tell him where we're headed in case he needs me."

Several minutes later, we walked about a half block down Riverdale Avenue and turned into Maria's Luncheonette. It was a rather simple place, with Formica tabletops, hard chairs, and a limited menu. It was run by a somewhat elderly couple. The wife, Maria, was famous in the neighborhood for the wonderful donuts and crullers that she baked from scratch in the kitchen out back. We each had a chocolate cruller and coffee.

"So I have to ask," Father Sedgwick said as he dunked his cruller, "do you have anything to report to me, any new thoughts about what happened on that golf course?"

"Not really. I mean, I understand what you are hoping for, that some other logical explanation may have occurred to me. But I have to report that I am still stuck with what I saw and heard."

"Well, I have been doing some research about your case."

"Research?"

"Yes. I telephoned Mr. Rothschild and explained to him who I am, and he agreed to send me a copy of the transcript of your case. It is public knowledge, so there was no problem as far as any kind of privilege might be concerned."

"And you've read it?"

"Yes. Fascinating stuff. Kept me up all night. I was particularly struck with the expert testimony of Dr. Ingersoll from Columbia University."

"About the meteorological evidence."

"Yes."

"And?"

"And he convinced me that not only Sister Mary was struck by lightning, but you were too."

"I know. I imagine the jury came to the same conclusion."

"I agree. Let me ask you a few questions."

"Okay. Shoot."

"I assume you heard the voice after the lightning struck. That had to be the case. Right?"

"Yes."

"Has it not occurred to you that the rather heavy jolt of electricity that you experienced must have affected your senses, your brain? We know people hear voices when there are no voices. Strictly from within their heads. Could that have been the case with you?"

"I have thought about that possibility, but you can't imagine how real this event is in my thinking. Can I ask you a question?"

"Of course."

"How do you explain the fact that there was absolutely no evidence of a lightning strike on the green at that time? None—no radar, no satellite of any nature. And what about the nature of the strike? Dr. Ingersoll said it was as though the lightning was searching for its target. Doesn't that suggest that I witnessed an actual act of God? Isn't that a possibility?"

"I thought Ingersoll explained it quite well."

"And the jury bought it. In the end, as far as I was concerned, the jury got it right but for the wrong reasons. It was as though they gave me a reprieve. In fact, they actually got it wrong. I was guilty. God barely missed me and hit Sister Mary."

We were whispering because other people had come in, but my whisper was practically a shout. A few people looked in our direction.

I continued, trying to whisper more quietly. "I mean, I did constantly swear. I did promise Sister Mary I wouldn't. I did say, 'May the good Lord strike me dead.' I have felt ever since then that I am being punished."

"Punished."

"Yes."

"By God." His eyebrows were arched questioningly.

"Yes."

"God is punishing you because He made a mistake."

"Yes ... Well, not so much because he made a mistake as I was the intended target."

"Why would he be punishing you? If you were the intended target and he missed, why hasn't he devised some other means of striking you dead? Why go through all this rigamarole?"

I leaned back in my chair and paused for some time. "I hadn't thought of that. It's a good question. Why am I still here?"

"Exactly." He leaned forward, "I believe that you have your answer. You are still here because what happened on that golf course was a meteorological event. Nobody missed anything."

I sat up straight. "So you are saying I was hearing things in my brain, my consciousness, when I heard that voice saying, 'Damn, I missed again.'"

"That is what I believe. You did, after all, keep repeating that phrase on the golf course. It was definitely in your consciousness. You are not daft. It may take a while for you to fully grasp what we have been discussing, but you should now be able to go on with your life without any sense of guilt or doubt about your faith."

I left some money on the table, and we headed back to St. Ann's. We were silent until we came to his car in the parking lot. As he got into his car, I thanked him.

"Understand, Iggy, that I am always available to you if you need. It will probably take a while for everything to settle in your mind."

"I will. And thanks again."

I watched as he drove off and wondered, *Am I really through with this? I have so much going through my head. Will it ever end?*

I headed into the church and to Father Clancy's office.

"Ah good, you're here," he said. "Jimmy's a bit under the weather. Nothing serious. But can you substitute for him? He's supposed to be conducting Mass this evening, and I can't see him doing it."

"Sure," I said. "Would you like to hear what went on with Father Sedgwick?"

"Yes, that would be good. I trust you're basically back in the saddle?"

"He thinks I should be. He told me to feel free to contact him if I need any more help. But at least for now, I guess we're done. He added that it will probably take a while for me to fully appreciate that I am healed. But I have to say that this whole affair is solidly in my mind. I hope I can finally get rid of it."

"You mean the trial and the cause of it?"

"Yes, I suppose that's the way to put it. I mean, I have this whole missed target idea going through my head. I know it makes no sense, but I can't seem to get rid of it."

"But Father Sedgwick gave you reason to believe it will go away."

"Logically he made perfect sense. But sometimes logic isn't enough, I guess. In any case, I'll go prepare for Mass."

He smiled at me, and I smiled back and left his office.

As I headed back to my room, I had no idea why, but a thought suddenly came to me. *Why don't you call Dr. June Noble?*

Chapter 24

✝

Two days later I entered Dr. Noble's apartment. "It's good to see you," she said with a smile. "I was hoping to learn how you're doing. I followed the trial in the papers and on TV. It was an awful grueling they put you through."

"It sure was."

"But at least now you are free of it."

"If you mean of the legal situation, then yes, I am. But I'm not so sure I am free of the rest of it."

"What do you mean?"

When we arrived in her office, she went to the chair behind her desk. I sat down across from her and said, "I am still struggling with what brought the whole thing on. Sister Mary being killed by lightning that was meant for me."

"So you are still carrying that sense of guilt?"

"I suppose so. But it's more than that."

"Can you explain?"

"I probably should first tell you that I have been having some counseling from a priest who is also a psychiatrist at the archbishop's offices."

"Ah. So you were able to confer with someone within the church after all. Did you tell him your full story about hearing God speak?"

"Yes, I did. I had to, really. Otherwise, what would be the use of seeing him? And the legal thing was out of the way, so I didn't have to worry about it coming out and messing things up. Now I could seek guidance as to how to deal with it within the church. Also, I saw it—and still see it—as more than a question about my sanity. If I kept harboring this memory I had of it, then I was also questioning my faith. Father Clancy suggested I see him, and it seemed the logical thing to do."

"And?"

"And he gave me good reason to try to leave it all behind me and go on with my life as a Roman Catholic priest at St. Ann's."

"I sense, however, a but …?"

"But I don't seem to be able to shake myself of it. Father Sedgwick, that's his name, said it might take a while but he felt that, with me having seen the logic of his argument and getting back into my normal daily routine, after time it would all fade away."

"May I ask what the logic of his argument was?"

"Basically, it was quite simple. I was carrying around this sense of guilt and of God punishing me, as you know."

She nodded.

"But then he asked me why God would have been punishing me all this time. If I was the intended target, then why hadn't God found some other way to accomplish my demise? Why go through all this rigamarole, as he put it."

"Interesting question."

"He also felt that during my golf game with Sister Mary, I had been saying, 'Damn, I missed again,' many times and that it was in my head when the lightning struck. He suggested that I was hearing it in my own head. Not surprisingly, that might have been the case, given the fact that I, too, was struck by the lightning. He noted that we know of many people who hear someone speaking to them when there is no one actually talking."

Dr. Noble sat back in her chair. She had a slight smile on her face. I couldn't help but think that she was very cute. The expression on her face was somehow reassuring and a bit more than just professional.

"He sounds very intelligent, as though he does know his business," she said.

"I agree."

"How much time did you spend with him?"

"Maybe an hour at the archbishop's headquarters in downtown Manhattan, and then a couple of days ago, he dropped in at St. Ann's completely unexpected. He said he wanted to get a sense of where I worked and what my surroundings were like."

"Did you chat with him then?"

"Yes. We went out for a bite to eat at Maria's. You know it?"

"I love it. Delicious food and inexpensive."

"It is. I like it a lot. We probably spent an hour there, and that was where he gave me his analysis."

"And you agreed with him?"

"I did."

"But you are here now."

"Yes."

"Because?"

"It's hard to explain. I'm not sure I know why I am here, other than it sort of came to me to see you." I looked at her and felt my face getting hot. My God, was I blushing? I hurried on. "It's like this. I have to wonder why I keep this idea in my mind that God said he missed, meaning that he is not infallible. I understand now that the voice probably was only in my head. But if it was there and if I keep harboring the notion, then …? And there's also my last visit with you when you got me thinking about Carl Jung and his theories and what seemed to be notions about God that I never thought about before. And that idea about the universe being conscious! It's all swirling around in my head. The trial put all such concerns out of my mind. But now …?"

"Have you told Father Clancy about your concerns?"

"No. I can't see myself doing that."

"And that is because?"

"Because I have to wonder if I really am questioning my faith. And there's no way I can present him with that question. All these years being raised as a Roman Catholic, going to seminary, becoming and then being a fully committed priest, hearing confessions, saying Mass, visiting patients in the hospital—all of it. Am I out of my mind?"

"Iggy, you are not out of your mind. You are certainly not the first person to question his or her faith within whatever discipline he or she may have been raised. In fact, I would suggest that this questioning of your faith is quite healthy. We, all of us humans, follow various courses throughout our lives, be they religious, social, personal, or whatever, and I would argue that it would be unhealthy to *not* question these things from time to time. Either we come out of such questioning more firmly convinced of the path we are following or we change course. And there is nothing wrong with that. In your case, of course, I can certainly understand your concern. Your entire life and even your livelihood depend on your faith. But let me ask you. Are you absolutely certain that your priesthood depends on an inflexible belief about God?"

"Inflexible?"

"Well, maybe that's not the right word. Dogmatic? Does that work? What I am saying is that there are tens of millions of Roman Catholics in the world. And I suppose tens of thousands of priests and nuns. Right?"

"I don't know the exact numbers, but yes."

"And don't you suppose that, while they all may participate in the same rituals and sacraments, each individual, including each priest and nun, has his or her own understanding of what I suppose you would call the church's tenets?"

"No. I can't say I ever thought about that possibility. To me, the Roman Catholic Church and its teachings have always been what they are, and that has always been enough for me."

"And yet over the centuries those teachings have evolved to where they are today."

I leaned back in my chair. "That is correct, of course. And I suppose that evolution is bound to continue, considering the way this world is going."

"I would imagine so."

"So what does this mean for me?"

"What comes to me is that you should return to your work, hear those confessions, perform those masses, visit the sick, and in the meantime, let your own thought evolve. Don't fret over it. Don't do a lot of conjecturing. Just let it go. As we said before, 'Be still and know that I am God.'"

She smiled warmly at me. I returned her smile and rose from my chair. She stood and went over to a rather large set of shelves jammed with books. I watched as she perused them for a moment and then pulled out a volume.

As we walked down the hall to her front door, I thought to myself, *Know that I am God. Right, okay, but ...*" She opened the door for me, looked me in the eye, handed me the book, and said, "Do keep in touch, will you? I'd like to see you again."

"Yes. Thanks. For sure. I will."

She closed the door behind me, and I headed down the hall to the elevator. What had she meant, I wondered. Professionally or …? I probably shouldn't have, but I had to admit that I would enjoy another session with Dr. June Noble.

I looked at the book cover while the elevator descended. It was called *Quantum Enigma: Physics Encounters Consciousness* by Fred Kuttner and Bruce Rosenblum.

Chapter 25

✝

O ver the years, I had developed the habit of reading myself to sleep when I went to bed. It usually took me three or four pages. I normally read various religious tomes. The book handed to me by Dr. Noble, however, kept me up until one o'clock in the morning, at which time I decided I really needed to stop and get some sleep.

In our first session before the trial, Dr. Noble had suggested that physicists were beginning to question whether something was going on in our physical world that defied our normal way of believing; some even posited that the universe was conscious.

That concept blew my mind at the time, and I began thinking of God in a somewhat different way from my normal teaching. But then the trial had intruded, and all thought of such things had disappeared.

It took me three nights to finish the book. It was written for the scientifically uninitiated, so it was easy to read. Even though the concepts were sometimes difficult to grasp, I was hooked.

I became rather consumed with thinking about what I had read, such that Father Clancy asked me what was going on.

"You seem quite excited," he said. "Looks to me as though you are doing well. Back to your normal self."

We were having breakfast together, as we often did.

"Yes," I said. "I think you're right. I am much less concerned than I was."

"Any idea why? Seems rather sudden to me."

I told him about my last visit with Dr. Noble and about the book she had given me to read. "It's utterly fascinating," I said. "It's called *Quantum Enigma: Physics Encounters Consciousness.*"

"Excuse me? What?"

"I know. I never would have thought. But it is a really interesting explanation of what an incredibly complicated universe God created. Full of all sorts of quandaries I never knew existed."

"Can I see it?"

"Sure. I finished reading it last night." I brought it to him after I finished with breakfast.

Father Clancy handed the book back to me the next morning.

"Interesting," he said. "I'm afraid it's a bit outside my normal comprehension of things. I'd like to make an observation to you, though: I hope you won't let yourself get too carried away with your fascination. Don't allow yourself to lose sight of your real purpose."

"Sorry?"

"You are a Roman Catholic priest. You have answered a calling and are following it. Don't lose sight of that. Don't lose sight of your faith. I'm sure you won't, but I felt I had to say it." He smiled at me and returned to his office.

I was dumbfounded. My experience at the golf course had made me wonder if I was losing my senses. Father Sedgwick had pretty well settled the losing my senses thing. But losing sight of my faith? Was that happening?

I had been raised in a large Roman Catholic family, gone only to parochial schools all the way through high school, and gone directly into seminary. I couldn't be more steeped in my faith if I tried. I couldn't imagine even the possibility of losing my faith in God and Jesus, who brought the true faith to earth.

As the days went by, however, I found myself at a loss trying to find something of interest to read. I couldn't get that physics book out of my head.

Finally, I phoned Dr. Noble. "I'd like to return your book to you. Is there any time that would be good for you?"

"Did you enjoy it?" she asked.

"I can't get the thing out of my head. It was fascinating."

"I'm glad. You can bring it back anytime, although I wouldn't want to interrupt a session with my clients. I'll tell you what. How would you like to come by one evening when you're free? Perhaps we could discuss things about the book. No formal session. We could have a glass of wine while we talked. Would that work for you?"

"Yes, I'd like that."

"Is there any time that would be best for you?"

"I have a day off coming to me this next Thursday."

"That would be perfect. Say five? Stay long enough and I could also come up with some supper for the two of us."

"Are you sure? I wouldn't want to put you to any trouble."

"I am positive."

I was stunned. It had never occurred to me that my therapist would invite me over for some wine and supper. This had to be out of the ordinary. But I said, "Okay. Great. I'll see you this Thursday at five."

"Wonderful. See you then. I'm looking forward to it."

"Me too. And thanks."

As I put my cell phone back into my pocket, I couldn't help but feel intrigued. Was it about the chance to learn more about various studies we might discuss? Or was it something else?

Chapter 26

✝

W hen she opened her door the following Thursday, I was confronted with a very different Dr. June Noble. She wore no business outfit. Instead, she was dressed in a close-fitting black creation that was demurely fastened right to her neck and fell below her knees. Her arms were bare, and she had on some makeup—something I had not seen her wear during our sessions. With her large dark eyes outlined and her black wavy hair, normally back in a bun, falling to her shoulders, she was, to put it bluntly, stunning!

I was dressed in tan chinos and a short-sleeved dark blue shirt. As I entered, I could smell some kind of garlicky supper. I hadn't been entertained in any way by a woman since before I entered the seminary. It was a little scary, but her welcoming smile put me immediately at ease.

"Hi, Iggy. Come on in." She led me to her living room, where a coffee table was set with two wine glasses and two bottles of wine, one red and one white, and a tray with some cheeses and crackers on it.

I handed her the book.

"Oh thanks. I'm glad you enjoyed it. Help yourself to something." She pointed to the tray. "What do you prefer? I have a pinot Grigio and a pinot noir."

"I'm no connoisseur of wine," I said. "But I think I'd like the red, thanks."

"Red it is." She poured a full glass for me and another red for herself. "I wasn't sure what you would enjoy, so I put out both a white and a red. I generally like the red wines too."

We clinked our glasses together.

"Here's to some pleasant conversation," she said. "Have a seat." She pointed to the couch behind the coffee table. We both sat, she at one end and me at the other.

She reached over to the tray, sliced off a piece of cheese, and put it on a cracker. As she started to bring it toward her mouth, she said, "So you have me very interested. Can you tell me what you found so fascinating in the book?" She stuck the morsel in her mouth.

I was getting hungry, so I followed suit. Before I ate my cracker and cheese, I said, "It's really hard to say. I mean, I could hardly put the book down. I read it every night before going to sleep and ended up staying awake long after I should have. The whole thing was fascinating." I stuck my cracker into my mouth and started chewing. "And now I'm at a loss for something equally interesting to read."

"I might be able to help you with that. This"—she pointed to the book on the coffee table—"is only my most recent read. I have many more that I have consumed. I am no physicist or even a mathematician, so I can't say I fully grasp what physicists are coming up with these days. But I believe I get the gestalt of it, and I find it fascinating."

"Gestalt?"

"It's a psychological term. In essence it means the overall meaning of a subject. In this case, each of the books I have read and all of them taken as a whole. Does that make sense?"

"So while one might not understand the math involved or

even some of the examples given, one can still get the basic drift of the thing?"

"Yes, exactly. The drift of it. I like that. I'll have to remember it."

"Well, I'm not sure I got the gestalt of this book." I pointed to the table. "But I wasn't able to put it down either. So something held my attention."

"Any idea what caused your fascination?"

I thought for a moment. "I guess maybe it was my first introduction to the world of physics and cosmology beyond what I had in high school physics, which I only barely passed and which never touched on the stuff in this book, as near as I can recall."

"When did you take physics in high school?"

"I think it was in my senior year? And I really don't remember much about it."

"Do you remember studying anything about Albert Einstein?"

"Well, of course. He was, is, very famous, but I can't say I recall any discussion about him in class. He was responsible for relativity, I think. But I didn't have a clue what that meant until I read this book. And, truth be told, I really don't know what it is all about now either."

"Had you ever heard of Niels Bohr?"

"No. Not until reading this." I pointed at the book again.

"Well, those two were responsible for establishing the foundation of where physicists are today, in my opinion. Of course, they both died around the middle of the twentieth century, and so much has been discovered in the decades since. But when you read biographies of these two, you get a wonderful sense of what it is like to be a genius of their caliber. Something most of us can hardly imagine."

"So you've read their biographies?"

"Yes, several."

"You must be really hooked on this stuff."

"I have to admit I am."

As I reached for a refill of my wine, I said, "I have to ask. Has this had any effect on your practice as a psychologist?"

"Yes, definitely. My attempting to understand a client's issues has been greatly influenced."

"Including me." I said it as a statement, not a question.

"Most especially including you." She gestured with her almost-empty glass as if pointing to me.

"I don't suppose you could say in what way?"

"I don't suppose I should. But what do you say we take a break? I took a chance that you might be tempted and cooked some chicken piccata and linguini and a tossed salad. Have I succeeded?"

My mouth started watering. "You have indeed tempted me, and I am willing to give in."

"Excellent!"

Chapter 27

Dinner was delicious. Everything had been prepared from scratch, she told me. Dr. Noble was a wonderfully talented person, it seemed. As we headed back to her living room, I spied a spinet piano.

"Do you play the piano?" I asked.

"Yes," she said. "I also play the flute. A few friends and I get together every now and then to play together. We're a small ensemble. I usually play piano. There aren't that many pieces that call for flute, violin, and cello. Do you play an instrument?"

"Not really. My mother made me take piano lessons when I was in grammar school. And I hated it. I'll never forget one time when I was sitting at our upright piano doing nothing. Just sitting there. Suddenly she whacked me on my back! Not hard. But it sure startled me. 'Just sitting there won't work, Iggy,' she declared rather firmly. 'I'm not hearing any scales coming out of that piano!'"

"What did you do?"

"I don't remember. I suppose I practiced my scales. As much as I hated those lessons, though, my mother and I would play duets sitting together at that piano. There was a music magazine my mother subscribed to for me. Maybe for her too. And every month there was a new piano piece in the centerfold. Sometimes

Robert Y. Ellis

it was a duet, and she and I would play it. She used to play that piano a lot, as I recall. I wonder how she learned to play? She was pretty good at it … Good Lord, I haven't thought about that for decades. Anyway, I haven't sat at a piano in years. I doubt I could even play a scale today."

"Oh, I imagine you could if you set your mind to it. I don't suppose you have a piano at St. Ann's?"

"Actually, there is one in the Sunday school. And there's the organ. But I can't see myself disturbing the peace there."

"I would think, though, that you can read music?"

"Sort of. I understand it to some extent when the hymns are played."

"Do you sing?" She was smiling broadly as she asked.

We were back on the couch, sipping wine. But what were all these questions about? I thought we were going to discuss the stuff in that book. Nevertheless, I answered, "Yes, if you want to call it singing. My mother once told me I had a nice tenor voice. And when I was in high school, I joined the school chorus. It was fun. We had a tough director. But she took us all over the Philadelphia area to sing in various venues. Especially at Christmastime. Man oh Manischewitz! I haven't thought about this stuff in forever! Why do you ask?"

"It's just idle curiosity. You asked about my piano, and it got me going. I don't suppose you sing in any choral group now?"

"Never crossed my mind. Why do you ask?"

"We have the Masterworks Choral Society, and they can always use tenors."

"And I have to believe you are a member. Right?"

"Right."

"Is there anything you don't do? You cook, you play the piano and flute, you sing. Anything else? I suppose you are an artist too."

"I'm afraid I have to admit to that as well. A number of the paintings you see on my walls are mine."

I stood up and walked about the room and hall with my glass in my hand. "I bet the more abstract ones are yours," I said over my shoulder.

"Yes," she said. "You'll find my initials in the lower right corner. Do you like them? Or are you not into abstract?"

"Actually, I do like them. I have no idea what you are saying in these," I said as I sat back down on the couch. "But I hardly ever do with abstracts."

"Sounds like you have some knowledge of art?"

"Some. I took an adult education course in art appreciation one semester. No idea why. It just seemed like a good idea. And that brought me to the museums here in New York. One visit to MoMA was to see an exhibit of art inspired, if that's the right word, by the holocaust. Those paintings were abstract, but they sure spoke to me. Gave me nightmares."

"I hope mine won't give you nightmares."

"Not at all. I get a sense of joy. Like the artist was smiling, having a good time."

"I was. I paint when I feel a need to relax. It's not as though I am trying to say something important. Your sense of joy is correct. I find myself smiling a lot while in front of the canvas."

"Did you take lessons? Or are you self-taught?"

"Like you, I took some adult ed courses at the School of Visual Arts here in New York. But only to get some instruction in the basics of how to deal with oil, acrylic, and watercolor and some understanding of composition. But not in art appreciation. I just wanted to be able to give it a try on canvas, and these are as far as I've gotten."

I remained silent for a spell. I was chatting with an amazing person. She was full of energy, constantly exploring.

"And then you have your interest in physics and cosmology. I couldn't believe the books you have on your shelves in your office and the one you handed to me. Is there anything you're not interested in?"

"Not interested in? Hmm. It's true I do find myself fascinated by all sorts of things going on around me. I love to be in the woods, for instance, and stay still and watch all the activity that goes on around me. If you stay still long enough, most everything that went still when you first arrived comes alive again. Birds, insects, animals, creatures you probably wouldn't notice if you just went walking by. I sometimes walk through Van Cortland Park. It's a big area and full of lovely woods. So I guess there's not much I am not interested in, at least in the broad sense of the word. How about you?"

"I'm not sure how I should answer. You've opened up a whole line of inquiry for me. I sort of feel like I've been in a bit of a rut up to now."

"No, no, Iggy. You mustn't feel that way. You are an intelligent guy who has been through one hell of an experience."

"Yeah, but—"

"No buts about it. You're not stuck in a rut. You have followed your conscience, which has led you to go into the priesthood and to minister unto people, bringing succor and hope to many. No one could ever fault you for that. Add to that an open mind that's willing to explore various ideas? You are where you are right now, but who knows what may come to you going forward. Which, it occurs to me, brings me to the reason I believe you are here. That book." She pointed to the coffee table.

"Right." I sat back down on the couch after refilling my glass. I was feeling very relaxed, sitting and gazing at my hostess at the other end of the couch. "So where do we begin?"

"I'm not sure. As you said, I have all those books in my office, many of which deal in one way or another with contemporary physics and cosmology. But I find that when I try to start a discussion with my friends about what I like to think of as my newfound knowledge, their eyes glaze over rather quickly. So far, though, your eyes appear anything but glazed over. It's occurring to me that maybe I've found someone with whom I can explore some of the revelations of current science. Not the actual mathematical concepts, but perhaps the meaning they might have for us humans on this earth."

I didn't know what to say. Did I really want to explore concepts that possibly would change my understanding of what I believed to be reality? Had my experience on that golf course brought me to such a possibility? That experience definitely had brought me here to this apartment and to a very pleasant evening with Dr. June Noble. No question about that. But where was this heading?

On the other hand, why not? My lifetime schooling gave me the understanding that God had created everything. And *Enigma* had given me a sense that we had no idea what that word— *everything*—meant. It had given me a brief glimpse into the world that scientists had been exploring for eons. And they were just beginning to develop an understanding of how incredibly complex everything was. Everything that God had created. Why not look further? Try to get some understanding of what the amazing world of God's creation was all about? Why fear that my faith was being threatened?

"You look like you're in deep thought," June said. "Are you, perhaps, having second thoughts?"

"Second thoughts?"

"Yes. About continuing our discussion. Are you okay?"

"Yes, yes. Sorry, I was being rather rude. I didn't mean to. It's just that I was trying to figure out how my delving into this subject might affect my faith going forward. Father Clancy warned me not to lose sight of my mission as a Roman Catholic priest."

"Why did he do that?"

"I showed him the book after I finished reading it. He read part of it, became uninterested, it seemed, and then cautioned me."

"Iggy, the last thing in the world I would want is to cause you to question your faith. Do you feel that's a possibility?"

"That's what I was just stewing over. But, no, I don't. It seems to me that the sciences are uncovering all kinds of what they call conundrums in the world of physics. But that says to me that God created an amazing world, an amazing universe. And my curiosity has been piqued. I'm no physicist. So there's not much hope I might actually grasp some of this stuff. But still ..."

"But still?"

"But still, I am fascinated. I mean, about their suggestion that physics has encountered consciousness. They say it's a huge problem for them since consciousness is anything but a physical entity.

"You have been thinking a lot about this."

"I have. And it's all rather mind-boggling."

"And challenging?"

"Challenging?"

"Yes. Do you think, possibly, that Father Clancy is right in cautioning you?"

I went silent. I had my glass of red wine on the way to my mouth, and it stopped before it got there. She had a slight smile on her face, and her gaze was almost drilling into mine. Finally, my glass finished its trip to my lips, and I took a sip.

"That's an interesting question," I said. "And I suppose that might be why he spoke to me."

"I suppose, then, that you might want to consider what, if any, effect this kind of thinking, exploration, might be having on your … I'm not sure how to put it. I suppose we are talking about your faith?"

"My faith. Hmm. No. What I think I am seeing is that we are talking about the universe and what runs it. When I stop and think about it, I realize that *Enigma* says that scientists are performing experiments and their *consciousness* has caused the experiments to be performed and, therefore, caused the results. That suggests to me that there has to be some kind of universal consciousness that must be at work. And I can only think of one name for that, and that is God."

"Why do you say that?"

"All material entities, large and small, end up somewhere all the time. That's how things come together and become recognizable entities. So some kind of universal entity—God?— must be thinking or be conscious and, therefore, causing these actions. Oh boy, is this making any sense?"

"Yes. You have asked some very interesting questions."

I was in somewhat of a dreamy state, possibly because of the wine but also perhaps because I was looking at her and she at me across the distance of the couch. Then I spied a digital clock sitting on the end table behind her. It read 10:18 p.m. "Oh my Lord, look at the time!" I declared. "It's getting late."

She turned her head. "So it is," she said. "I guess it's true that time flies when you are enjoying yourself."

"Very much so," I said. "But I have a busy day ahead of me tomorrow, so I'm afraid I must go. But …" I almost called her by her first name, which didn't seem quite right. I wasn't sure I should. Would that be crossing the line from seeing her as my counselor or therapist to something different?

"But what?" she asked after I paused.

"But I have to say I've had a wonderful time this evening.

Quite a change for me. Dinner and the libations were great. And the conversation ..."

"And I have to say to you that I have enjoyed myself immensely. It's not often that a patient of mine turns into an interesting friend. Someone with whom I enjoy conversing. Even on topics most friends find eye-glazing. I hope you don't mind my saying that."

"Absolutely not. You've opened some doors for me that I never knew were there. And I'd be unbelievably stupid if I didn't consider you a friend, June." There. I took the step. "I am so glad Mr. Rothschild recommended you to me."

"So am I," she said as she stood. "Let's be sure to keep it going."

"I'd love that." As I stood and began to take a step, I realized I was a bit unsteady.

"Are you okay?" she asked. "Are you going to be able to walk back to St. Ann's? Should we call a cab?"

I took a few steps. "No. I'll be fine. It's just a short distance. I'm actually feeling fine."

She walked me to the elevator. When the doors opened, she patted me on the back. "Keep in touch," she said.

"For sure, I will," I said as the doors closed.

As the elevator descended, I leaned against the rear wall, watching the floor numbers blink by. I felt as though I was descending from paradise. It was a strange feeling for me, probably greatly induced by the wine. But there was definitely more to it than that. I, a Roman Catholic priest, had a new, wonderfully attractive friend. I had to wonder where this was heading.

Chapter 28

✝

I awoke the next morning slightly hungover. I couldn't deny it. I was not normally a heavy drinker. A glass or two of wine at dinner was my usual dosage. But I knew the hangover was the result of a very unusual experience for me that I had enjoyed immensely, so I decided to get up and get on with my duties without any self-condemnation. A shower, breakfast, and several cups of coffee had me feeling like my normal self, and I was able to greet Father Clancy with a smile on my face.

"You look like you had a nice time last night."

"I did. A very nice time. Dr. Noble is a very interesting person and a fine cook. And we also had some good conversation. Quite enjoyable." I wasn't quite able to call June by her first name. That might sound ... I wasn't sure what.

"Well, good. After all you've been through, I'm glad you were able to have some time away from all that."

"Me too. I am feeling much freer today."

"Excellent. I'm heading downtown to headquarters for a conference. Probably won't be back until four or five. And I assume you are on your way to the hospital."

I said I was and that I was looking forward to it. It was a part of the priesthood that I especially enjoyed. I spent perhaps two hours at the North Central Bronx Hospital. It was good to be back there in my proper place and not as the confused patient I had been.

During the thirty-minute drive back to St. Ann's, I found my thoughts wandering back to last night and to the conversation June and I had had.

While I was feeling much freer from my recent golf experience, I still had questions running through my head. Father Sedgwick had fairly well dispelled any questions I had regarding our Lord making mistakes, but now I was confronted with questions regarding our Lord's creation. And I found myself concerned about Father Clancy's admonition. Was I, in some way I couldn't see, finding issues with my faith? Was I somehow losing track of my mission as a priest? I absolutely did not want that to be happening. But …

And then there was the question of my newfound friend, June Noble. I kept mentally denying it, but if I was honest with myself, I knew deep down that my enjoyment last night was the result of more than a meal and some conversation.

As I pulled into the parking lot at St. Ann's, I felt I needed to come to grips with these questions. I started toward Father Clancy's office but remembered he was at the diocesan offices downtown. I felt a kind of relief that I wouldn't be able to bare my soul to him once again. Surely he would begin to think I really was losing my senses.

So I went about the rest of my churchly duties for the day and tried to put it all aside.

But that night, all these questions kept going around and around in my head. I had felt so good that morning. Now I was in a turmoil again. I finally fell asleep and had strange dreams involving what I thought were college professors or bearded scientists. I was trying to find my way down a long dark hallway toward I didn't know what, and these people kept locking their doors as I approached. It was incredibly upsetting to me. When I awoke, I discovered that I had been perspiring. My sheets were wet. My brow was covered in droplets.

"What is this all about?" I asked myself as I got up.

I showered, shaved, dressed, and headed down to breakfast. Father Clancy was there sipping his coffee.

"My Lord, Iggy, you look awful. Are you well? You look positively haggard."

"I hardly had any sleep last night. And when I did, I had what I have to think were nightmares. But I'm okay. Not ill or anything like that. Just sleep deprived."

"What brought it on? Do you know?"

"Not really. Or at least not specifically."

"What do you mean?"

"I think it means I'm not really healed, if you will, of everything that's happened."

"What does that mean?"

"I honestly don't know except maybe to say that when you cautioned me after having a look at that book I showed you, it set me to wondering whether or not I did need to be careful."

"Careful of …?"

"That's exactly what I mean. I don't know what. My faith? My mission? Am I in danger of corrupting them? I don't believe rationally that I am. But the question keeps coming to me."

He stayed silent for a while and looked off to one side as he often did when thinking.

Finally, he said, "When I tried to read that book, I found it rather dense. That's the only word I can think of. It was exploring concepts that I have never been interested in. We see various programs on PBS and other channels that attempt to explore similar concepts, attempt to explain what scientists are discovering about the cosmos. But they tend to leave me cold. I prefer to look into the human soul. That's mysterious enough for me. And when we witness human behavior that we see almost daily on TV, there's so much need there for our attention that I find this science stuff sort of beside the point. Or perhaps it would be better to say that I see it as a distraction from what I consider to be important, especially as a priest."

He turned toward me and said, "That, I believe, is what I was saying to you. I believe my concern was that you might stray from that all-important mission. I don't recall that I was concerned about your faith."

I stayed silent.

"Should I be concerned regarding your faith?" Father Clancy's eyes zeroed in on mine.

A few more seconds went by. Then I said, "I honestly don't believe so. But I am thinking maybe I need to do some of my own soul-searching. I'm thinking that I am developing a very different understanding of my faith than I have always relied on."

"In what way? Can you tell me?"

"It's hard to say. That's my problem. I found those explanations about physics confounding yet fascinating. I can't deny it. And I have the feeling that it is challenging my own long-held understanding of … I guess you'd have to call it reality? But I understand what you are saying. I, too, love our mission. It's what I wake up to every morning. It's what I live by. But still …"

"But still you are wrestling with doubts."

"Doubts. Hmm. I'm not sure I want to go that far. I don't believe I am wrestling with doubts about my faith. It's something else that I don't seem to be able to put my finger on."

"All because you read that book. What is it called?"

"*Quantum Enigma: Physics Encounters Consciousness.*"

"And despite my disinterest, you are interested."

"I am. It's not as though it's all-consuming. But I do find it fascinating."

"Have you shared this interest with anybody else?"

"I discussed it with Dr. Noble when I returned the book to her." I couldn't call her June. Not to Father Clancy.

"Is she as into this subject matter as you?"

"She's really into it. You should see her library. It's full of books on physics, cosmology, you name it. The one you and I saw is only the last one she had read. I'm nowhere as knowledgeable about these things as she is."

"When you discussed this with her, was that when you had dinner with her? After which it seemed to me you were sort of on a cloud the next morning?"

"Yes. I was on a cloud, as you say. But now ..."

"But now you're having doubts. What about? Is there no possibility you can put your finger on it?"

"I guess at this moment it's whether or not I should follow this interest. Is it even right or proper for me to do so? Will it interfere with my true purpose as a priest? Will it become a distraction, as you put it?"

"Time is flying by here, Iggy. We both have duties to which we should attend. But I wonder if you might want to consider some more counseling. I have a feeling that everything that has gone on in the past few months has created a cauldron in your mind, making it very difficult for you to sort things through."

"You mean see Father Sedgwick again?"

"I hadn't thought of anyone in particular. But he might be just the person. Let's call a halt to this for now. But think about it, okay?"

I nodded, and we went our separate ways.

Chapter 29

I had more than a week to think about it before I could get an appointment with Father Sedgwick. And think about it I did. A lot. I had several sleepless nights thanks to all kinds of ideas going through my head. One that kept occurring was, Why not call June Noble? But I felt that she, her very presence—and yes, her attractiveness—was an important part of my mental cauldron. I also couldn't help but wonder if Father Clancy suspected that she figured into my mental gyrations.

Some ten days later, I found myself in Father Sedgwick's office again. Neither he nor his office had changed. He still had that Redford look about him, and but for the crucifix above his desk, the room still was bare.

"So what brings you back?" he asked as he rose from his chair and we shook hands across his desk. "I was hoping that those issues we last discussed were behind you."

"I'm pretty sure I'm done with the lightning thing," I said as I sat. "I'm here for a rather different reason, though I guess it stems from that experience."

"And?"

"And I have been trying for the last week since I called you to figure out how to explain things. And that's the problem. If I could explain, I probably wouldn't be here. I had a discussion with

Father Clancy, and he said that, putting together my experiences over the past few months, I probably had a cauldron going on in my head and maybe I ought to seek some assistance in trying to sort it all out."

"Sounds like something has happened since I last saw you."

"Yes."

"Anything to do with the trial?"

"No. Not really, though if it hadn't been for that, it wouldn't have occurred. Have I ever mentioned Dr. June Noble to you?"

"I don't believe so."

"Well, she's a psychotherapist that my lawyer, Mr. Rothschild, suggested I see during the trial. Her office is just a couple of blocks from St. Ann's. I had a couple of sessions with her, all in an attempt on her part to get me to relax and trust in the process of the trial. Her mantra was 'Be still and know that I am God.'"

"So she's a Roman Catholic?"

"No. I'm pretty sure she's not. I never asked her, and I have no idea what religion she has, if any. But she, of course, knew I was a priest, and so she tried to get me to use my own religious thinking to help me through the experience. At least I believe that was her process."

"Sounds very sensible. But it also sounds to me as though there might be something about your experience with her that brings you here? Is that why you mention her?"

"Yes."

He nodded with his eyebrows elevated, waiting for me to explain.

"Where to begin? I suppose I should start by explaining why Mr. Rothschild recommended her. He said she had been trained as a Jungian psychotherapist and that might make her more sympathetic toward me and the issues I was dealing with when I went to see her."

"A Jungian. Interesting. You mean your concerns regarding God missing the mark, I suppose."

"Yes. She explained to me that she was, indeed, trained in Jungian theories but that psychotherapy had come a long way since Jung died, and she was fully cognizant of the progress made. She even said it had gotten to the point that psychiatrists tended to treat mental illnesses with a pill. And she said that often was the correct diagnosis. But she was also still simpatico with Jung's mystical side."

"Did you describe your experience to her, including hearing what you believed was God?"

"I did."

"And?"

"And she was basically dumbstruck like everybody else who heard my experience."

"Including me."

"Yes, including you. But, like you, she accepted the fact that I thoroughly believed it had happened. As I recall, however, we didn't dwell an awful lot on that. She was helping me get through the trial."

"Can you describe how she did that?"

"You mean other than the quote from Psalms?"

"Yes. I assume you spent some time with her. What led up to that send-off, if you will?"

I looked over his shoulder, trying to think. How had June talked to me? It was, I had to admit to myself, June who had introduced concepts I had not pondered before I met her.

Finally, I said, "I don't think I can describe in any kind of order how our session went. It lasted for at least an hour."

"Don't worry about the chronological order of things. Just say what comes to mind."

"I suppose the most interesting thing that she introduced to me was what she called synchronicity. Do you know what that is?"

"Yes, of course. It's one of Jung's most well-known theories. I suspect most psychiatrists today more or less debunk it. But I find it still interests me."

"She told me about Jung's saying synchronicity was evidence of some kind of principle that somehow operated without any cause? Something like that?"

"Jung called it an acausal connecting principle. Yes, no cause or effect. Most what he called meaningful coincidences are brought about by this principle, he said."

"Right. I asked her if Jung meant this was God."

"Ah! So are you struggling with your faith? Is that why you are here?"

I was startled by his question. And I was sure he could see it in my face. But I replied, "No. I don't believe so. But the idea did make me wonder a bit about God. Made me wonder if I needed to, in some indefinable way, broaden my concept of God."

"Do you think that was Dr. Noble's intent?"

"No. I don't think so. This all came up as a result of lots of conversation. She was trying, I think, to get me to trust the process regarding my trial. She left me with 'Be still and know that I am God,' which really didn't work at all for me. I was that stressed out. I definitely was not at that time thinking about anything as esoteric as synchronicity."

"But you are thinking about it now."

"Well, yes. But mainly because I am attempting to describe how my sessions with her went."

"Sessions. So you had more than the one."

"Yes. I'm not sure why. But one day after the trial and after seeing you and our working out the lightning issue I was still struggling with the whole God making a mistake thought. Why was it still working its way through my consciousness? And it just occurred to me to call Dr. Noble. So I did."

"And how did that go?"

"Actually, I have to say I was glad I had gone to see her. She was glad to see me, she said. She was curious as to how I was doing after the trial, which she had followed in the paper. We had an interesting chat during which we touched on synchronicity again, as I recall. I was still hung up on God making a mistake. I told her about your question of why God would go to all this rigamarole, as you put it. She thought that was a brilliant question. Anyway, one thing led to another, and we ended up talking about consciousness."

"Consciousness?"

"Yes. And whether or not there is some kind of universal consciousness."

"Ah. So we are getting into quantum physics? My, my!"

"Yes. She has a bunch of books all about the subject. I wondered if she was talking about God. She said she wasn't suggesting that but sort of left the question open. This was far from my thinking. But we had talked for some time. In any case, as I left, she handed me a book from her extensive library of books to take home."

"What sort of book? What's its title?"

"It was called *Quantum Enigma: Physics Encounters Consciousness.*"

"I know the book."

"You do?"

"Yes. I have a copy at home."

"Really! I never would have thought."

"Why not?"

"Well, I mean ..."

"You mean why would a priest have an interest in such things?"

"I guess that is what I mean. And I guess that's why I am here."

"Explain."

"I found myself fascinated by the book. I really didn't understand a lot of it. I mean, I have had absolutely no education in the field of physics beyond my high school training. But some of the concepts the authors described basically blew my mind."

"Why would that make you feel you had to see me?"

"Well, I think it's because I showed the book to Father Clancy, and after reading some of it, he cautioned me not to lose sight of my mission as a priest."

"Did he say why?"

"When he said it, I was rather excited about what I had read, and I guess he was concerned that I might lose sight of my mission as a priest. He told me he watched programs on TV about cosmology and such things and felt that they were a distraction from what he considered the mysteries of the human soul. That is where he feels a priest should be devoting his energies."

"I can understand why he, as a parish priest, might feel that way. But in general, I can see no way in which the reading of such tomes, even the study of them and the subject in general, should be a problem for you."

"You can't? I mean, you don't see it as a distraction from living the true faith?"

"I am afraid I do not understand why you might suspect that. There isn't a Roman Catholic university that doesn't include such studies in its curriculum. To do so would be to bury one's head in the sand. Look at Manhattan College in your neighborhood. They have a department devoted to quantum theory, as well as a number of other seemingly esoteric studies."

"I hadn't thought of that," I said.

"It's not surprising that you hadn't. You've only recently

become aware of the subject. Here's the thing, Iggy. It does seem that, as Father Clancy said, you have a cauldron going on in your mind. I sense there is more going on than a concern for learning about some previously unheard of concepts about the universe we live in. Does that sound right?

"Yes."

"Is it something you can articulate?"

"No. I don't even think I know what is really bothering me."

"Would you be willing to try a little experiment? Nothing arduous."

"I suppose so. What is it?"

"I'd like you to lean back in your chair, close your eyes, and try to relax. Just let things go."

"Are you going to hypnotize me?"

"Absolutely not. I only want you to try to relax and let that cauldron have a rest. Maybe think of something normally very pleasant to you. Or try to think of nothing at all. Although that's an impossibility. But just lean back, close your eyes, and let some good thoughts come to mind. I'll stay silent too. If something comes to you that you'd like to say, no matter how unrelated it may be to our discussion, say it."

"All right. I'll give it a try."

I leaned back in my chair and closed my eyes. It was not the most comfortable chair I had ever sat in. But I found that cauldron churning around in my head, revealing the golf course, a bolt of lightning, Sister Mary's scorched body, my mother, my father, my brothers and sisters, Detective Folger, the ninth hole, Sister Mary staring at me, her scorched body, Mr. Rothschild, Father Clancy, Jimmy, Paul, Judge Johnson's slight smile, Mr. Waterman, the jury, two what I supposed were atoms smashing into each other, the physics book cover flashing across my mind, a glass of wine, spaghetti, a chocolate creation in front of me, Dr.

Noble sitting behind her desk, her bookshelves filled with books, June Noble in her clinging black dress. All flashed in front of me. And then, filling my vision, June Noble's smiling face and dark eyes with her eyebrows raised in a question. I woke suddenly with what must have been a startled expression on my face. I had no idea how much time had gone by.

"I get the feeling you saw something." Father Sedgwick said.

"I saw a whole bunch of stuff."

"But something caused your eyes to pop open rather suddenly. Can you say what?"

I was feeling stunned. "I don't know what to say," I said.

"Can you give me some idea of what thoughts crossed your mind?"

"It wasn't thoughts. It was images."

"Ah. Interesting. What sort of images?"

"I saw my parents and my brothers and sisters. And the golf course and Sister Mary's scorched body." I went on with the list. But I left out June.

"Sounds as though your life history went by."

"I suppose you could say that."

"But there was more, wasn't there? It wasn't only history. Was there perhaps some kind of suggestion about the future? Perhaps something that is at the root of things?"

I remained silent, looking at the blank window behind him. He didn't say a word, just waited. After some time, I said, "I suppose there was."

"Are you able to say what it was? I sense this is absolutely no joke for you and it might be difficult for you to say anything right now."

I stared at him. "I saw a glass of wine, some spaghetti, and a chocolate dessert."

He had a puzzled expression on his face.

"I know it doesn't make any sense to you," I said. "I haven't told you everything. I think I have been afraid to."

"Can you tell me now?"

"I think I have to … I haven't told you about my third time with Dr. Noble."

"You had three sessions?"

"Yes. But the third wasn't really a session."

"Not a session," he said with a questioning look.

"No. I phoned her to find out when I could return the book. She said anytime. But then she said she wouldn't want me to interrupt a session with one of her clients. So she invited me to come over one evening so we could chat about the book." I described my visit with June, leaving out no details.

When I finished my story, I looked at Father Sedgwick and said, "And what I also didn't tell you was that the last image I saw and what woke me out of my trance just now was one of Dr. June Noble. Just her face. It was smiling and had a questioning look on it."

Surprisingly, at least to me, Father Sedgwick smiled. "And so," he said, "we now have gotten to the root of the problem."

"You think so?"

"Pretty sure. Iggy, you are a priest. I am a priest. We have both taken a vow of celibacy. But that doesn't change the fact that we are men. Now, we both know that many priests down through the ages have violated that vow, some in dreadful ways. And there's no denying that fact. There's no question that it has been revealed as a great problem for the church these days. But I assume that in your case, and I know in mine, no violation of that vow has taken place."

I nodded in agreement. In fact, I was practically as innocent as a newborn. I'd had a few flirtations during high school, but nothing ever came of them. And from high school I had gone directly into seminary.

"But we are men. Being men, we can't help but find the opposite sex attractive. Would you agree?"

I only nodded.

"Iggy, there's no sin in appreciating the glories of the women in our lives."

"Right. I understand that. But …?"

"But? You're saying there's more to this than you've told me?"

"Not in any physical sense, no. But …?" I shook my head back and forth in a questioning way. He must have seen a quizzical expression on my face.

"In other words, there's more than a simple appreciation of her womanhood." It was a statement on his part.

"I have to admit she was exquisitely lovely that evening. I was very much attracted to her, and I am pretty sure my feeling was reciprocated. Though she never once expressed that toward me. It's just a feeling I had."

Father Sedgwick leaned back in his chair and stared off into space. I waited. Then he said, "You're not the first priest to come into this office with, I'll call it, a similar set of circumstances. I'd like to ask you a few more questions. Rather personal, in a way. You can say you don't want to answer if that occurs to you. Will that be all right?"

I had a dreadful feeling that I was in for it. "I suppose a refusal to answer will be construed as another potential issue?"

"Yes. That's a possibility. But so far we've had some good discussion. And please feel secure in the knowledge that whatever transpires in this office is strictly confidential. Shall we continue?"

"Okay."

"When you say you found Dr. Noble attractive, was this from the very beginning at your first session?"

"I recall that I thought she was attractive, even cute, the first time I saw her. But I was so caught up in the lightning thing that I don't believe it went any further than that."

"How about your second session?"

"That was after the trial. I was feeling relieved about that, but still, as you know, faced what I suppose we can call those religious questions."

"These sessions, I presume, were held in an office?"

"Yes. She was very professional, even down to her attire. I will say that I did note that she was petite, feminine, and cute. There's no denying it. But it was rather like seeing an attractive woman in church. If I felt anything beyond that, I don't remember it."

"So it was during your third visit that something more than an appreciation of her womanhood occurred."

"Yes."

"How did that feeling express itself?"

"Express itself?"

"Yes. Was there, perhaps, some kind of physical manifestation?"

"Physical manifestation?"

"Yes. Look, Iggy, I am not immune to appreciating a woman's qualities. Or, to put it more succinctly, her sexuality. I, like you, am a man."

"Right. I get it. And yes, there were some physical manifestations, as you put it. But I wondered if they, to some extent, were thanks to the wine. I had consumed much more than I normally would, and I was feeling a kind of glow as she walked me to the elevator and while I descended. It was pleasant. I remember thinking I had had a very pleasant evening with June and wondered if more such evenings might be in the offing."

"June."

"Yes. That's her name."

"I know. But until now you have called her Dr. Noble."

"I guess that's right."

"I know it's right."

"Is that significant?"

"You tell me."

I knew, of course, that it probably was. I had been avoiding saying June. I wasn't sure why. Perhaps I thought it might somehow indicate … I wasn't sure what. But I thought I might know if I was completely honest with myself. Still, I wasn't able to say anything. Father Sedgwick just watched me with a calm but questioning look on his face. I could only return it.

Finally, he broke the silence. "I suspect, Iggy, that there is a lot more to this relationship you have with Dr. Noble than you may have realized up to now. And I think you would be wise to ponder the extent to which you should let it continue. I am not one of those priests who condemns other priests who allow themselves to fall into these kinds of conundrums. In the end, one needs to follow one's true conscience, not just the dictates of the church."

He continued, "But what one needs to know is what is one's true conscience? I'd like to suggest that you go back to St. Ann's and immerse yourself in your priestly duties. But I also suggest that you see if you can take some time off, even if for only a few days, and leave your normal environment. Go someplace, perhaps with a friend or two, where it would be possible for you to feel free of all entanglements. I know this sounds like a tall order, but do you think you could give it a try?"

When Father Clancy suggested I seek counseling and I thought of Father Sedgwick, I had never dreamed it would come to this. I had never thought I would confess my feelings for June. In fact, I hadn't believed I had such feelings. Now I was beginning to believe I did and that they were, in fact, at the root of my sense of unrest. And what Father Sedgwick was now suggesting without saying it outright was that I should avoid June.

I replied, "It does sound like a tall order for me. But yes, I will give it a try."

"Do you think you could get a few days off?"

"Father Clancy has been very good to me through all this. I have no idea where I might go, but I imagine he will be receptive to the idea."

"Good. Then let's call it a halt. I have another appointment due here momentarily. But please keep me posted. I don't mean to include myself in your list of entanglements. At least not yet." He smiled broadly at me, and I laughed, which broke the rather depressing spell I was feeling.

Still, as I walked back to the subway station on my way back to St. Ann's, I couldn't help but wonder what was in store for me.

It was late afternoon when I got back to St. Ann's and nearing time for me to say Mass, so I had no time to fill Father Clancy in on my trip downtown other than to say I'd had an interesting talk with Father Sedgwick and that I would fill him in tomorrow.

Father Sedgwick had suggested that I immerse myself in my priestly duties, and I couldn't think of a better way than by saying Mass. That and other duties kept me busy until bedtime. I was rather glad that I was unable to think about anything that had transpired during my visit downtown. But as soon as my head hit the pillow, the cauldron returned, but this time with this afternoon's developments added to the mix. And worse, that image of June Noble smiling at me was foremost.

Chapter 30

Despite the swirl of thoughts, I slept well and woke feeling refreshed. I'd had a number of dreams but could only remember that they were pleasant. In a few cases, I remember telling myself I would have to remember this one. But it didn't work. None came to mind after I woke.

Once again I found Father Clancy in the kitchen, having his breakfast. He had a coffee mug to his lips as I entered. He gulped down his sip of coffee as I sat with my mug in hand.

"Well, you're looking rested," he said.

"I am. I'm feeling quite well," I said.

"So your trip downtown was well worth it?"

"I believe so, though actually the cauldron you describe is still with me but with yesterday's visit added to the mix."

"Good Lord. What does that mean?" He began to dig into his bacon and over-easy eggs—his standard breakfast. "I trust your visit helped sort things out?" he said as he lifted a forkful of egg to his mouth.

I added cream and sugar to my coffee, stirred it, and then took a sip while thinking of a response. "In a way, yes," I said. "What I mean by that is that Father Sedgwick managed to get me to sort of list everything that had been going through my head—I mean mentally, not on paper—and to begin to at least try to make some kind of sense of it all."

"And did you succeed?"

"Succeed?"

"Yes. In making sense of it all."

I got up to get my bowl of Cheerios and some milk. As I sat back down, I said, "I have to say no. But while everything was going through my head last night when I went to bed, I nevertheless fell right to sleep and slept through the night."

"Interesting. Sounds as though any sense of guilt or worry you might have had is now gone."

"I believe that is true. What he did was assure me that whatever questions I might have been harboring or am still harboring are not abnormal. That I had no reason to carry any sense of guilt over my as-yet unanswered questions."

Father Clancy stuck a last forkful of eggs into his mouth. After he swallowed, he said, "Can you describe these questions to me?"

"That's the thing. I can't even describe them to myself." I knew I was skating on thin ice. The main issue was, of course, June Noble. But I didn't dare tell him that. Not now. Not before I could get my own sense of reality sorted out. Why bring her up to him when she might just be a passing fancy?

"But you said you had a list."

"I did. But it's strictly mental. I haven't written anything down. And it keeps changing." More thin ice. As I began to scoop up my last spoonful of Cheerios, I said, "And that brings up a suggestion Father Sedgwick made."

Father Clancy began to rise out of his chair. "What's that?"

"He wondered if I could get a few days off to go somewhere completely free of my normal environment, as he put it, to try to relax and let God speak to me. He didn't put it that way, but that's what he was saying." More even thinner ice?

Father Clancy sat back down. "God can't speak to you in his own church?"

"Father Sedgwick was saying that even St. Ann's is a part of the cauldron going through my head. I believe he was suggesting I go somewhere that is free of any connection to anything and anybody that has been a part of my experience during these past several months."

He leaned back in his chair. "Hmm. It does make some sense, I suppose. Where would you go?"

"I don't know. I haven't really thought about it. Maybe a retreat house somewhere?"

"I know of a very nice retreat house in Gloucester, Massachusetts. They specialize in silent retreats. No talking for the entire time you are there. I attended one some time ago. It's rather strenuous at first. But then you get into it. Would something like that work, do you think?"

So it appeared Father Clancy would have no problem with me leaving him short-handed yet again.

"I don't know. Might, I suppose. As I say, I haven't given it any thought. For now I think I should concentrate on my work here. That was Father Sedgwick's first suggestion. And I'll see if something comes to me. If that's all right with you."

"Of course it is. Glad to have you fully back on board. But if you come up with an answer to being away for a few days, let me know. We'll work it out here." He rose from his chair, cleared away his dishes, and headed to his office.

I gulped my last swallow of coffee, returned my dishes to the sink, washed them, set them to drying, and started the first of what I trusted would be many full days as a priest with no more major distractions.

The images in my cauldron kept coming to mind from time to time, but as the days went by, they began to fade. Even June's pleasant smile came upon me less and less. Yet, I knew Father Sedgwick was correct. Each time I was reminded of why I had gone to see him, with some recollection of the trial or of the ninth hole or of Mr. Rothschild (there was no rhyme or reason for the sudden popping up of these images), I knew I probably should find a way to follow his suggestion to get out of my normal environment.

Then, mixed in with the cauldron, I began to think about my family. Why such thoughts came to me I did not know. They were simply there. I saw my mother and my father. Each of my fourteen brothers and sisters kept coming to mind. I had not given them much thought over the last several months. I had not wanted, under any circumstances, to let them know what I had gone through. They were in Philadelphia, and I hoped they had not heard about my being on trial.

But now I began to think about going home. To my roots. To where I knew I was loved unconditionally. Where I was completely safe.

Chapter 31

A week later, after conferring with Father Clancy, I packed my small bag, left St. Ann's, took the IRT subway to Penn Station, and boarded the train to Philadelphia. It was half-empty, and I located a seat next to the window. As the train pulled out of the station, I found myself beginning to unwind. There was something about trains that had always been soothing to me.

When we came out of the tunnel under the Hudson River, I watched the train yard speeding by. Soon the countryside came into view. Houses, factories, farms, gardens, and highways filled with cars whizzed by. I gave in to the soft sound of the wheels on the tracks. They used to click on the spaces between the rails, but now I knew that the rails were welded together. The relaxation I had longed for began to come over me.

Too soon we pulled into the Thirtieth Street Station in Philadelphia, and I departed the train. I caught a cab, and thirty minutes later I was at the front door of my childhood home. My mother and father still lived here even though all my brothers and sisters had left, were married, and had their own homes and children. I was glad my parents had not moved. I would be able to go to my room, which I had shared with two of my brothers. Now I would have it to myself.

My parents were expecting me. I had phoned them once I decided I wanted to take my break at home.

As I climbed the four steps to the porch, I heard a dog yipping in the house. I opened the front door, and there was Cherry, a small black short-haired dog with a tail wagging impossibly fast. She had white toes, a white chest, and soft floppy ears. People often asked why the name Cherry. It was because she was a rescue dog and had been found starving under a cherry tree.

She took one look at me and started running circles around the room in what I could only interpret as sheer joy. I called her to me, and she jumped into my arms and licked my face as I squeezed her and scratched her tummy with my one free hand. My parents had rescued her from a shelter some eight or nine years ago, and every time I visited, she had welcomed me in this effusive, affectionate way.

My parents heard the commotion and joined me and Cherry. I put her down, and both gave me huge, long-lasting, very comfortable hugs. Cherry stood next to my mother, still wagging her tail and staring up at us.

"It's been so long since you've been to visit," my mother said. "Cherry's so happy to see you, and so are we. You look well. Maybe a little thin?"

"But you're not wearing your collar," Dad said.

"No," I said. "I don't wear it when I want to be anonymous. If I were to wear my clerical clothes while on the train, I would get all kinds of stares from people. I know they mean no harm, but I'd just as soon do without the attention."

"I guess I can understand that," he said. "But it does bring you a certain amount of respect, I would think."

My father was very proud that his son had become a priest. He thought a priest should get the same kind of attention and respect that a member of the armed forces might get. It was rather old-school. But I understood it. He and my mother had raised fifteen children, all of whom had done well. They had good reason to be proud. Now my dad was retired. He was receiving a pension from the union he'd been a member of for all the years he had delivered mushrooms to the city. They owned their home outright, and he and Mom both had their social security. So without having to support all those kids, they were reasonably comfortable, for which I was very grateful.

"I suppose so, Dad," I said. "Although nowadays things are not quite the same as in yours."

"What's that supposed to mean?"

"It means, Mom and Dad, that I have been given a few days off by Father Clancy, so I have come home to see my parents and relax a bit. I have a lot to tell you about. But for now I'd like to leave such questions for later."

"It sounds like you are seeking some solitude," my mother said.

"Not from you two. But yes, from a lot of stuff in the Bronx, New York."

"At church?" my father asked.

"Not at St. Ann's. At least not really. St. Ann's and Father Clancy have been a refuge for me."

"Good Lord. What are you talking about?" my mother asked.

"Nothing for you to worry about. All is very well with me. It's just that a lot has happened since I last saw you. Things that I never would have dreamed. They are for the most part behind me. Father Clancy agreed that it would make sense for me to take a few days off and come to see you guys. I promise I will fill you in."

I leaned over and petted the top of Cherry's head. Her tail started wagging again as I said, "But you know, I haven't even been upstairs to my room. What do you say I go up, freshen up after my trip, maybe take a brief nap, and then come down? It'll be close to dinnertime by then. I assume you each have your glass of wine and some cheese and crackers before you sit down to dinner. How about I join you then?"

"Of course, you are tired from you trip," my mother said. "We should have given you a chance to freshen up. I'll start getting things ready in the kitchen, and Dad can read his *Inquirer*."

My father loved the *Philadelphia Inquirer*. He read it religiously every day. Apparently, though, the *Inquirer* had not picked up the story about a priest being accused of manslaughter in the death of a nun on the ninth hole at the Van Cortland Park Golf Course. Thank God for that.

"Great," I said. I picked up my bag, called to Cherry, and she and I headed upstairs.

My room had not changed, as I suspected would be the case. Being the youngest of their children, I had been housed in this bedroom with my next two youngest brothers. All three of our beds were still in the same positions. The wallpaper was the same, as were the Eagles and Phillies pennants. I assumed I should sleep in my old bed and found, sure enough, that my mother had put on clean linen and left a towel and washcloth folded neatly at the foot of the bed.

I suddenly realized that I was very tired. I had relaxed on the train, but a lot of the tension had returned. I stretched out on my bed. Cherry jumped up and settled in next to me. I scratched her tummy again. It was nearing four o'clock, and I knew my folks liked to dine around six, so I looked forward to an hour and a half of sleep.

Suddenly, I heard a knock on the open door. I woke to find my father in the doorway, leaning over and patting Cherry on her back. He looked up at me. "You really were sound asleep," he said. "Are you sure you're okay?"

"Yes. I'm fine," I said a bit groggily. "What time is it?"

"It's 6:15. Your mother sent me up to make sure you're okay. We're about to have some wine and then dinner."

"Oh boy," I said as I swung my feet over and sat on the edge of the bed. "I'm sorry. I had no idea. I'll be right down."

"See you there. I'll pour you a glass." He turned and headed back downstairs with Cherry following.

I sat for a few minutes with my elbows resting on my knees. I was feeling a bit disoriented. Finally, though, I got up, grabbed the towel and washcloth, went into the bathroom off the hall, and freshened up. As I looked at myself in the mirror, I thought about how quiet it was. This bathroom used to service a whole bunch of kids. It had been tumultuous at times. Now I was alone. In a way it was unnatural, strange.

Well, I thought, *you wanted solitude. To get away from it all. You have it. At least in this room. But what are you going to say to your parents?*

Chapter 32

Many people think the name Costello is Italian, but actually, it is Irish, and my father is the personification of a dark-haired, dark-eyed Irishman. He was born in Philadelphia, but his grandparents, my great grandparents, had immigrated here from Ireland during the potato famine. They were from County Cork, which I was told many times was the southernmost and largest county in Ireland. Worse, they were from a village called Skibbereen, which for some reason had suffered most from the famine. You can, to this day, I was told, still see the now-grassy mounds under which hundreds of bodies were buried. Dad had never been to Ireland but often said he'd like to go see where his roots were one day.

My mother was Irish too. Her parents, who were from Dublin, had immigrated here. Being my mother and the mother of my fourteen siblings had been Mom's entire role in our household. My father was the provider, hauling those mushrooms for some forty years. He was a good man, a gentle man who loved his wife and his children and their little dog.

I loved him in all his seeming gruffness, which I was sure came from his relationships with all those truck drivers he must have befriended over the years. He was not a tall man. Perhaps five foot eight or nine. But he was broad shouldered and muscular.

Those pallets full of mushrooms were heavy and kept him trim and in good shape. As I looked at him today, I realized he was still trim. There didn't seem to be a bit of fat on him. His once black hair had turned steel gray, but his clean-shaven face was mostly free of lines. He was still a handsome Irishman even in his late sixties.

Neither he nor my mother had gone beyond high school, yet they somehow made sure their children went to college and a few to law and medical school.

Mom was petite at no more than five foot two. How she ever bore all us kids I'd never know. And even with all those births, she was able to maintain her girlish figure. I'd noticed in my ministry that a lot of women seemed to go to pot after their first children. Not so with Mom. She, too, was in her sixties, a few years younger than Dad, yet her hair was still as dark as I had always known it to be. I doubt if she had it colored, though perhaps she did. She wore only a bit of lipstick, which she always said she needed to stop her from looking like death warmed over. I never understood that. She was my mom, and I always thought I understood why my father had been attracted to her.

As I entered the living room, Dad handed me a glass of red wine, and I sat down in one of the easy chairs. Cherry jumped into my lap, tail wagging. I scratched under her chin, and she settled down. Cheese and crackers were on the coffee table in front of the couch, where my parents sat.

"So how are you guys?" I asked as I leaned back and took my first sip.

"We're just fine," my mother said.

"And everyone else?"

"Well," said my father, "they, like you I'm afraid, don't keep in touch as much as we might like. But as far as we know, everyone is doing well."

"Jeanie's pregnant with her third child," Mother filled in. "Everyone is doing well. They all seem to be quite busy with their lives and their families. They do try to keep in touch as much as they can."

Dad gave a brief nod. I wasn't sure he agreed with Mom. "But," he said, "we have not heard from you in months, it seems."

"I guess it has been a while. There's been quite a brouhaha that has had me rather preoccupied. I thought you might have heard about it or read about it in the *Inquirer*. But I guess the news didn't get this far."

"Good Lord!" my father exclaimed. "Something involving you that would make the news?"

"Yes. In fact, it made the papers and TV in New York. But it's all in the past for the most part. On the other hand, it's the reason Father Clancy thought getting away for a few days would make sense."

"I think you had better explain," he said with a rather perplexed expression on his face.

"I have something in the oven I need to check," my mother interrupted. "Dinner's probably ready. Let's sit at the table."

I was glad for the break in conversation. I still didn't know how I was going to bring my parents up to date. I wasn't sure I knew what up to date really meant. But we got up. I brought my wine glass to the table, which was at the other end of the room, and sat down. Cherry understood what was happening and curled up on her cushion that perfectly fit her small body. Mom and Dad went into the kitchen. I heard the sound of plates being assembled, the oven door being opened and then closed, and whispered conversation going on between them. I couldn't understand what was being said, though I could imagine.

Mom had set the table, and soon Dad came out with a beautiful

Robert Y. Ellis

prime rib of beef roasted to what I was sure was perfection. It was surrounded by roasted potatoes. Mom carried in a bowl of veggies.

How many times had I sat at this table with my brothers and sisters and watched my father carve a roast? We were never all together at this table. It only seated twelve if we jammed enough seats in. But the older ones left home to follow their own lives before I and my next oldest brother and sister ever came along. When we were all together at celebrations such as Christmas, the youngest children had been seated at a separate card table covered with a tablecloth. And we had all watched our father carve the turkey or beef. It was something of a ritual for us.

Mom and I handed our plates to Dad in turn, and he placed a cut of beef on them. He knew Mom preferred it well done. So he gave her an end cut. I received the next cut, which was perfectly medium rare. He took the next for himself. He added potatoes to our plates and handed them back to us. Mom passed the bowl of spinach mixed with celery and carrots cooked together. She always liked to add a little color to her meals, hence the carrots. I knew she had inserted bits of garlic into the roast before baking it, but I had no idea what seasonings had gone onto the potatoes and veggies. Whatever their preparations, I immediately dug into my meal. Meals back at St. Ann's were fine, but this was like a little bit of heaven.

We ate in silence for a few minutes. Then finally, Dad said, "Iggy, I have to tell you that you have us wondering what's going on."

"I understand," I said. "And I want to tell you all about it and why I am taking this holiday." I shoved another bite of meat into my mouth and chewed for a bit. Still chewing, I said, "It's a rather long story." I swallowed and then continued, "But first, you must understand that I am fine. St. Ann's is fine. Father Clancy, who has been a huge help to me, is fine. There is no reason to

198

concern yourselves over my well-being going forward. Just about everything is back to normal."

"Just about?" said my father.

"Okay. Everything. There may be a few loose ends that need to be resolved. But I'll get to that." I took a last bite of my potatoes. "Could I have another potato, Dad? These are delicious, Mom. So is everything else."

"Thanks," she said. "I have discovered a seasoning I never knew about that I love to add to my roasts and the potatoes. It's called Montreal steak seasoning, but I like to add it to a lot of things. Lends some flavor and a little bite to things, if you know what I mean."

My father landed two more potatoes and another slice of beef on my plate, and I started to dig in again. "Are they starving you at St. Ann's? Is that what it's all about?" Dad had a smile on his face.

"No, no. Nothing like that," I said. "Let me finish this and then I'll fill you in." I took my time as I squirreled away my second helping. Finally, though, I had practically licked my plate clean and could wait no longer. "I suppose dessert is in the offing?" I asked. Both Mom and Dad had finished their meals.

"Yes," my mother said. "But let's wait for a bit. Let our meals settle. You go ahead with your recitation."

My recitation. "Okay. I am going to start by telling you what will seem like the worst thing to have happened. I'm glad you are sitting down. But please be assured it now is in the past."

"Good Lord!" they exclaimed simultaneously.

"Are you ready?"

"For God's sake, get on with it!" my father said.

"It was all a huge mistake, but I was indicted for second-degree murder last April."

"What!" came another simultaneous exclamation.

"You heard it right."

"Second-degree murder?" my mother almost whispered.

"Yes. But as I say, that has all been sorted out and I was found not guilty."

"You mean you had a trial?" my father asked.

"Yes. As you can imagine, it was very stressful."

"And you never told us!" Dad said.

"I know. I didn't want to and hoped you wouldn't find out until it was all resolved. I didn't want you both to get all worked up over what I knew was not true. I had not killed anyone."

"But someone was killed?" Mom asked, again in almost a whisper.

"Can you fill us in? Who died and why were you brought into it?" Dad asked.

"Yes. It's rather a long story. Should we have dessert first?"

"I don't know about Mom, but you have me on pins and needles. I'd like to get to the end of the story and then have dessert and probably another glass or two of wine."

My mother nodded in agreement.

"Okay. Hold onto your seats."

I spent at least the next half hour telling them the story, starting with my wanting to play golf, not being able to find a partner, and finding Sister Mary. I went on to describe everything that we did and said, including my swearing. But I left out the part about God saying he had missed his target. I described Mr. Rothschild's friendship with Father Clancy and his representing me, and I mentioned having therapy with both Father Sedgwick and Dr. June Noble. I only briefly mentioned the fact that I had therapy. I did not describe the sessions. I let my parents come to their own conclusions that the sessions had been designed to help me get through the trial and the stress.

I also described the trial, the prosecution's presentation, as well as Mr. Rothschild's defense, including his calling Professor Ingersoll to the stand and his analysis of the lightning. And I mentioned my bent putter on the green.

Dad interrupted, "One day, my son, you will have to get that golf temper of yours under control."

"Boy, do I know that now!" I said. Then I continued describing the character witnesses Mr. Rothschild had called.

"How is Paul?" Mom asked. "We haven't seen him in years."

"He's fine," I said. "And I believe his testimony sealed the deal as far as the jury was concerned. In any case, the jury found me not guilty, and the judge—her name is Marion Johnson, and I will never forget her—told me I was free to go home."

"You'll never forget her?" Mom asked.

"No. Because throughout the trial, I had a sense that she was not convinced by the prosecution, and at the end, when she told me I was free to go, she had a nice smile on her face. She was clearly glad the jury returned a not-guilty verdict. At least that's the way it seemed to me."

"I think it's time we had some dessert and some more wine!" my father exclaimed. "My Lord, Iggy. What a story and what an ordeal for you. I can see why you must be exhausted and feel in need of a break."

I had not said anything about my religious quandary. Nothing about God missing a target. Nothing about my sessions with June, especially nothing about our dinner together in her apartment. Those issues were the reason I was here seeking some solitude, some distance from it all, some time to let my thinking calm down. But I felt no need to burden my parents with such issues.

"How long ago was this, Iggy?" my mother asked.

"A few weeks," I said. I couldn't tell them it was more like a couple of months.

"And you never told us," Dad said. "How about your brothers or sisters? Have you told any of them?"

"No. I didn't want to involve any of you in this if it wasn't necessary. And it wasn't, as it turned out. I even swore Paul and the others who knew you to secrecy. They knew I would fill you in in good time. And that's why I am here now."

"Well, okay. Let's get some dessert," Dad said, and he and Mom went into the kitchen. Soon they came out with bowls full of sliced pound cake, vanilla ice cream, and hot fudge sauce. Mom knew it was one of my favorites.

"Oh wow!" I said. "I'll have to come home more often."

"That would be nice," Mom said.

Chapter 33

✝

Mom and Dad always liked to watch the nightly news, so after dessert, we retired to the living room and little more was said. Soon I excused myself and headed back upstairs. Cherry followed me. I changed into my pajamas, hopped into bed, and lay down with Cherry snuggling very comfortably against me.

I had gotten a lot off my chest, and it had felt good. But as I went to sleep, the unmentioned questions filled my consciousness. It must have been rather briefly, though, since I woke the next morning feeling greatly refreshed.

It was nine o'clock in the morning by the time I finally headed downstairs.

"Your father and I have had our breakfast," my mother said. "You don't normally sleep this late, do you?"

"No. I can't believe it's so late. I'm usually up and at 'em by six. But I slept like a log last night, and it felt wonderful."

"And that's why you are here. After what you told us last night, it's no wonder you need some time away."

"Where's Dad?"

"He's gone shopping. I discovered we're low on eggs, cream, and milk. He should be back soon. What would you like for breakfast?"

"I usually have a bowl of Cheerios and some orange juice. But

I was thinking something different would be good for a change. But if you're out of eggs …?"

"No, no. I still have a few. And some bacon and toast?"

"That would be fantastic. Are you sure it's no problem?"

"After all these years, young man, how can you ask such a question?"

"Mom, I'm thirty-three. Young man?"

"I know. And a respected priest in the Roman Catholic Church. What more could a mother ask for? But you are still my last and youngest child and my youngest son. I can't help it." She was smiling broadly.

I smiled back at her. As she went to work on the eggs, bacon, and toast, her words "respected priest" ran through my mind. Was I? Should I be seen that way? Did Father Clancy see me that way? Our parishioners who witnessed in one way or another the trial? Mr. Rothschild? Even my close friend Paul? And how about Jimmy? What about all of Sister Mary's fellow nuns? What did they think of me? And then there was June Noble.

"There you go," my mother said as she placed a full plate before me.

She handed me some silverware and a large paper napkin. I dug in.

"You looked like you were deep in thought just now."

"I suppose I was."

"Anything you'd like to share? I'm pretty good at listening. You have fourteen brothers and sisters who have trained me well."

"There is a ton of stuff going through my head these days. But it's hard to describe. Hard to pin anything down."

Suddenly, the kitchen door opened and my father came in with a paper bag full of groceries.

"Well, you will be here for a couple more nights. Let me know if you'd like to talk," Mom said.

"Hello, son." Dad greeted me. "Hope you had a good sleep."

"I did, Dad. Wonderful, in fact. And I'm just finishing one of Mom's fantastic breakfasts."

He sat down at the kitchen table across from me while my mother put the groceries away.

"Any idea what you're going to do for the next couple of days?"

"Not really. The trial left me very stressed out, and that's a big reason for my being here. But then there are all kinds of things going through my head. Thoughts that never would have occurred to me but for my experience on the golf course and during the trial."

"What kind of thoughts?"

"That's the thing. I was just explaining to Mom that I can't even describe them clearly to myself."

"I suppose then that's the real reason you are here?"

"Yes. I have to say it is. Telling you about the trial took a huge load off my shoulders, not only because you needed to know about it but also because it is the first time I have actually told anyone else about it. I mean, Father Clancy and my lawyer and others who went through it with me, know about it. But telling the story the way I did to you felt quite therapeutic."

"Well, don't let us stand in the way of your doing whatever comes to you," he said.

"Thanks. I won't." I looked over to the corner of the kitchen where Cherry was perched on her cushion, looking at me with her dark, almost black eyes. Her tail wagged briskly, and her flappy ears were almost erect.

"You know," I said. "I think I'd like to take Cherry for a walk in the park. Would that be okay?"

"I've already taken her for her morning walk. She's taken care of all her business," Dad said. "But of course. I'm sure she'd love it."

"Great. I'll get my jacket."

I dashed upstairs. Cherry followed me up and back down. I reached for her leash, which was hanging on its normal hook next to the back door. Cherry waited patiently but with her tail wagging furiously as I attached the leash to the ring on her collar.

"See you in a little while," I said.

"Better take a doggy bag just in case," Mom said.

"Right. Thanks," I said as Mom handed me the bag and we headed out.

Cobbs Creek Park was a long narrow park that followed Cobbs Creek for some distance. I never knew how long the park was, but it had to be a couple of miles at least. Our house was one block away. I kept the leash short as we walked to the park. It coiled up into the handle, and when we got to the park, I let it extend for its full twenty or so feet.

There were very few people out and no other dogs that I could see, so it felt as though we had the grass and foliage to ourselves. Cherry had a wonderful time running back and forth with her nose to the ground, sniffing all kinds of mysterious but seemingly important smells. Every now and then she would dash over to me for a quick pat on the head and then continue her search for whatever it was dogs sought as they prowled. It was a joy to watch her, to be with her.

After we had walked a fair distance, I found a bench in the sun and sat down. Cherry understood and settled down next to me. I leaned back and stared into space; Cherry leaned against my ankles and stared at I knew not what.

Her presence, what I felt was silent counsel, had a reassuring effect on me. I would never forget how that little trusting dog soothed my consciousness.

The sounds of the city were muted by the park. It was very quiet. Only Cherry and I were there.

My eyes closed but not for sleep.

It was one of those rare moments when my mind stayed quiet. They say the mind never stops thinking. But when I thought about it later, I felt it had actually stopped. I was aware of the sound of birds, the insects buzzing, the breeze—nature behaving as it should, I was sure. But actually thinking? Not for some moments.

Then it was as though I heard a voice: "You are not the same person you were before that golf game. Too much has happened since then. That sense of routine and equilibrium you had is gone. It's time to take stock. Get a sense of how to proceed, how your life is going to open up for you going forward. You can do it. One way or another, the therapists have shown you your power of reason and opened up new worlds for you. Have the courage to look at those worlds."

"But," I interrupted myself, "does that mean I have to change my career, leave the priesthood?"

"Not at all," the voice within me said. "You just have to open your thoughts to all possibilities in order to become thoroughly grounded in the path you are going to follow."

I opened my eyes with a start. Cherry stood erect and stared at me.

"What was that?" I said out loud. "Where did that come from?" I looked around me to be certain no one else was there.

A sense of peace descended upon me. I let it wash over me. Finally, I stood up, and Cherry and I continued our walk. It was getting later in the morning, and people began to show up with their dogs. That little dog somehow knew something had happened to me. Instead of returning to her sniffing and furrowing in the grass, she stayed by me no matter how much leash I gave her. After a while, she and I turned around and headed home. It really did seem like a joint decision. She stayed near me and looked up at me every now and then with those dark eyes and with her ears as erect as they could go. When I looked back on it, I had to say that I was in somewhat of a trance, and that little dog brought me home.

Chapter 34

We came back in through the back door. I removed Cherry's leash, hung it up, poured a cup of coffee, stuck it in the microwave to reheat, and sat at the kitchen table. Cherry returned to her cushion, rested her chin on her front paws, and stared at me. Her ears were now calm, and her tail was still. The microwave beeped, so I retrieved my coffee, added some cream and sugar, and took a sip. Then I set the mug on the table and, with my hand still holding it, stared into space.

My parents were not home. I knew they had their own lives to lead and errands to run. They would be back for lunch around noon or one o'clock. It now was about quarter after eleven. I realized that when I arrived here yesterday I was full of myself and my own problems. I thought little about my parents and how they were doing. My eyes traveled around the kitchen, and I spied an iPad on the counter. My parents had cell phones, but I had never thought that their acquaintance with the digital world would have gone further than that.

I got up and wandered into the combination living and dining room. There in a corner was a small desk with a desktop computer on it. Next to it was a stack of letter-size papers. It looked as though my parents (I wasn't sure which) had printed a document or documents. I didn't feel that I should study what they had printed. It was private. Maybe I would learn later. I wandered some more around the house, my home, which I had not lived in for some time. In their bedroom was another desktop computer. The screen was on, and an article from the *Wall Street Journal* was displayed. I had no idea my parents were so "with it."

Just then the kitchen door opened and my parents came in. They saw Cherry, and Mom said, "Iggy must be back."

I returned to the kitchen.

"Ah. There you are!" she exclaimed.

Dad grabbed a mug of coffee, stuck it into the microwave, sat down across from me at the kitchen table, and asked me how my walk with Cherry went.

"It was quite wonderful," I said. "That little dog and I had a really nice time. There was hardly anybody in the park. We walked for a while and then sat in the sun on a bench. She and I just sat there, soaked in the sun, listened to nature all around us. It was peaceful, quiet."

"Did you get any answers?" Mom asked.

"Did I get any answers?" I repeated. "I think maybe the better question might be do I know the questions for which I need answers. Worse, do I want to know the questions?"

"What is that supposed to mean?" my father said as he stirred his coffee. It was one of his favorite questions. But in this case, he was right on point. What did I mean?

"I was going to keep it to myself for a while," I said. "But I had an experience in the park that I can't possibly describe but that left me with what I think was the sense of peace I have been looking for and maybe a sense of direction."

"And what would that direction be?" Mom asked very quietly relative to Dad's booming question.

"It's occurring to me that I went through that trial, I went through all the counseling from my attorney, I went through therapy sessions from two therapists—one at the archdiocesan offices and one a woman recommended to me by my attorney—all for a reason. These events didn't just happen accidentally. There is a reason that I need to try to discover. It occurred to me that a new world of opportunities may be opening up for me."

"A new world of opportunities," my father said. "You're sounding like your brothers and sisters. They're always looking to expand their business horizons. Doesn't sound very priestly to me."

"I know what you mean, but I didn't mean it in that sense. I even wondered, sitting on that park bench, if leaving the priesthood was a possibility. And the answer came to me in the form of a resounding no. Rather, I think what was occurring to me was that I should explore the possibility of expanding my experience, my knowledge beyond what has become rather routine in my daily life. Father Sedgwick even pointed out to me some of the branches of study being pursued at many Roman Catholic universities, including Manhattan College in my own neighborhood."

"What kind of studies?" Dad asked.

"The sciences."

"Sciences?"

"Yes. Mostly physics and cosmology."

"Really," Dad said. "How did that come about? Doesn't sound very theological to me."

"And yet, Dad, there are many priests who are studying in these fields. Even Father Sedgwick has an interest. And I have to say my own interest has been piqued."

"This is very interesting," Dad said. "I never thought I would be having a conversation right up my alley with my son who is a priest. And I have found that, but for one, your brothers and sisters have no interest. But I have found myself intrigued with the sciences. You may not have noticed, but I have quite a few books on my shelves that have absorbed me on the subject. Your mom thinks I'm a bit crazy to be so entranced with the stuff. Nevertheless, I am."

"I don't think your father is crazy. I just don't get it," Mom said. "I believe I've lived my life as a good Roman Catholic, and I see no reason to delve into such things."

"And there's no reason for you to do otherwise, I keep saying!" Dad said. "There's no reason for you to stop going to church or confession, to stop praying, to stop saying your Rosary. That has nothing to do with having a curiosity about how things work in the universe. As far as I am concerned, it's all God's creation. And now I believe I have just heard our son, the Roman Catholic priest, confirming what I've been saying."

"Wow!" I exclaimed. "I had no idea. And you guys are almost at loggerheads over this."

"Not at all," Mom replied. "Your father goes his way, I go mine, and we meet every night in bed. It's quite convenient."

"You haven't stopped going to church?" I asked my father.

"No. Not at all. We are both regular, faithful attendants. That'll never change."

"You said but for one. Do you mean one of my brothers also has an interest?"

"No. One of your sisters."

"One of my sisters! Who would that be?"

"Charlene."

"Charlene?"

"You know she teaches science at her school. She somehow started looking beyond the normal curriculum. Way beyond her curriculum, in fact. She told me about it and got me hooked."

"Unbelievably hooked," my mother said. "You wouldn't believe how boring their discussions can get when they are together."

"What kind of discussions?"

"Oh, they talk about Albert Einstein, of all people. Or some fellow named Bore? A very apt name if you ask me."

"His name is Niels Bohr, spelled *b-o-h-r*. Mom knows that but loves to make that play on his name. He is generally considered an early guru, if you will, of quantum theory. And Einstein, as you probably know, enunciated relativity."

"Well, actually, Dad, until very recently I had never heard of Bohr or about Albert Einstein, although, of course, his name is well known."

"Yes. Bohr is not very well known generally. Funny how Einstein became a hugely famous public figure even though he was a very modest, rather quiet man. How did you come to know about him?"

My mother interrupted, "Don't tell me you two are going to start talking about this stuff!"

"I am just asking Iggy how he got into it."

"Hmph," my mother said.

"It was thanks to my therapist."

"Father Sedgwick?" Dad asked.

"No. The first person I went to, Dr. Noble."

"Why would she have mentioned Einstein to you?" my mother asked.

"She didn't. It's kind of complicated. But my lawyer, Mr. Rothschild, suggested her to me because she was trained in the theories of Carl Jung."

"Who's he?" Mom asked.

"He was a psychologist well known in the first half of the twentieth century. And he had what I can only call sort of a mystical side to him. Mr. Rothschild thought that, given what I had been through on that golf course, a therapist who wasn't strictly materialistic might be able to help me."

"I'm afraid I don't understand," my mother said.

"Nor I," said my father.

"This has to do with the one part of my experience that I haven't told anyone except my lawyer, Father Clancy, Father Sedgwick, and Dr. Noble, all of whom agreed I should not relate it to anyone else."

"Good Lord!" my father exclaimed.

"What on earth are you talking about?" my mother asked.

How in the world was I going to tell my parents what was at the root of all my misgivings but had hoped was behind me?

"You can't even tell your parents?" Dad said.

"Yes. Why can't you tell us?" Mom asked.

"The problem was, and I suppose still is, that if I told anyone about it, they would think I was daft. That's why I haven't mentioned it. Also, Father Sedgwick and Dr. Noble pretty much convinced me that what I thought happened was a figment of my imagination. It didn't really happen even though I believed very deeply that it did."

"Pretty much?" Dad repeated my words.

"If I am honest with myself, I have to say that I am still somewhat haunted by it."

"Haunted?" My father squinted at me.

"It's not something easily forgotten."

"Don't you think it might be time for you to let us know what in the world you are talking about?" Mom's slight smile told me it was time.

"I suppose it is." I decided to plunge in and describe my experience on that ninth hole. When I finished, both Mom and Dad stared at me with what I could only feel were dumfounded expressions on their faces.

"You thought you heard God speaking to you," Dad finally said.

"Yes."

"And saying that he had 'missed again' I believe is what you thought you heard."

"Yes."

"So you thought God had spoken and said he had missed and this wasn't the first time."

"Yes."

"And you went through your entire trial believing that."

"Yes."

"But didn't it occur to you that God used the exact same words you had used?"

"You know, it did. But you had to be there. You had to see the cloud, hear the wind, get struck by the lightning, and see Sister Mary lying there horribly scorched and dead to get a sense of where I was coming from. It was an awful experience. But you're right. Father Sedgwick asked me the same question. He suggested those words were in my consciousness when the lightning struck and that it was my consciousness that spoke, not God. Dr. Noble agreed when I told her about my session with Sedgwick, and she thought it made sense too."

"I'm trying to understand why you had to see two therapists. Why wasn't Father Sedgwick adequate for the task?"

"He probably was, as it turned out. But at the time, it seemed to make sense for me to see a therapist who would have no theological ax to grind. Someone who would be able to hear my story totally free of any theological considerations. That was Mr. Rothschild's sense of it, and Father Clancy agreed."

"So you saw Dr. Noble." Throughout this conversation, my mother only nodded along to my father's questions.

"Yes. On Mr. Rothschild's suggestion. He and Father Clancy are close friends. They went to grammar school and high school together and lived in the same neighborhood in Riverdale. So Father Clancy trusts him implicitly."

"So you went to see Dr. Noble. Can you tell us about her? Did you like her? Was she as helpful as Father Sedgwick? It does seem strange that you would see two therapists at the same time."

"I suppose it would seem strange, but I saw Dr. Noble first for the reasons I've explained. Father Sedgwick didn't enter the picture until it didn't seem necessary to avoid the theological issue anymore."

"The theological issue."

"Right. You need to understand that I believed I had heard God and that he had missed his target. It threw me. Along with everything else, I was unbelievably confused. Father Clancy now suggested I see someone in the church. It was time, I think he felt, that I dealt with what he believed was a question about my faith. Was I questioning my faith?"

"Good Lord! Were you?"

"I didn't believe so. But—"

"But what?" my mother interjected quietly.

I looked at her but said nothing. Neither parent said anything. Looking back on it, I would later realize that this was the moment I had begun to be honest with myself.

My parents waited patiently as I tried to collect my thoughts. We were sitting at the kitchen table, the two of them across from me. Cherry quietly came over and leaned against my left leg. I reached down reflexively and petted her gently.

"I think it's really good that I came down here to be with you both. You're causing me to think things through as I haven't before, and I am beginning to see things or admit things to myself that I haven't until this moment."

They both continued to look at me, each with what I could only describe as an encouraging expression. I would have thought, given my very strict raising in the church, guided by my parents, that they might have been alarmed at the way the conversation was going. But I got no sense of that. Rather, they seemed to want me to be able to express whatever I was thinking with no fear of judgment on their part. I would never forget that sense of support they gave me.

"There's another area of experience I have had that I haven't told you about." I tried to choose my words very carefully.

Mom and Dad continued to stay quiet.

"It involves the sessions I had with Dr. Noble. There is more to them than I have mentioned."

"Ah," said my father.

"Don't get me wrong." I looked at Dad. "Nothing at all untoward went on."

"But?" Dad asked.

"But ..." I paused then. "I had three sessions with her. The first two were in her office and strictly professional. The third was a bit different."

"A bit different," Dad repeated. He was clearly getting suspicious.

"Yes. Don't get the wrong idea, but it was more of a social event than a professional one."

"You are getting very obtuse, Iggy," Mom interjected. "Can you by any chance stop beating around the bush?"

"Okay. It's like this. After my second session with her, Dr. Noble handed me a book that she thought I might find interesting. It's what got me interested in the sciences," I said as I looked at Dad.

"What was its title?"

"I can't recall exactly. Something to do with physics and consciousness?"

"Maybe *Quantum Enigma: Physics Encounters Consciousness?*"

I was startled. "Yes, that's it! You know it?"

"Yes. I have the book. It's over there." He pointed to the shelves next to his computer.

"Really?" I looked toward the shelves.

"Yes. And it's very interesting."

"I had no idea you might have read it. And you found it interesting?"

"Yes very much so."

"Well, it was very interesting to me too."

"Please, you two," Mom said. "You are getting off the subject."

"Right. Sorry," I said. "Anyway, I needed to return the book to Dr. Noble, and when I phoned her about it, she suggested that I come over one evening and we could talk about it rather than have an official session."

"Let me ask you a question," Dad said. "I have to ask. Is this Dr. Noble attractive?"

I paused for a second or two and then said, "Yes."

"Very attractive, maybe?"

"Yes."

"I think I am beginning to get the picture," Dad said. "Does this Dr. Noble happen to have a first name?"

"Yes. June."

"So my son, the celibate priest, is seeing a very attractive psychotherapist by the name of June Noble."

"No. You are taking this much too far."

"Really?" Dad stated, perhaps a bit sarcastically.

"Yes. Let me continue. Okay?" I paused.

They both nodded.

"I returned the book to her a couple of weeks ago. It was in the evening. She had wine and cheese and crackers set out. We sat at opposite ends of her couch in her living room and chatted about a lot of stuff, including the book. She also served me dinner and then dessert and more wine. I probably had too much wine. She even wondered if I was okay to walk back to St. Ann's when I got on the elevator. It was one of the most pleasant times I have had in a long time. The next morning, Father Clancy even said I looked better than he had seen me look in a long time. And that's it."

"That's it," Dad repeated. "You only sat on the couch together."

"Yes, Dad. Really. At opposite ends of her rather long couch. I promise you that's my entire experience with June up to this point."

"So she is June, not Dr. Noble? And 'up to this point?'" my mother said.

"Yes. She is June, and I have to say that I consider her a friend, though I haven't seen her since. But I also have to say I hope I will see her again. She's quite a fascinating woman. What they call a renaissance woman these days."

"What do you mean by that?" Mom asked.

"She is unbelievably talented. Not only is she a therapist but she also is an artist, plays the piano and flute, and is a vocalist. She's a member of the Masterworks Choral Society. She suggested I might want to join it. They need tenors, she said. But I said there was no way I could do it."

"So where is all this headed?" my father asked.

"I don't know. I talked a bit about it with Father Clancy, and he suggested I see Father Sedgwick again, which I did."

"You told Father Clancy about your June?" Mom asked.

"She's not my June. But no, I don't think I mentioned her. It's just that he saw that I was having problems still stemming from everything that has gone on."

"And how did your meeting with Father Sedgwick go?" Dad asked.

"I told him about my apparent new interest in the sciences and wondered if that was appropriate and also about June."

"And?" both parents prompted.

"And he pointed out to me that most all the Roman Catholic colleges and universities have science departments that study such things as relativity and quantum theory. He told me he has an interest in the subject as well and that it was perfectly fine for me to want to explore the subject."

"Oh dear," my mother said.

"What about your involvement with June?" Dad asked.

"Dad, there's no involvement. But, to put it bluntly, he reminded me that while he and I are celibate, that doesn't change the fact that we are human and men and find members of the opposite sex attractive."

I looked across the table at my parents and saw only blank faces. They were attempting to absorb everything I had said, I supposed.

Finally my mother said, "But still, after all these conversations with Father Clancy and Father Sedgwick, you felt the need to get away from it all. In fact, Father Sedgwick suggested you do just that, and that is why you are here."

"Yes."

"So you still are unsettled in your thinking," my mother said.

"Yes."

My father interjected, "Stop me if I'm wrong, but I think there are two things, two issues or conundrums, that are at the root of your being here."

"You do?" I asked.

"Yes. Shall I continue?" He looked at me and then my mother.

"If you think you should," my mother said.

"I'm not sure I should because I could be way off base. And I don't want to influence your mental process improperly," he said, looking at me.

"I can use all the help I can get, Dad."

"Okay. Here's what I think is going on. Number one, no matter how you slice it, no matter how much you may deny it, I believe you are struggling over your faith. Your exposure to scientific thought has made you wonder about things. You've had it explained to you that scientific exploration is perfectly okay within the church, but your experience on that golf course has complicated things for you, and you are still having to deal with that. Put the two together and we find an understandably very confused priest.

"Number two—and I don't want to seem condemnatory when I say this—you are a man, as your Father Sedgwick rightly has explained, and it's normal for you to appreciate the joys of womanhood. I certainly understand that, being a man as well. But I suspect there's more to your finding your June Noble attractive than you are willing to admit, even to yourself. That's what I think."

Dad's declaration was stunning to me, even though I knew deep down that he had hit the nail on the head. I rose from the table without saying another word and took another walk in the park with Cherry. My parents were rather nonplussed, but they, too, didn't say another word. There were many more people in the park, but I nevertheless was able to calm myself with Cherry's help. It was amazing how calming an effect a little dog could have.

When we returned, I found that my mother had prepared a salmon salad for lunch.

"I hope we haven't upset things," she said as Cherry and I came through the door.

"I suppose I have to say you have." I said as I removed Cherry's leash and she settled into her bed. "But not in a bad way, if that's what you mean. Yes, you have caused me to be more honest with myself. And that seemed rather upsetting when I left with Cherry.

But I now understand that I have some serious contemplating to do. And I think the best place for me to do that is back in Riverdale and at St. Ann's. It's time I face these questions head-on and get on with my life."

My father was sitting at the table, sipping what had to be at least his third cup of coffee. "What issues?"

"The ones you outlined. To put it bluntly, how solid is my faith? Does the fact that it was shaken by that experience on the golf course, no matter how irrational the cause may have been, mean that I am not as solidly founded as I should be as a priest? And then there is June. You put it very well. I need to decide if there is more to my attraction to her than is healthy for a celibate priest. There's no more beating around the bush. I've decided that I need to get back to where I belong and to where the action is."

"The action," Dad repeated.

"Yes. St. Ann's is my home and headquarters. And Riverdale is where June Noble is. It all centers around those two."

"You're not going to give up your faith, Iggy, are you?" My mother looked as though she might be close to tears.

"No. I see no question of that happening, Mom. It's not so much a question of that as it is of the priesthood."

"So bottom line, it comes down to June Noble," Dad said.

"In a way you could say that. But what she has done, and to some extent Father Sedgwick, is caused me to think about things I never thought about before. I am beginning to think my faith has been founded on a rather narrow sense of things regarding our creator."

"Narrow sense of things?" Mom asked.

"You know," I said. "I have no idea how many times I have looked up at the heavens on a clear night and seen all those stars and thought how beautiful they were. But I never wondered what they had to say about my God. How do the stars in our Milky

Way fit into my understanding of heaven? How did those stars get there? And our moon. What keeps it revolving around our earth so constantly? I'd never thought about those things. But now I do. And it's rather mind-boggling."

"I see what you're saying," my father said. "And you think that you need to go back to St. Ann's to, what, explore your new thinking?"

"That's what came to me in the park. I need to fill Father Clancy in, tell him everything. I trust him implicitly to help me go forward. But he can only do that if he knows everything. And I mean everything."

Chapter 35

✝

I left Philadelphia on the 4:33 p.m. train out of Thirtieth Street Station and spent the two-hour ride watching the scenery go by as I tried to collect my thoughts and figure out just how I should approach Father Clancy. From Pennsylvania Station, I took the IRT subway up to 242nd Street and walked the mile or so back to St. Ann's. I had phoned Father Clancy to let him know I was returning. By the time I walked into the rectory, it was approaching eight o'clock, but a meal had been saved for me, and I dug in. Father Clancy joined me at the table with a cup of tea in his hand.

"So you are back. And a day early," he said.

"I am."

"And you are well, I trust."

"Yes. Very well. It was good that I went to see my parents. They have always been supportive of me and all my brothers and sisters, and this time was no exception. We had some good conversation, and I had some good walks alone, or almost alone. I had their little dog, Cherry, with me. Believe it or not, having her with me, trusting me implicitly, was wonderfully therapeutic."

"Sounds very nice."

"It was. But I decided to come back early because I came to

a decision that I would like to share with you, if that would be all right."

"Of course it would be all right. About anything in particular?"

How could I explain? Finally I said, "Yes. In a word, about my future."

"Sounds … I'm not sure what. Ominous?"

"No, no. Don't think that. Nothing like that. It's just that so much has happened, so many experiences I never believed could happen, so many ideas expressed to me that I would like to fill you in on and get your opinion as to how I should proceed. I can go to all kinds of therapists or what have you. But when push comes to shove, I would rather talk to you."

He took a sip from his tea. "Are you talking about a confession?"

"Actually, no. I don't think so. I just would like to bounce all this stuff off of someone I trust. And I can't think of anyone else but you. I hope you understand."

"Well, thank you for that." He looked at his watch. "It's getting rather late. Shall we talk in my office after breakfast tomorrow?"

"That would be great. Thanks so much."

"No need to thank me. As you know, a good part of my job is to make sure my priests are okay in their mission. So I'll say goodnight now and see you tomorrow.

The next morning after breakfast, Father Clancy and I brought our cups of coffee with us to his office. I sat in the same chair I had occupied a number of times during the past several weeks, and he sat behind his desk. He sipped at his coffee and then put the cup on his desk and said nothing but looked at me with a slight smile.

I took a sip of my coffee, put it on his desk, and proceeded to relate everything that had happened during my visit to Philadelphia. I even included many details about Cherry and the comforting company she had provided. Halfway through my dissertation, Father Clancy slowly swung his chair partially around, leaned back with his elbows resting on the arms, and touched his steepled fingertips to his lips. His eyes were almost closed.

After I finished my story, I held my breath. Father Clancy remained in his pensive position and said through his fingertips, "Your father sounds like a very intelligent man."

"I've always thought that," I said. "You know, he only finished high school, never went to college, but he constantly reads rather esoteric tomes. He knows a lot. I've often thought he is smarter than a lot of college-educated people I've met."

"I know what you mean. My father and mother are the same. I rely on their counsel often." He turned his chair back to face me. "So your father suspects you have an attraction for Dr. Noble that goes beyond mere friendship."

"Yes."

"And he thinks you should or could expand your understanding of the, shall we say, stars without necessarily impinging on your faith but that you are struggling over that as well."

"Yes."

"Is he correct in his thinking?"

"Yes."

"Including about Dr. Noble?"

"I haven't seen her since that evening when I returned her book to her, so I have had no further experience with her. But I can't deny that something draws me to her. Something wants me to get back in touch with her. Is that something more than friendship? I don't know. But I do wonder about it. So I guess I have to say the answer is yes."

Suddenly I discovered I was breathing easier. I had finally

gotten things off my chest with Father Clancy. But where were we headed?

After pausing for some time, Father Clancy said, "You know, Iggy, you are not the first priest to feel an attraction toward a woman. Down through the centuries, the history of the church is rife with incidents where not only priests but members of the hierarchy were not only attracted to women but violated their celibacy and fathered children. So as far as you are concerned, your story is not at all unique. The question remains, however: What are you going to do about it going forward?"

"I understand. And I, at this instant, don't know what I am going to do. Should I treat her as simply a friend and get back in touch? Or should I stay away?"

"I cannot answer that question for you."

"You can't?"

"No. And here's why. The last thing in the world I would wish is to have you leave the priesthood and our parish. As you know, I consider you a valuable member of our little family here at St. Ann's, and the last thing the church at large needs right now is to lose a faithful priest. We're having a hard enough time finding new priests as the older ones retire without also losing someone like yourself. You know that, of course. But the key word in what I just said is *faithful*, and I'm not referring to church doctrine. I'm talking about a priest going about his duties without distractions, to put it mildly. No. This is a matter of conscience, and the only person who can decide the correct path to follow in your case is you."

I had known for some time Father Clancy was a wise man. But his words still were a huge relief too me. I felt a tension in my shoulders fade as I said, "I had a feeling you would say that, but I wanted to be sure you knew where I am coming from."

"I appreciate your confidence and your keeping me up to date.

It means a lot to me. It also confirms my confidence in you. I've told you before, and I'll repeat it now: you are a good man, Iggy. I know you will do the right thing."

"Thanks. I have to say I have no idea what that right thing is. But …"

"Well, why don't you go about your chores here at St. Ann's and let God be your conscience."

"Be still and know that I am God."

"Exactly."

"You know who reminded me of that?"

"I suspect Dr. Noble."

"Yes."

"I've never met her, but from everything you've told me, she's a good person. Something that is also occurring to me, Iggy, is that you might be harboring a sense of guilt regarding any attraction you may feel for her."

"Yes. I suppose that is true. I hadn't thought of it in that way but …"

"Well, Father Sedgwick spelled out very well how that works among us celibate priests. Take that to heart and get rid of the guilt. You are who you are. You are only trying to follow the correct path, to do the right thing. One can ask for no more than that."

He stood. "Now I have things I need to attend to. You are home a day early, so why don't you take the time to do some serious praying and get an understanding of what your next move should be."

Chapter 36

✝

About four blocks south on Riverdale Avenue, just beyond Public School 81 where Father Clancy went to grammar school, is a small park called Vincent Veteran Park. Next to it is Hackett Park, which borders the Henry Hudson Parkway. It could be noisy, but Vincent Veteran Park could be quiet, even with all the traffic going by on Riverdale Avenue. So I dressed in my civvies and headed there. I couldn't have Cherry with me, but I could still sit on a park bench and enjoy the small amount of foliage in the park and listen to the few birds chirping in the trees.

As I sat there, it was rather strange to me how much I missed that little dog. She had in some way helped me to let go. To get quiet. To stop thinking about all this stuff.

"Well, so be it," I thought. *"There's nobody else around. You are alone. Make the best of it."*

So I did. I just sat there and let whatever might come to me come to me. The whole business about the trial and everything else began to intrude, but I managed to cast those thoughts aside. Finally, I found myself concentrating on June.

I guess it's inevitable, isn't it? I thought. *In the last analysis, she got me thinking about all this science stuff. Add to that the fact that she is very attractive and I enjoy being around her. That's where it's at. Admit it.*

So I let myself dwell on Dr. June Noble. I reviewed my sessions with her in her office. I remembered how cute I thought she was even with her hair pulled back and dressed in her professional business attire. I remembered how blown away I was when she greeted me that evening when I went to return the book. She was devastatingly beautiful with her dark hair down, dressed in that close-fitting though modest black dress. Her bright smile as she looked at me.

Yes, I thought. *I am a man, and she is wonderfully attractive.*

My eyes opened. I felt I had been daydreaming. The sounds of the park came back to me. The traffic noise on Riverdale Avenue came back. But it had been a very pleasant daydream indeed.

"Okay. So now what?" I asked myself. *"Let's try to be rational, to think things through logically."* It occurred to me that I was actually being unfair to June. Yes, she was very attractive to me, and I believed she had dressed up for our evening together.

But it wasn't her fault that I was so attracted to her. And besides, it wasn't only her physical attributes that I found appealing. *"She's a very intelligent, creative person."* I thought. *"What's wrong with wanting to get to know her better? As a friend. Forget the attractiveness thing. Think about what she has to offer as a friend."* I paused for a moment.

I got up and started walking along the path with my hands clasped behind my back.

"So," I then asked myself out loud, "what's your next step? She hasn't reached out to you. Maybe she's thinking it would be best not to maintain a relationship. Maybe she doesn't even want to maintain a relationship. After all, you are a priest. What could there be in it for her?"

That stopped me cold. Of course. I had been thinking only of myself. Worrying only about myself. But what about her? She undoubtedly saw no future in any relationship with me, at least not in any romantic way. But what could I offer her in any friendship way, I wondered. Not an awful lot. She had all the smarts.

So I decided then and there to try to drop the subject and get on with my life as a priest.

Chapter 37

✝

B ut, as I was walking back to St. Ann's, my cell phone rang.
It was June Noble. I had not heard a word from her since I
last saw her and now she was calling. What could this be about,
I wondered.

"Hello?" I said.

"Hi, Iggy. It's been a while. I've been wondering how you are
doing," she said.

"I'm doing well," I said. "And you?"

"I'm doing very well. But I do have a reason for calling."

"What's that?" I tried to sound very noncommittal.

"Well, the Masterworks Choral Society has started rehearsals.
We had our first one last Monday evening, and there's a real
shortage of tenors. Our conductor asked us all to see if we knew
anybody who might join us. I know you didn't think it would be
possible for you to join, but I thought I would give it a try. Any
chance you could join us? We're doing Handel's *Messiah*."

"It's funny. I was just thinking about you," I said.

"You were?"

"Yes. I don't know why," I lied, "but you popped into my
head. And now here you are phoning me."

"Interesting. Do you suppose it's that synchronicity business?"
She chuckled a bit.

"Could be, I suppose. As far as the choral society is concerned, you know I'm no musician. Except for hymns in church, I haven't sung a word since high school. We did do *Messiah* back then. A couple of times. In fact, I believe I still have a copy that I saved. So I'm somewhat familiar with it. But I don't know about being very helpful. And I doubt I'd ever pass an audition."

"We don't have auditions. Anyone who wants to is welcome to join. We have an incredible conductor who is very patient and somehow gets us to produce a wonderful sound at our performances. Can you think about it? We rehearse every Monday night."

"I'd have to clear it with Father Clancy. Where are the rehearsals?"

"We perform at the Hayes Auditorium at Mount St. Vincent, and we rehearse in one of the Hayes rehearsal rooms. What do you think? Can you do it?"

"I don't know. Let me think about it. Can I get back to you?"

"Of course. Let me hear from you. I'll look forward to it." She hung up.

"Now what?" I asked myself as I continued the few blocks to St. Ann's.

"You'll never guess who just phoned me," I said as I entered Father Clancy's office. He was just hanging up his phone.

"June Noble," he said.

"How did you know?"

"She called here. Said something about wanting to reach you about joining a chorus? I told her you had gone out and gave her your cell phone number."

"I wondered how she had my number. Yes, that's what she called about. There's a Masterworks Choral Society of which she is a member. They have started rehearsals for a Christmas concert doing Handel's *Messiah*. They need tenors, so she called me. She had mentioned it last time I saw her, but I told her I couldn't see myself becoming part of such a thing. But I guess they are desperate for tenors, so much so that their conductor asked them to cast about for them."

"When do they rehearse?"

"Monday evenings at the Hayes Auditorium at Mount St. Vincent."

"Mondays are our least busy evenings. Why don't you give it a try? Could be a nice departure for you. Broaden your vision."

"You think so? What about June?"

"What about her? They need tenors. She thought about you and gave you a call. Why make it any more than that? How big a chorus is it? Do you know?"

"I think she told me that they have something like one hundred members."

"What voice does she sing? Do you know?"

"No, I don't."

"Well, it doesn't matter. It's a good-sized chorus. You'll be among the tenors, and she'll be among the sopranos or altos. Never the twain shall meet. At least that used to be my experience when I sang at DeWitt Clinton High School."

"Mine too in high school now that I think of it. Maybe I'll do it."

"Go ahead. Give it a try. It'll be good for you."

"You really think I should?"

"I wouldn't say so if I didn't. You must know that by now."

"You know, the more I think about it, the more I like the idea. I'll do it." I turned around and left his office. I still had the rest of the day off. It was lunchtime, so I went into the kitchen, found myself something to eat, and sat at our communal table.

Jimmy came in and saw me. "You're back. I thought we wouldn't be seeing you until tomorrow."

"Me too, but I wanted to get back here. Don't ask me to explain. It's a long, boring story. How are things going?"

"Fine. It'll be good to have you back, though. We've been a bit short-handed."

"Then I'm really glad I came back sooner." I paused and then said, "You'll never guess what I've just decided to do. Father Clancy even encouraged me."

"I have no idea. What? Go get an advanced degree in something?"

"No, no. Nothing like that. I've decided to join the Masterworks Choral Society."

"Really? Whatever made you do that? They're a really good organization. I've been to a couple of their concerts, and they are very good. They're quite a large group. Put out a fantastic sound. Kind of overwhelms you when you hear their first notes."

"I had never heard of them until I met my therapist. You know, Dr. Noble?"

"Oh yeah. Are you still seeing her? I thought you were all over that business."

"I am. She called me today out of the blue. Told me they need tenors and wondered if I would join them. After talking with Father Clancy, I decided I would."

"Sounds like it could be fun. I'd do it myself if I could carry a tune. But I'm the old poor Johnny One-Note. Only with me it's Jimmy One-Note."

"Right. I've noticed."

"You have?"

"I have indeed."

We both burst out laughing. My Lord, it felt good to be back and to be having a plain old normal conversation with my good friend Jimmy.

After lunch I decided to head up to my room and take a nap. I was feeling very relaxed. I was so glad Jimmy had come in and sort of brought me back down to earth. I stretched out on my bed, decided to phone June after dinner that night, and fell fast asleep.

Chapter 38

✝

June picked me up at St. Ann's on the next Monday evening promptly at 6:30. Rehearsals started at 7:30 p.m. on the dot, she had told me, and she liked to get there a half hour early to check in and do whatever else members had to do. She also wanted to introduce me around, especially to their conductor.

I had found my rather dog-eared score for *Messiah*, which for some inexplicable reason I had decided to take with me when I first moved to St. Ann's from Philadelphia. After making our appointment for Monday, I had gone over the score. It was no easy piece to learn, especially the tenor part, which bore little relationship to the melody that the audience heard. I surprised myself by feeling somewhat familiar with it.

So I was feeling reasonably comfortable with the idea of attempting to participate in the Masterworks Choral Society's performance of *Messiah*. And, to be honest with myself, it was wonderful to see June again and to sit next to her as she drove us to Mount St. Vincent College, only a few miles up Riverdale Avenue.

"It's wonderful to see you, Iggy," June had said as I climbed into her gray Honda Civic.

I was dressed in gray slacks and a short-sleeve shirt. She had on black slacks and a loosely fitting but somewhat revealing sweater. Her black hair fell loose to her shoulders. I also noticed some lipstick.

Oh boy, I thought. *Is this going to work?* But I only said, "Me too."

"So you are in your civilian garb. How do you want me to introduce you?"

"Just call me Iggy Costello. Or Ignatius, Iggy for short, I suppose. Something like that. That usually gets a chuckle from folks, which will be fine."

"Okay. I can imagine you would rather not have folks put two and two together and remember the trial."

"Exactly. I'd just as soon be anonymous for now."

We soon pulled onto the campus and into a parking lot next to Hayes Auditorium. We got out, and June led me into a side door that brought us directly to a small lobby area where a bunch of folks were signing in prior to entering the rehearsal hall.

June took me by the hand, which was a pleasant sensation, and brought me to a table where several women were seated. She introduced me to them and explained that I was a new tenor.

"Hurray!" they exclaimed. They explained that new members, especially tenors (said with a big smile) were exempt from dues for their first semester. I had not thought about having to pay dues, and June had not said anything, probably since I was a new member.

June brought me into the rehearsal hall and introduced me to the conductor, Mitzi Templeton. She was young, slender, and quite vivacious and greeted me with great joy. June then pointed out the tenor section, where a number of men and a few women were already seated.

"Grab any chair you want," she said. Then she left and headed over to what I soon learned was the soprano section.

I grabbed a seat on the aisle next to another man, who said

hello and told me his name. "Nice to meet you," I said. "I'm Ignatius Costello. Most folks just call me Iggy."

"Nice to meet you, Iggy," he said with a huge smile.

His greeting was welcoming. The conductor's greeting was welcoming. The entire place felt very welcoming.

Ms. Templeton called us to order and had all new members stand, and we were applauded. She warned us new members that many of the regular members knew *Messiah* well and that we should not concern ourselves if we found it difficult. "Give it a few weeks," she said, "before you allow yourselves to be discouraged."

We then spent the next two hours rehearsing various sections from Handel's *Messiah*. We would not perform the entire piece, which lasted some four hours, but enough sections, including, of course, the "Hallelujah Chorus," to fill about a two-hour program. Ms. Templeton, who everybody called Mitzi, worked us very hard. We sang our parts over and over until she was satisfied that we were getting it. By the end of those two hours, I was exhausted, and I could see many others were too.

As we started to exit our seats, June came over. "How did you like it?"

"I haven't worked that hard on something for two hours in a long time. But I really did enjoy myself."

"So do you think you'll continue?" She wore a somewhat concerned expression as if she feared I might not.

"Absolutely," I said. "This has been a great change of pace from my normal routine and from all that I have been through. I can't thank you enough for inviting me to join."

"Oh, I'm so glad," she said. "I have to admit, I was a bit nervous."

"Have no concern. It was an experiment on my part, but I'm totally hooked."

"Excellent. A few of us usually head over to the Riverdale Pub for a drink or two. Would you like to join us? If not, I can take you right home."

"Yes. I think I'd like that."

"Great. Let's go."

The Riverdale Pub was only a couple of blocks from St. Ann's. It was a full-service restaurant, but at this hour, which was around ten o'clock, all they were offering was pizza and drinks. Six or seven folks were already there when June and I entered.

"Hi all," June said. "Meet our new tenor, Ignatius Costello, who goes by the name of Iggy."

"Hi, Iggy," they all responded.

We found a couple of chairs next to two women who, I learned, were altos. They were older folks and during our conversation explained that they had been members of the chorus for more than twenty years!

"So you all have been singing for a long time," I said.

"Yes," one of them said. "In fact, some of our members have been with the chorus for its entire existence, which is more than fifty years. Mitzi is our second conductor. She's been with us about five or six years, I guess."

"My Lord!" I said. "I've been living in this neighborhood for close to ten years and I had no idea."

While we were chatting, a waitress came over, and June ordered two glasses of red wine for us. When the glasses arrived, she said, "Last time I saw you, you preferred red. You were so involved in chatting that I figured that would work for you."

"You're right. Thanks. But I had better have only the one. Last time it was all I could do to walk home."

"So you two know each other well?" one of our table mates asked.

"Reasonably well," June said. "We've only met a few times, but the last time was at a small gathering, and let's say Iggy seemed to enjoy the red wine that was being served. I had to make certain he could make it home okay. It was only a short walk."

"Oh, I hate that feeling," one of the ladies said. "There's nothing worse than that morning-after feeling."

"You know," I said, "I know what you're talking about. I was a little hungover the next morning, but I quickly recovered and, in fact, told my boss I had a very nice time and was feeling great."

June looked at me with a lovely smile. She had nicely explained our relationship without actually saying anything. I had no idea whether or not these people knew she was a therapist.

A short while later, folks began to say goodbye, and we followed suit. We were only a couple of blocks from St. Ann's, so I told June she needn't bother to drive me.

"Okay," she said. "See you next Monday?"

"For sure."

"Shall I pick you up?"

"Why don't I pick you up?"

"Okay. I'll be waiting downstairs at six thirty. See you then."

We parted. I wasn't sure what I had expected, but I felt a bit disappointed.

Chapter 39

✝

I got back to the rectory around eleven o'clock and felt hungry, so I headed to the kitchen to see if there was something I could munch on before going to bed. Lo and behold, there was Jimmy finishing what looked like a piece of chocolate cake. He saw me staring at his dish and pointed to the kitchen counter, where the remains of a cake was waiting to be devoured.

"Do you suppose there's any ice cream?" I asked.

With his mouth full, he pointed with his fork to the refrigerator. I opened the top freezer portion, and there sat a large container of vanilla ice cream. There was nothing better than a piece of chocolate cake and vanilla ice cream, I thought. I cut a large piece of cake, scooped out a sizable portion of ice cream, grabbed a fork, and sat down opposite Jimmy.

"So what has you up so late?" I asked.

"I might ask you the same thing," returned Jimmy.

"I just got back from rehearsing with the Masterworks Choral Society."

"Oh, right. I forgot about that. How did it go?"

"It was exhausting but good."

"Exhausting?"

"Yes. Two hours of almost nonstop rehearsing. Going over and over lines."

"What are they doing?"

"Handel's *Messiah*."

"Oh, that is a tough one."

"Yes and no. I mean, it's a gorgeous piece of music, and I am somewhat familiar with it. But, yes, there are a lot of notes to learn. And some really tricky passages. So what has you up so late?"

"Nothing really. I was reading and began to feel hungry and came down to see what I could find. So how did you know to go to the chorus?"

"Remember? I told you my therapist told me about it?"

"Oh yeah. I forgot. But if she's your therapist doesn't that feel a little strange?"

"Strange?"

"Well, yeah." He said. "I mean couldn't that make your sessions a little weird?"

"I'm not seeing her as a therapist any more. That's all over and done with. At least I hope it is. And I don't think I would go to her again as a therapist. She's become a friend, and it probably wouldn't be appropriate."

"A friend."

"Yeah. I mean, I don't really know her that well, but we've been to rehearsal together and we also went out with a few other choristers after the rehearsal for a drink. So, yes, I'd say she's a friend."

I headed up to bed, fell fast asleep, and woke the next morning feeling very well and ready to take on my duties at St. Ann's. At breakfast, I thanked Father Clancy profusely for encouraging me to go to that rehearsal.

I kept telling myself that I was so enthused about rehearsing for *Messiah* because of the experience I'd had at the first rehearsal: going over all those lines of music, learning again all those notes, beginning to grasp just what Handel in the eighteenth century had wanted from us singers in the twenty-first century, and also meeting a few more of the choristers afterwards and getting to know some new faces.

At the same time, I kept mentally denying that I also was looking forward to seeing June Noble for any reason other than to take her to rehearsal.

Chapter 40

I had always loved the Christmas season. As a child and the youngest, the Christmas tree and all the decorations and presents had been magical. Our neighborhood in Philadelphia had always been wonderfully lit up and decorated.

Riverdale and St. Ann's were no exception. From the crèche out front to the tree in the vestibule and all the holly and candles, it was magical. A lot of Jews resided in Riverdale alongside all the Christians. Between the two, Riverdale was incredibly lovely, especially in the evenings prior to December 25 with all the menorahs in people's windows and the various Christmas displays.

This year was especially memorable. June and I had spent the last ten or eleven Mondays commuting together to rehearsals for *Messiah*. Finally, on the Sunday before Christmas Day, the 120 voices of the Masterworks Choral Society performed in front of a packed Hayes Auditorium. Together with a chamber orchestra, including timpani and trumpet—to accompany "The Trumpet Shall Sound"—and four incredible soloists, and ending with the final, unbelievable "Amen," we brought the house down. I thought the standing ovation would never end. What a joyous way to end the weeks of rehearsing.

Several of our chorus members were Jewish, and one of them who lived in Fieldston invited all us choristers to her house for an after-the-concert party. Fortunately, she lived in a large house. While not everyone attended, a lot did. It had been my turn to drive, so I drove June to the party. Our hostess had gone to a lot of trouble to decorate her living room, dining room, and even her kitchen with menorahs, a large Christmas tree, wreaths, and mistletoe. It was an ecumenical decor.

We had a wonderfully festive time singing Christmas carols and even a few Hebrew songs for which sheets of music were provided. The food was excellent. I was just plain blown away. June told me that this party was an annual event and was always held at this home.

By the time we left, it was approaching ten o'clock and a lovely, gentle snow was falling straight down. There was not even a hint of a breeze. The sidewalk was beginning to get slippery as we walked back to my car. June had changed out of her practical standing-on-the-stage shoes into fairly high heels, and she was finding the sidewalk a bit tricky. Without saying anything, she tucked her hand under my arm and took hold. I looked at her, and a lovely smile met my eyes. With the gentle snow, the crisp cold air, and our walking together arm in arm, I couldn't help but think, *What could be more romantic?* And for the moment, I didn't care.

I held open the door to the passenger side of my car as June thanked me, gave me another smile, and climbed in. I went around to my side, climbed in, started the car, and drove to her apartment. I pulled up in front of her building.

"I'll walk you to the door," I said. "It's getting quite slippery."

"Okay. Thanks," she said.

I walked around and opened her car door. She climbed out, smiled at me, and took my arm once more. We walked the thirty feet to the entrance of her building.

"I don't suppose you'd like to come up for a last glass of wine?" she asked as I opened the lobby door for her.

"I probably shouldn't, but I'd love to," I said. "This has been an incredible day and evening for me. The best time I have had in a long time. And I'd love to cap it off. As long as it's no trouble for you."

"No trouble. Come on up."

Our only socializing for the last eleven weeks had been taking turns driving each other to rehearsals and joining a few folks after. June, I felt, had become a good friend. I had not been in her apartment since the third time I saw her.

As we came off the elevator, I saw a holly wreath with a welcome sign below it hanging on her door just below the peephole. We entered her apartment, took off our overcoats, and hung them in the hall closet. I followed her into the kitchen, where she grabbed two wine glasses from a cabinet and poured red wine from an already open bottle. She handed me a glass, and I followed her into the living room. We once again sat at opposite ends of the couch.

"It has been quite a day, hasn't it?" she said as she put her glass to her lips.

"It sure has," I responded, taking my first sip. "Hard to believe it's over. All those rehearsals culminating in today."

"And no more Monday night rehearsals for two months. I hope you are expecting to continue."

"I am. Do you know what Mitzi has planned for the next concert?"

"I believe she said Brahms's *Requiem*."

"I'm not familiar with it. Is it a toughie?"

"It's an incredible piece, and you'll certainly recognize some of it. It's not your normal Catholic Latin Requiem Mass. Rather Brahms wrote it in German and in memory of his mother, who he must have loved very much. The first time we did it, which was maybe five years ago, it was difficult for me at first. But as the rehearsals continued, I finally began to get it. We sang an English translation, and I imagine we'll do that again."

"I guess I'm a bit relieved we won't be having any rehearsals for a while," I said. "Christmas is almost upon us, and we will be very busy at St. Ann's. So it's probably just as well at least for the next couple of weeks. What will you be doing over the holidays?"

"My brother and sister and I will be joining our parents in Upstate New York. My brother is married and has two youngsters. They're a lot of fun."

I'd had no knowledge of her family until now. "So you have a brother and sister."

"Yes. My brother's the oldest. My sister's a couple of years younger than I am, and neither of us has taken the plunge … yet." She smiled at me.

"Yet? Someone in the offing?"

"No. Here I am, thirty-one years old and haven't clicked with any of the guys I have met in the past." She shrugged and smiled broadly. So she was a bit younger than I was.

I smiled in return. "I can't be with my family at Christmas, as you can imagine. But we used to have a blast. You can't imagine what it's like to have fourteen brothers and sisters all together. And they still do it, except without me. They, with all their spouses and kids, congregate at my mother and father's home. It's the same home we all were raised in. Then, a few days after Christmas, I'm usually able to join my folks and whoever else is still there."

"Are you able to visit your parents often?" she asked. "I am ashamed to say I only see mine at Christmas and maybe in the summer. They live on a lake, and I sometimes head up there for a few days."

"No, I don't see them as often as they would like." I had not told her about my last visit to Philadelphia. Should I? Would I?

Having what I guessed was my third glass of wine of the night gave me some concern. I was feeling very mellow, and I did not want to get any more mellow like the last time I was here. All kinds of thoughts ran through my head as I looked at June sitting at the other end of the couch.

At some point during our rehearsals, it had become known that I was a priest. With that knowledge, I knew people saw nothing more than the friendship that existed between June and me. We commuted back and forth to rehearsals on Monday nights and that was it. I went about my church activities and she about her practice the rest of the time. And I believed that.

Still, here I was enjoying myself immensely and regretting that we would not be seeing each other until rehearsals started up at the end of February.

And I did not want to leave. But why? What was it about this relationship that was so compelling?

"… do you?" June was saying to me.

"What? Sorry. I'm afraid I was lost in thought there. I'm feeling really good right now and was sort of wondering … I don't know what."

"I was saying that I suspected you wished you could see them more often."

"My parents?"

"Yes."

"Yes, I probably should try to see them more often. My last visit with them was one of the nicest I have ever had. I learned a lot about them that I never knew before."

"Good things?"

"Yes. Very good things. And a bit startling."

"Startling? About your parents? Like what? Do you mind my asking?"

I had to wonder if June the therapist was asking these questions. But she was refilling my glass, which was in my hand once more. And looking into my face. *Oh boy! How much more of this stuff should I drink? Is this heading somewhere?*

"No, I don't mind your asking. I found out my dad has an interest in the same things you introduced me to—physics, cosmology. To the extent that, it seems, he sort of drives my mother to distraction. She can't understand the fascination. He says one of my sisters is also into the same stuff. My mother says that when they get together, their conversations are unbelievably boring. That's how she put it. She even made a play on the name of Niels Bohr. Thought his name was very apt."

June laughed out loud, and I followed suit. For some reason, we both couldn't stop laughing. Tears came flowing from my eyes. It almost became painful. Finally, we got ourselves under control.

"My God, I haven't laughed like that in I don't know how long," June said.

"Me too. What brought it on, I wonder?"

"It sounds like your mother has a real sense of humor."

"She does. They both do. But I didn't think it was that funny. I really lost it there."

"Well, we've both had a fair amount to drink. That can loosen things up," she said. "And we've had a wonderful day. And if you are anything like me, we're tired."

"I am. Really tired, in fact. I guess we should call it a halt. Though I have to say I don't want to. I have been enjoying myself so much."

"Me too. But you're probably right. We better call it a day … or night … or whatever."

We both started laughing again.

Finally, I said, "Okay. It really is time for me to go. But, June, let me say this. I can't possibly thank you enough for everything. For all your help during those difficult days and weeks, for getting me to join the chorus, and for your friendship. You are a very special person, and I am so glad you have come into my life. I suspect the reason I don't want to leave is that I don't want it to end."

"Iggy, thank you for saying that … It's not going to end. For me you are a special guy. You have a quality about you of gentleness and decency that is rather rare in a man, in my experience. And I certainly consider you a very good friend. There's no way we are going to let it end. At the very least, we'll be starting rehearsals again in a couple of months. And who knows what may bring us together in the meantime."

We headed to her hall closet, and she pulled my overcoat out and helped me put it on. Then she patted me on the back, took my arm, and walked me to the elevator.

"You are going to be able to drive home, right?" she asked.

"Yeah, I will. The snow stopped falling outside your windows, so I doubt it's very deep. No problem there. The wine? Well, it's only a short drive. I'll be okay."

The elevator arrived, and the doors opened. I stepped in and turned to face her. She had such a lovely, somewhat wistful smile on her face as the door closed.

When I stepped outside, it had stopped snowing, and the air was very crisp. The snow was maybe two or three powdery inches deep, and the stars were shining brightly. All the Christmas lights were glowing. It was, indeed, a magical evening. I had to wonder as I drove the couple of blocks back to St. Ann's what might bring June and me together in the meantime.

Chapter 41

✝

The Christmas season was upon us in spades. The preparations leading up to the midnight mass kept us busy. Finally, the mass was upon us. Father Clancy was clad in his finest clerical garb, as was I. Jimmy and I assisted him as we went through the ritual. The church was full unto overflowing. It was interesting to see all the family members who never came to services during the rest of the year suddenly here dressed in their finest.

Toward the end of the mass, I spied June Noble way in the back of the congregation. To my knowledge, June was not a Catholic. But there she was. Of course, she was looking in my direction, but I didn't think she was aware that I had spotted her. I kept watching her out of the corner of my eye as the service proceeded, and it seemed clear to me she was unpracticed in the ups and downs expected of congregants. But she kept up well, obviously not wanting to stand out.

After the service, it was dark and cold outside, but we priests went to the front of the building and greeted as many parishioners as we could, wishing all a Merry Christmas. Suddenly, there was June.

"It was a lovely service, Father," she said as she shook my hand.

"June, what a pleasant surprise. And it's Iggy to you." Then I turned to Father Clancy and Jimmy. "Father Clancy and Father Conan, I'd like you to meet Dr. June Noble. She's the therapist who helped me through all those troubles last summer."

"Oh, Dr. Noble, I'm so happy to meet you," Father Clancy said. "I've heard so much about you from Iggy. You were a great help to him." He shook her hand. "It's so nice of you to come out on this rather frigid night."

"Me too," said Jimmy. "He's told us how much you helped him."

"I am not a regular church goer," she said. "But knowing Iggy, I somehow felt impelled to come. And I am so glad I did."

Father Clancy and Jimmy turned to other parishioners who wanted to thank them and wish them a happy Christmas.

"I saw you in the congregation," I said. "What a surprise. I thought you would be with your family."

"Me too, but I had a patient in crisis. I spent the early hours this evening at the hospital and left around eleven. I was at a bit of a loss for what to do. Then I thought, why not go to St. Ann's for their midnight mass? I've never been to one and Iggy will be there. So here I am."

"Is your patient okay?"

"Yes. I'm pretty sure we're over the crisis. I expect to head to my parents' tomorrow."

"Well, it sure was a surprise seeing you here. A very pleasant one. Hope it didn't show."

"Not at all. I wasn't sure you even saw me. But I'm glad you did. And I'm glad I have met your cohorts. They seem very nice."

"They are. I'm fortunate to have gotten this appointment. And being here made it possible for us to know each other."

"I suppose that's so. But actually, it's your penchant for golf that brought us together."

"Right. That's true. Well, I really must pay attention to other folks here. But let's try to get together sooner than later. How about we get some coffee or something after the holidays?"

"Yes. Let's do that. Give me a ring when you're free. Okay? I'll look forward to it." She smiled, walked down the steps and headed in the direction of her apartment.

I spent the next five or ten minutes greeting parishioners. Then we three priests went back inside, took off our vestments, headed to the kitchen, and grabbed a snack before heading to bed.

"I think the service went well," Father Clancy said.

"Very well," said Jimmy. "Everyone seemed to be especially grateful for it. It really is a wonderful time of the year and reminds one of why we do what we do."

"Well said." Father Clancy nodded and turned toward me.

"Absolutely. It was very nice," I agreed.

"And what a surprise to see your non-church-going therapist here," Father Clancy said.

"No kidding," I said. "I had no idea she would even think of going to a midnight mass. She's never said anything to me one way or another about her religious leanings, if she even has any."

"Well, it was certainly nice of her to come out on this frigid night. And now I am going to hit the sack." Father Clancy rose from his chair and left the kitchen.

"Me too," said Jimmy. "I'm beat." He left as well.

I was now alone with my thoughts and couldn't help but think how nice it had been to see June, and so unexpectedly. Why had she come to the service? Was it just curiosity? Wanting to see me at work? Maybe that was all it was. But then, why?

Finally, I rose and headed off to my room, changed into my pajamas, and crawled into bed. I had suggested to June that we get together for coffee one day. I had never met with her without there being a reason. Therapy, rehearsals, returning books, or some such thing. Now we would simply be meeting for the purpose of meeting. Was that a good idea? Well, why not? We were good friends. Why not just get together, sip some coffee, and chat? If she were a man, I wouldn't even be thinking about it. I fell asleep with those thoughts going through my head.

Chapter 42

✝

We never did get together for coffee. Before we knew it, rehearsals started up again. We would be doing the Brahms's Requiem, an incredible oratorio. June and I continued our commuting schedule, alternating who drove. Nothing changed in our routine during the next several weeks, including our after-rehearsal drinks at the Riverdale Pub.

Finally, sometime in April while June was driving us to the Hayes rehearsal hall, I blurted out, "June, would you mind my asking you some questions?"

"Questions? What sort of questions?"

"Questions about issues I am having to deal with."

"What sort of issues? Are you still struggling over last summer?"

"No, no. Not at all. Rather, it's about what I guess I might call current events."

"Current events."

"Yes. Within the church."

"Such as?"

"It's hard for me to broach the subject. But, well, I might as well cut to the chase. Father Sedgwick brought it up during one of our sessions. He noted that Catholic priests take a vow of celibacy but that down through the ages, as he put it, many priests have

263

broken that vow, some in dreadful ways. He also noted that it's a great problem for the church these days. We didn't really discuss it. Sort of brushed it off. But truth be known, it's an issue that has been bothering me for some time."

"Ah. You mean the sex scandals within the church that we keep hearing about?"

"Yes."

"I have to admit, Iggy, that I have been wondering about that too. I mean, I know you. And I find myself wondering how these reports are affecting you. But I didn't know how to approach you. It has to be a very troubling problem, I would think. But this isn't something we can talk about now, in the car."

We were pulling into the Hayes parking lot. "No, it isn't but—"

"You know, we never had that cup of coffee you suggested on Christmas Eve. Why don't we follow up on that idea? There's no way we could meet in my office anymore. You're a friend, no longer a patient. Does that make sense?"

"Yes, it does. Where and when?"

"I have a fairly full schedule of appointments, so it would be best for me if we could maybe meet late in the day. Maybe sometime after four?"

"I definitely do not want to have to ask Father Clancy for time off or anything like that. Not given what we will be talking about."

"Very understandable. Do you have a day off coming up?"

"Yes I usually get Tuesday's off. So tomorrow. Does that work?"

"I can't do tomorrow. But how about next Tuesday?"

"Fine. Shall we say four thirty? How about at Maria's?"

We finalized the time and place and headed into the rehearsal. But the following Monday evening as I was driving us to Hayes, June said, "I've been thinking about our appointment tomorrow, Iggy. And I've been wondering just how easily we'll be able to talk at Maria's. It is a rather public place. What do you say you come up to my place? I make a good cup of coffee. We'll chat in my living room and will be completely free to say anything we want without fear of being overheard. Does that make sense?"

"Yes. That does make sense. Okay. Let's meet at your place. And I'll get some goodies from Maria's. I love their chocolate crullers. How about you?"

"I love their chocolate crullers. Great for dunking."

The next day, just before four thirty, I rang June's doorbell. She opened the door, and I greeted her with a bag of four chocolate crullers. I could smell coffee brewing. If nothing else, we were in for some tasty treats. Soon we were seated on her couch with a pot of coffee, containers of cream and sugar, and a plate of crullers on the coffee table. I was in my civvies, and June was dressed in her normal business attire, with her hair pulled back in a bun and no makeup. *Well*, I thought, *she has been seeing clients all day after all, I suppose. But she still is lovely.*

After we prepared our coffees, dunked our crullers in them, and took our first bites, June said, "I'm rather curious about the reason you're here. One can't help but wonder, given all the publicity going on that even appears to reach up to the Pope, how the average clergy in the Roman Catholic church are dealing with all these reports. How does one keep going?"

"It's a legitimate question. And I can only speak for myself. I mean, we have discussed it at St. Ann's around the breakfast table. But only to the extent that we seem to say it has nothing to do with us personally and we should just keep soldiering on, so to speak."

"But …?"

"But I find it troubling. I guess things are sort of coming to a head for me. During my last session with Father Sedgwick, we touched upon the subject. But only in terms of admitting that we were men, human, and therefore understandably celibacy could be a challenge. His point was that neither of us had violated our vow of celibacy and that was what mattered."

"Can I ask why you were having this discussion with him? What brought it up?"

Oh boy. Was I going to tell her the real reason? I paused, dunked my cruller again, took a bite, and tried to use that time to figure out how to answer her.

I tried to hedge the question by saying, "It was a long interview, and it's hard for me to recall the context."

She smiled at me. I was pretty sure she knew I wasn't being completely honest.

"You said things were coming to a head for you?"

"Yes. I mean, how does one simply soldier on when we know all our parishioners are aware of the same news? How can we just keep on going? I know that within the St. Ann's staff, no one is involved in any of this stuff that's being reported. I'm absolutely certain of that. But there's this kind of cloud hanging over us, or at least me."

"Can I ask you a very direct personal question?"

"I guess so."

"You don't have to answer if you'd rather not."

"I know. Go ahead."

"Have you ever contemplated leaving the priesthood?"

There was the question of all questions. I stalled while dunking another bite of cruller. I was glad we each had two crullers, allowing for lots of stalling on my part.

"I have to ask you," I said, "why do you ask?"

"I think, given everything you have been through and now this questioning, it's a logical question."

"I suppose it is. My parents even asked me if I was contemplating such a thing. I told them categorically no. But ..."

She remained silent for a bit. Then she prompted, "But ...?

"But ... I suppose I have, though I have always not wanted to admit it to myself. If that makes any sense."

"It makes sense. We all stew over things and then deny to ourselves the very stewing. So there have been moments when you have wondered about seeking a different career?"

"That's a different way to put it. Interesting. Doesn't sound quite so ominous, does it? But I don't think it's that easy to contemplate. After all, we priests take a vow. It's a very serious one taken after long study and thought. It would not be easily broken. At least not by me."

"Good point. But let's get back to the earlier question. You said things were coming to a head. What did you mean?"

"I guess I'm trying to figure out this 'soldiering on' concept. How do I pretend none of these horrid conditions exist within the church, are probably even going on right now? How can they not affect me and my ministry, to say nothing of my fellow priests at St. Ann's?"

"Something's occurring to me, Iggy."

"What's that?"

She took a sip of her coffee and then looked off into space. "It's been occurring to me that there's much more to this."

"Much more," I repeated.

"Yes." She looked at me. "It's coming to me that this is not so much a question of soldiering on, though I don't question that that is important. But I have to wonder if what's really at the root of the problem is your faith."

"My faith," I repeated again.

"Yes."

I responded with a questioning look.

"Perhaps I haven't put it correctly. I think I am wondering if, with everything that has gone on for you personally over the past almost year and with the constant news of scandals within the church, you are having second thoughts about your religion or, perhaps more to the point, your belief in your religion."

I poured myself a second cup of coffee, added some cream and sugar, and sat back against the couch. I looked at her piano, perhaps avoiding looking at her. *How should I answer this question?* I wondered.

Finally I said, "First of all, I was raised from birth, through my very early years, through kindergarten and elementary school, through high school, and finally through seminary as a Roman Catholic. It's in my blood, my head, my bones, my body. I believe unquestionably the catechism taught in the Catholic church. I believe our Lord Jesus Christ is our savior. That much I can say unequivocally.

"Second, however, I have to say I am not happy with the way everything I have lived by for all my life is being projected by some of the governing entities of my church. I hasten to say that I do not include St. Ann's. If all churches and all members of the hierarchy of the church emulated what goes on at St. Ann's, we would not be having this discussion."

I looked at her. She was almost staring at me. It was a bit unnerving.

"You actually have given this a lot of thought, haven't you? You've been struggling for some time, it would seem," she said.

"Yes. I guess I have. For quite a while now. And, truth be told, I haven't come up with any solutions to my quandary."

"And so you came to me."

"Yes. Want to know why?"

"Yes, please."

"Because I trust you. I trust your judgement. And I consider you a very close personal friend who would never betray that trust. That's why."

"Thank you, Iggy. And I consider you a very close personal friend. And I will never betray your trust." She looked at me with what I could only describe as a very earnest expression and a light smile.

"So," I asked, "where do I go from here?"

She had tucked her legs under her body on the couch. I couldn't help but feel very drawn to her. There was something more than just good friendship here. Something I couldn't pin down. Something I probably didn't want to pin down.

"I honestly don't know," she said.

"Neither do I."

"Maybe we should take a break," she said. "It's approaching dinnertime. Would you like to have something to eat?"

"I am feeling somewhat hungry, I suppose. But please don't start thinking you need to cook something up."

"I couldn't if I wanted to. I don't have anything beyond some frozen Lean Cuisines. And I wouldn't want to inflict something like that on you."

"Actually, that would be no problem for me. But how about some pizza? We could have it delivered."

"That's a great idea. And while we're waiting for the pizza, I have some cheese and crackers and some very nice red wine. We could take a break from all this serious stuff and have ourselves some supper. Then if we're still up to it, we can go back to the discussion at hand. Or, if we feel we should, we can put off any further talk until another time."

"That sounds really good to me," I said.

Chapter 43

✝

Perhaps an hour later, around seven thirty, we had finished our pizza, cleaned up, and were back on the couch with our wine glasses and an unfinished bottle on the coffee table.

"So how are you feeling?" June asked me as she took a sip of wine. "Are you up to continuing where we left off?"

"Yes. But I can't say I quite remember where we left off."

"I believe we had established that you are troubled over the idea that one should soldier on in the church in spite of the very disturbing revelations that have come out in the news. You are uncomfortable, I suppose, with attempting to ignore what everyone knows is out there. And I suggested to you that, while that is important, you are also possibly struggling with your Roman Catholic faith. You, however, outlined to me your very deep faith. Does that sum up where we are?"

"Yes, I suppose it does."

"So if I am not mistaken, what you are struggling over is much more than just the question of how you can soldier on. Perhaps your question is whether you *should* soldier on. Is there some step you should be taking in the face of present circumstances?"

"Like what?"

"I'm not sure. Let me ask you something else just coming to

me. Do you believe your concerns are affecting your work? Are you able to minister as effectively as you should?"

I took time to reach for the wine bottle on the coffee table and refill my glass, but only halfway. This, I decided, should be my last drink for the evening. I then leaned back against the couch, took a sip, and looked for an answer.

"I honestly don't know," I finally said. "I certainly try to perform my job as conscientiously as I can. There are times, I suppose, when I ask myself your question. So am I, in a way, being a hypocrite? If I am so concerned with, even angry at, the miscreants, how can I bring meaningful solace to our parishioners in the confessional, in the hospital? I guess it's a question I have been avoiding."

"I suppose," June said, "the soldiering on gambit is doing that? Avoiding accepting that there might be undesirable results if one addressed the issue head-on, at least in one's own consciousness?"

"Undesirable results?" I repeated.

"Mmm." June's lips were pressed together as she looked at me with a raised eyebrow.

"I wonder what they might be. Any idea?"

"You have to answer that one," she said.

"I don't think it's anything I want to contemplate right now."

"Perhaps not. I get the sense that there's an awful lot for a priest, especially a highly principled priest like yourself, to agonize over. I hate to use that phrase, but that is what you have been doing for some time, isn't it?"

"Agonizing over?"

"You, Ignatius Costello, have been having an incredible inner struggle for almost a year now. And, yes, my impression is that it has seemed like sheer agony to you much of the time."

"It's true. I can't deny it. Never in my wildest imagination could I have dreamed up the year I've been through." I suddenly broke into a huge yawn. "My God. Forgive me," I said.

"No need to apologize, Iggy. I'm close to doing the same thing. It is getting late, and we both have to get up early tomorrow. We probably should be thinking of ending this discussion for now. But we really shouldn't leave on a downer if at all possible."

"Believe it or not, I am not feeling depressed over what we have discussed. In fact, I am experiencing a kind of relief that I finally have gotten things off my chest. I feel as though I can begin to get a handle on things."

"Things?"

"Yes. I now have a sense of what I must sort out. I've not been able to even see what was really troubling me. This evening has brought important questions to the fore. I can see them, voice them. I haven't been able to do that until now. And I thank you for that. I can't think of anyone else I might have had this discussion with."

"I suppose it sounds rather trite, but … that's what friends are for."

"You are much more than that as far as I'm concerned."

No rejoinder came from June. She sat at the opposite end of that couch, legs tucked under her, wine glass at her lips, utterly silent. Had I said too much?

Finally, she said, "And I have the same feeling toward you. You have become a very close confidant. So far it has, for the most part, been going in one direction. Meaning you seeking counsel or solace from me. But I know that the roles could easily be reversed. Your parishioners must also trust you very much. You have a way about you that inspires trust."

She rose from the couch, put her wine glass on the coffee table, and came toward me. "Do you know what I would like right now?"

"No. Afraid not."

"I'd like a good hug. Hugs are good for people, you know. And I think you could use one too. Will that be a problem for you?"

"I have to say there's not a lot of hugging at St. Ann's. In fact, the only hugs I remember getting are from my family. My parents, brothers, and sisters are all good huggers."

"Well, shall we start a new trend in Riverdale?"

I felt a bit reticent, perhaps even a bit nervous. But then I said, "That sounds like a very nice idea."

She put her arms out in invitation, and I stepped into them. She clasped them firmly around me and patted me on the back. It felt wonderful. I returned the favor, patting her on her back. Except for my family, I didn't believe I had ever hugged another woman. And I had to admit that this particular woman was a wonderful hugger.

Finally, we parted.

"That was very nice, wasn't it?" June asked.

"Yes, it was."

"We'll have to do it more often."

What a very nice prospect, I thought. "Yes, we will … Well, I suppose I had better get going."

"Would you like to continue our discussion another time? Perhaps next Tuesday? Same time, same place?"

"I would. And I'll see you next Monday. I believe it's my turn to drive."

"Yes, it is. I'll see you then."

I had put on my coat and was heading out the door as we spoke. She walked me to the elevator. I entered as the doors opened and turned to find her smiling broadly as the doors closed.

Chapter 44

My father had warned me. I hadn't taken it quite that way, but he had warned me about June. It hadn't been an unfriendly warning, but as I looked back, I realized his alert had been the beginning of things I had not ever foreseen. Dr. June Noble was, in the last analysis, the root of my problem.

The next morning, I thought it was time I recognized that fact and dealt with it. I was fond of June Noble. Very fond of her. Was it more than that? *Truth be told, are you in love with her?* I asked myself. *Any normal man who was not a Roman Catholic priest, having been through all that you have been through and having come to know June as you have would be in love with her, wouldn't he?*

I had just wakened and was sitting on the edge of my bed as these thoughts streamed through my head. *What am I going to do?* I thought. *Nothing for now. I need to get up, get to work, and let it rest for now. Maybe things will become clearer as the day progresses.*

But they didn't become clearer. I had a fairly busy day of hearing confessions and visiting the hospital scheduled. In the middle of it all, I had a meeting with Father Clancy and Jimmy to work out our schedules for the next few weeks. It was a normal meeting, one we had from time to time. Everything went per usual. Except I could not get June Noble out of my head. At one point, Father Clancy asked me if I was okay.

"You seem a bit distracted," he said.

"No, no. I'm fine," I lied. Actually, I was feeling fine, but not in any way he would have wanted to hear about.

We finished our meeting, and I started hearing confessions. There were four parishioners. I did as expected, listening and administering absolution. But, between confessions, I had some quiet time to think, and a question suddenly dawned on me: *Is June in love with you?*

She had made it clear that she was very fond of me. But in love? She knew I was a priest, and she had said many times that she would never want to interfere with my faith. So ...?

I had no answer. How could I? Everything had been very circumspect. Even our hug last night had only been a friendly hug. At least that was the way I elected to take it. *But, Iggy, you really did enjoy that hug,* I thought. *It felt so nice having her in your arms like that. But then the question is did she have the same sensation.* I had no way of knowing. Other than asking her.

So what was I going to do? That was the big question. What *should* I do? Well, I analyzed, I wouldn't be seeing her until next Monday night at the rehearsal. Unless I decided I needed to break it off, in which case I could phone her and tell her I had to stop rehearsals. I'd say I couldn't do the Brahms after all; things had come up that prevented it. I'd tell her I was sorry, of course. But in that way, I'd break off the whole thing and not see her again.

How can I do that, though? I asked myself. How could I not meet with her and tell her all my concerns. Maybe she'd straighten me out. Maybe she'd tell me this attraction was only going in one direction. Maybe she had no romantic inclinations toward me. There, I used the word *romantic.*

You have a date with her, I kept ruminating, *to continue your discussion next Tuesday.* That would be the time to let her know my feelings and find out if she had any such feelings toward me.

Maybe she could help me figure things out. That's what she did for a living. But was it too personal? Would she be offended? I just didn't know what to think.

To add to my confusion on my way to the hospital I pulled over into a small rest area, turned off the engine, and sat there. I closed my eyes and waited, for what I didn't know. But eventually it came to me that there was nothing I could do now.

"You are a priest. You have duties, a job to do. At least for the rest of this week, let's drop all this mental stewing. Hopefully, your answer will come to you before next Monday. But for now, just get on with your normal life," I told myself.

The rest of the week came and went, and I succeeded in putting my concerns on the back burner for the most part all the way through Sunday Mass. But Monday night was looming, and no answer had come to me. Except perhaps that I should just let things continue. *When June picks you up, hop in the car as usual, go to rehearsal, go to the get-together afterward, and let June drop you off after as usual*, I told myself. *No problem. She'll probably ask if you still want to meet with her Tuesday. You really don't need to decide that for now. Just see how it goes.*

Chapter 45

A nd that's what I did. But getting through rehearsal and then the get-together afterward was not easy. I knew I would have to decide what to do about Tuesday. I was in a turmoil, so much so that I kept missing notes during rehearsal and constantly had to ask my neighbor where Mitzi wanted us to start again as we went over lines.

"Sorry," I had to say to him. "I have a lot on my mind, and I'm rather distracted."

"Are you okay? Anything we can do to help?"

"No, no. I'm fine. Just not totally with it today. Not to worry."

Nothing more was said.

After rehearsal, we went to the Riverdale Pub as usual. Then we hopped into June's car, and she drove to St. Ann's. As she pulled up, she turned to me and asked, "Are we on for tomorrow afternoon?" She had a nice smile on her face. Clearly she was not aware that there might be a negative answer coming from me.

"I'm not sure," I said.

"Has something come up?"

"No. Nothing has come up schedule-wise."

"Can you tell me?"

I suddenly blurted out, "June, I am afraid I am falling in love with you, and I don't know what to do about it."

Her smile disappeared, and her face went blank. Then slowly the smile returned, and her eyes crinkled. "Oh boy," she said. "I never saw that coming." She paused for several seconds before continuing. "But I'm not going to say it bothers me. I'm also not going to say it flatters me. I'm not going to say I don't welcome it. I can only say I don't know what to say."

"So now what?" I asked. "Do we still get together tomorrow?"

"I'm at a loss. I mean, Iggy, if you weren't a Roman Catholic priest sworn to celibacy, I have to admit I would probably be echoing your feeling. I hadn't thought of it in that way. You would think, knowing my profession, that I would know. But I've been trying to be so careful, not wanting to step on your toes. But now that you've explained things …"

"So if I was, say, an Episcopal priest, things might be different?"

"Yes. I suppose I have to say that."

"I had no idea I was going to say anything today, though I knew I would have to decide whether or not I should see you tomorrow. But I guess it comes down to this: Do we break it off? Do I stop going to rehearsals? Do I not see Dr. June Noble again? Or …?"

"Or? … What a question!"

"I know. I mean, I know what logic tells me."

"What's that?"

"It tells me I have spent my life being a Roman Catholic and all my adult life being a Roman Catholic priest. Should I even be thinking of giving it all up?"

"Iggy, please understand that I would feel terrible if I caused you to do anything you should not do. You have to be the arbiter of your decisions. But I do wonder if you would have to give all of it up. I'm wondering why you would need, in any case, under any circumstances, to give up your Roman Catholic faith."

"You mean I should give up the priesthood."

"I absolutely do not mean that. The operative word being *should.* That's something only Ignatius Costello can decide. I'm only saying that I see no reason why you should give up your faith."

"I wonder what my parents would say if they could hear this conversation. I wonder what Father Clancy would say or Jimmy or even Mr. Rothschild. And then there's Paul."

"Paul?"

"Yes. He's one of my closest friends. I believe his testimony at the trial clinched the verdict. He and I went through Catholic elementary school and high school together. I went on to seminary. He went to a non-Catholic college and then business school and is now a CPA. My point is that he has completely left the faith. Tells me he's an atheist. And we are still best friends. Interesting that he should come to my mind just now."

"So, Ignatius Costello, I have to ask the question. What are we going to do now?"

I couldn't help but notice that she said "we," not "you."

"I ask myself do I dare go up to your apartment tomorrow," I said.

"Do you?" she said with a very warm smile.

"I somehow don't think so. Not quite yet."

"Can you tell me what that means?" The smile still was there.

"No matter how I look at it, I am considering giving in to a serious temptation. Don't get me wrong. I don't see you as a temptress. On the contrary, over the past year you have been very strong in your desire not to influence me in my faith. But now it's not so much a question of faith, is it? Rather, it's a question of … I can't even bring myself to say it. But you know what I mean."

"I do. And I can't imagine the kind of anxiety you must be experiencing right now." She paused for a few seconds. "Okay, Iggy, I'm going to say something because I have to. I can't leave it up in the air. I have grown very fond of you. And if you give me permission, then I will say I have grown to love you. Very much. But the last thing either one of us wants is to learn to regret decisions we have made. Once the bloom is off the rose, things can get very testy. Believe me. If my practice has taught me nothing else, it has taught me that. So as much as I have been looking forward to seeing you tomorrow night, I think it might be best if we put it off."

She continued, "And here is what's very important for me. If, as you think about things, you come to the decision that you cannot leave the priesthood—and that is what we are talking about— then there will be no long-term regret on my part. Of course, I will experience regret in the short-term. But I will always consider you a wonderful friend. And if you do make that decision, then you will become a friend who I once loved very much but with whom things didn't work out. And you will remain a close friend."

She looked almost sad. Was she already regretting? Did she think she knew what my decision would be?

"June," I said, "you are a truly remarkable person. I wonder how many people could have said what you just said to me."

Her left hand was on the steering wheel, and her right hand lay on her lap. I picked it up and kissed it

"I'm going to leave now," I said. "But I'm not leaving for good. At the very least, we have next week's rehearsal to go to. But I am now going to get serious. An idea is coming to me about how to proceed. In my thinking, that is. So I'll see you next Monday. It's my turn to drive. Does that work for you?"

"Very much so. And I'll look forward to finding out where we stand. Although such a decision is incredibly serious, so it could take you quite a while. I understand that. But at least I'll see you next week."

I got out of her car. She started the engine and drove off with a wave. I waved back, turned, and headed into the rectory with a rather light step. I had just told a woman I loved her, and she had said she loved me. What more could a guy ask for? Unless, of course, he was a Roman Catholic priest.

Chapter 46

The idea that had come to me while talking with June in her car was to phone Paul and see if we could get together. He must have gone through some mighty soul-searching before deciding he was an atheist, having been brought up as I had in a wholly Roman Catholic atmosphere. How had he dealt with all the questions that must have gone through his head? What about his parents? How had they taken the news? How had he broken the news? Or had he even told them? He still went to church with them when he was home. How did that work?

When I phoned him, he was glad to hear from me and said that he was actually free that evening when I would have been visiting June. I told him that I was hoping he wouldn't mind if I bent his ear about something I was having to deal with. He had a favorite bistro that he liked to go to in his neighborhood, which was on West End Avenue on the west side of Manhattan near Riverside Drive, so we agreed to meet there.

I took the IRT subway down to the Eighty-First Street exit and walked over from Broadway and up West End a couple of blocks to the Roundhouse Bistro. A strange name, I thought, since I doubted if there had ever been a railroad roundhouse in this area.

Paul had wanted to bring his girlfriend, with whom he lived.

Normally, that would not have been a problem, but in this case he understood when I asked if we could dine alone.

"So," he said as I approached his table and sat down, "how are you? I haven't seen you since the trial. It's been quite a while. I guess you've given up on playing golf?"

"I wouldn't say that," I said. "Although I haven't been tempted to since then. But the police gave me back my clubs. On the other hand, I haven't replaced the putter, which they also gave me. Ugh. So I don't know where golf is going to go in my future. But that's not what I'm here for."

"It must be something serious since you wouldn't let me bring Carrie with me."

"Yes, it is. I'm sorry about that. You know normally I'd love to see her. She's a lovely gal. Which sort of brings me to why I'm here."

At that instant, a spritely young lady interrupted to hand us our menus, explain the specials, and take our drink orders. She soon returned with our glasses of wine and took our order for dinner.

"Okay, Iggy, why the hell are we here? You have me fascinated."

I took the bull by the horns and declared, "I've fallen in love with a woman, and I don't know what to do about it."

"Holy shit!" Paul said and fell back against his chair. "Are you kidding me?"

"No."

"Jesus Christ, man. Have I met her?"

"I don't think so. She's the therapist I saw during the trial and after. Her name's Dr. June Noble."

"You're serious about this?"

"Afraid so. And it has me in a serious quandary. I don't know what to do."

"With all due respect. I consider you a very close friend, Iggy.

But why are you asking me for advice? I mean, shouldn't you be seeing someone in the church?"

"I probably will have to. But this situation only came to a head last night. While I was with her."

"With her? What does that mean?"

"Don't get the wrong idea. I've joined a choral society in Riverdale, and she had driven me back from rehearsal, and we talked in her car in front of St. Ann's. Only talked. That's it, and that's all there has ever been."

"Christ almighty, Iggy. I don't know what to say. I still don't understand, why me?"

"Because, as you said, you are one of my closest friends, and you have left the church. I have to believe you went through some difficult thinking. I thought you might be able to give me some idea of what you went through. It might give me some idea of how to proceed."

The waitress arrived with our dinners.

We attacked our meals for a spell before Paul said, "My leaving the church is nothing compared to what you are contemplating. I wasn't a priest, for Christ's sake. Besides, are you thinking of leaving the faith?"

"No. In fact, we talked about that."

"Who's we?"

"June and me. She's said many times that she would never want to be the reason I left the faith, if I ever did. But here we are. I have to decide, I guess, whether or not I should break off any relationship with her and go back to being the faithful priest I have always been. Or …?"

Paul raised both of his eyebrows. "And you want me to help you make that decision. Are you kidding me? Does anybody else know about this? How about your parents? I bet they'd be thrilled to learn their son was leaving what is in their minds the most respectable profession on earth."

"Actually, I visited them last fall. Had a very nice time with them. And you wouldn't believe how things have progressed for them since their nest completely emptied out. You're probably right about Mom. She'd be really unhappy, I imagine. But Dad? He would never approve, but I suspect he would understand."

"I still can't get my head around this, Iggy. I mean, this is mind-boggling."

"Me neither. That's my problem. I can't get my head around it."

"What does Father Clancy say?"

"Nothing. I haven't told him. I haven't told anyone but you."

Paul leaned back in his chair. "Man! I don't know, Iggy. I mean, I never spent a lot of time stewing over leaving the church. It just sort of happened. I've never said anything to you because I didn't want to be disrespectful of your faith. But things kept happening. Stuff that made me feel like I just wasn't interested anymore."

"What things?" I asked.

"I'm not a theologian, as you well know. And again, I don't want to seem to be challenging your beliefs. But, well, for one thing, I stopped believing in the virgin birth. And the resurrection. I mean, where did Jesus go? As far as I'm concerned, NASA has pretty much demonstrated that there's no heaven in the universe they've explored. But these are theological issues, and I suppose a person can have different understandings upon which they found their faith.

"But the kicker for me, frankly, was the sex scandals. Not only that priests were being accused of such things but that the hierarchy of the church covered these sins up! And they are sins plain and simple! I still can't get over that. And to top it off, it's still going on today and seems to be only getting worse! There.

I swore I'd never raise these things with you. You're too good a friend and a good guy. I knew you would never be involved in all this crap. But you asked."

I remained quiet for a second or two, then admitted, "Truth be told, the scandals have become a problem for me too. I know that nothing like that has gone on at St. Ann's. At least that I know of. And I'd never suspect Father Clancy or Jimmy of any such thing. I've wondered, however, how we keep going on with our daily routine. Just soldiering on."

"I had no idea, Iggy."

"No idea what?"

"That these questions were bothering you. Have you always been worrying about these things?"

"Not so much worrying as wondering. It all started with the trial and all kinds of doubts that went through my head then and followed through all the therapy I had. Then it really came to the fore in my thinking a couple of nights ago when I brought it up with June. That, I think, is when I began to seriously wonder about my future."

"Your future."

"Yes."

"You're thinking of leaving the church?"

"Not the church. I don't think I could ever leave my faith. The faith itself has nothing to do with the good or bad governance of the church. Our Lord Jesus Christ, if he ever comes back to earth, will probably whip the priests, bishops, and archbishops the way he did the money lenders." I smiled at him.

"That's a good one, Iggy. I like that. But I still can't see myself attempting to give you any advice about your future."

"And I don't expect you to. You've already given me a lot of help. Helped me to focus things."

"So do you know what you're going to do?"

"Not for sure. One of the things that I can't decide is whether or not to go to Father Clancy. He's always been my confidant, my guide. He was fabulously helpful during my troubles last summer. But I'm not sure I want to seek his advice in this case. I just don't know yet."

"Maybe what you need to do, Iggy, is what you did with me. Just flat-out tell him you've fallen in love with a woman and out of love with the church. Not your faith, but the church."

"Suppose he asks me why. Which I know he will."

"Then tell him why. Lay it out for him. All of it."

"Oh boy," was all I could say.

We decided not to have dessert. Paul treated me to the dinner, and we agreed to walk to his apartment to have a last glass of wine with Carrie before I headed back to St. Ann's.

By the time I got back to the rectory, everybody else had hit the sack, so I did too. I lay on my bed, flat on my back with my hands clasped behind my head. What on earth was I ever going to say to Father Clancy? And when? Tomorrow? Was I going to tell him I was in love with June? Was I going to tell him I intended to leave the priesthood? Was I going to lay everything out for him as Paul suggested? I somehow managed to fall asleep with those queries going through my head.

I slept quite well. *Apparently*, I thought when I woke the next morning, *things are working out. You're not in such a frenzy.*

Chapter 47

✝

I have found, however, that I have a bad habit when it comes to facing something unpleasant. And I was very much concerned over what might transpire in Father Clancy's office. So, of course, I put it off. I didn't tell him or anyone else for the rest of that week. I just soldiered on. I was getting tired of that expression, but it was all I could hang onto. *Just keep soldiering on,* I told myself, *until something breaks. Something will break. You know it. Just keep soldiering on.*

It was a ridiculous stance, and I knew it. I had to fess up, not only to Father Clancy but to myself as well.

Pretty soon, it was Sunday afternoon. The fact that I would be picking June up for rehearsal tomorrow evening was looming. What was I going to say? What was I going to do? One thing was certain: June's presence was ever with me. There was no giving her up. Not now.

Finally, Monday morning as I sat at the table with Father Clancy and Jimmy, I asked Father Clancy, "Can I see you in your office once we're done here?"

"I suppose so," he said. "Nothing we can discuss here?"

"Not really. It's rather personal."

Jimmy's eyebrows rose with a questioning look. *I wonder what that's all about?* I could picture him thinking. He and I were good friends. But I didn't think he had any idea what was up.

"Well, all right," Father Clancy said. "I have a meeting downtown later this morning. Will this take a lot of time?"

"I don't know. I suppose it could. Would you rather put it off, maybe until this afternoon or tomorrow?"

"That might be a good idea. I should be back by no later than three o'clock. Will you be free then?"

"I think so. I might need to get Jimmy to cover for me." I looked at him.

"I probably can juggle things. Sounds kind of important. Anything I can do to help." Jimmy said.

"Well then, let's plan on that," Father Clancy said.

He returned at two o'clock and called me into his office.

"I got back sooner than I expected. Is this a good time for you?"

It was. But I had been dreading this interview and gulped a bit as I said yes.

"Okay, Iggy. What's going on?"

"I have to confess to you that I don't know how to begin."

"Why don't you just say what you have to say and let the chips fall where they may?" It sounded as though he suspected what was on my mind.

"I'm thinking of leaving the priesthood," I said in almost a whisper.

Utter silence followed. Father Clancy turned in his chair and, in his typical fashion, stared at the wall, with his elbows on his chair and his steepled fingertips touching his lips. The quiet lasted for some time.

Then he spoke. "I've been waiting for this for some time," he said. "It has been quite evident to me that you have never gotten over last summer and that events since then have done nothing to relieve you of that angst you have been carrying all this time.

I know you've had your ups and downs. But there have appeared to me to be many more downs than ups."

He continued, "But, Father Costello, I have to wonder if leaving the priesthood is your answer. How will that improve your situation going forward? Or is there more to this than I'm aware of? Are you troubled in your faith?" He turned his chair and looked at me. His brow was scrunched up, and his eyes were narrowed. "Are you able to answer that? Can you tell me what has brought you to this conclusion?"

I felt very uncomfortable sitting in front of his desk. I had always seen Father Clancy as a trusted confidant. Almost a father figure. Now, however, I felt like he was challenging me, calling for me to justify myself. He had called me Father Costello. That was a reminder of my present position in life, of my training, of the vows I had taken. I had the feeling that he could only see my assertion as an unforgiving and maybe unprincipled statement.

"Please tell me why we are having this conversation." He leaned back in his chair, his gaze on mine, and waited.

After a long pause, I finally said, "It has been incredibly confusing for me for a long time dealing with so many things that have come my way. But I'll try to explain. You know, of course, about last summer and all the questioning that went on in my head. Counseling with Father Sedgwick helped. But truth be told, I am still bothered by the idea that I was able to doubt the omniscience of God. That's still with me."

I added that I still held a fascination for the scientific issues to which I had been exposed and that I felt somewhat hindered by that as a priest. "But there's much more."

I went on to tell him how troubled I was concerning the governance of the church and how the sex scandals seemed not to affect the daily lives of us priests.

It took quite a while to fill him in.

"There's something else, though, isn't there?" he said when I finished.

"Yes," I admitted.

"You had better fill me in."

How had he known, I wondered. "I don't know how to say it."

"For Lord's sake, Iggy. Just say it."

This time, I sat back in my chair, put my elbow on the left arm, leaned my head against my hand, and stared back at Father Clancy. How could I tell him about June other than to, as he had admonished, just say it.

Finally, I sat up straight and said, "I have fallen in love with June Noble."

"Fallen in love … Does she know this?"

"Yes."

"So has she helped you to have all these doubts about your faith?"

"No. On the contrary, she has expressed real concern on that issue. I have to add that I have not lost my faith. That's not the issue. It is that I have become uncomfortable in what I feel would be the hypocrisy of my continuing as a priest. But I will never give up my religion, my Roman Catholic faith."

"How long has it been since you came to your decision?"

"Around a couple of weeks."

"And it's taken you that long to tell me. Rather, you have just been soldiering on, as you put it."

"I suppose that's right. Although, looking back, I'd say it was when I was in Philadelphia that I began to think about things."

"I thought your parents were solidly behind you going into the priesthood."

"They were. They are. They have no idea about this. But my father began to ask questions of me, knowing what I had been through. Questions that started me thinking. It's hard to describe."

"I suppose you have a rehearsal coming up tonight and that you will be going with Dr. Noble?"

Dr. Noble, not June. "Yes."

"I don't suppose you might consider missing this one, giving yourself a week to just be here and mull things over?"

"I suppose I could do that, if you thought it would be the best thing to do. But I have spent the last week knowing I should speak to you, and instead I did all kinds of mulling over. Truth be told, it's been agonizing."

"Agonizing!"

"Yes. I dreaded having this conversation. Dreaded finding out how you might react. You've always been my most reliable confidant, and now I have possibly ended all that."

"Mmm," was his response. Fingertips still at his lips, he said, "I would hope that would not have to be the case. You know I have valued your presence here. While I knew something was up with you, I did not realize how serious it was. I somehow trusted that things would work out for you. But not in this way. I certainly understood that you had a friendly relationship with Dr. Noble. But, again, not to this extent. I suppose you are sure your interest in her is reciprocated?"

"Yes. Very sure."

"All right." His fingertips were now supporting his chin. "You've given me somewhat of a shock, despite what I had suspected. This time I need some time to mull things over. Can you give me some time to think about how we should proceed?"

"Sure. But I am expecting to go to the rehearsal this evening."

"Yes, I understand that. That is up to you. There is a procedure for priests resigning. You're not the first, of course. But I want to give some thought to how to handle your particular situation.

And I'd like to give this whole thing a little time to brew, if you will. Let's give it a week. Okay? Who knows what might transpire in that time."

I supposed he thought I might change my mind. And that was okay. I doubted I would. But sure. Why not give it a week? A huge load had been lifted from my shoulders. I could be patient for another week.

"You mean I should continue my duties here?" I said.

"Yes. Please do. And let's keep this conversation to ourselves for now."

I said I would and left his office. Now I had to face the more difficult prospect of telling my parents. What would they say? Of course, some of my siblings had changed jobs. And that had been no problem for Mom and Dad. But this was rather different. How should I tell them that their son, the Roman Catholic priest of whom they were very proud, was leaving the priesthood? Oh boy! However, my visit with them last fall had given me some hope that they would understand. Meantime, it was nearing time to have dinner and go to rehearsal.

"How did your meeting with Father Clancy go?" Jimmy asked as we sat down to our dinners.

"Good," I said.

"What's going on, Iggy?" he asked.

"Nothing I can talk about right now. I'm sorry, but Father Clancy asked that of me."

"Humph," was Jimmy's only response.

"Sorry," I said, "but I kind of have to eat and run. I have to pick June up for rehearsal. I'll see you tomorrow morning." I stood, took my dishes to the sink, and left.

I went to my room. How long would this be my room, I wondered. I changed into my civvies and drove over to June's. As I was driving, it occurred to me that this soon would no longer be my car. It had been provided by the diocese. That was an interesting question. What would I do for a living, come to think of it? *I have no idea* was the answer that came to me as June hopped into the car.

"Hi," she said with a big smile.

"Hi," I replied as I pulled away from the curb. "I have some big news for you."

"Big news?"

"Yes. I met with Father Clancy this afternoon and told him about you and that I wanted to resign from the priesthood."

"Oh my God, Iggy! You really did?"

"I really did."

"I don't know what to say. I mean, this is a huge step for you."

"And for you, I trust."

"And for me. Yes. Absolutely." She smiled widely and leaned over to kiss me on the cheek. I nearly ran into the curb.

We soon were nearing the parking lot at Hayes Auditorium.

"Just one thing," I said. "Father Clancy asked me not to tell anyone about the conversation I had with him for a week So we probably shouldn't say anything tonight."

"Why doesn't he want you to tell anyone?"

"He wants to mull things over, he said. Figure out how to proceed. There is a routine to be followed when priests resign, but I think he is trying to buy a little time to see if I might change my mind."

"Is there any chance of that?"

"None. But I agreed with him. Just for the week."

We now were sitting in the car in the Hayes parking lot.

"Before we go into rehearsal I need to ask you a big question?"

"A big question?" She asked with a broad smile.

"Yes." I gulped. "Do you remember when I asked you if I was an Episcopal priest would things be different?"

"Of course I do."

"Well, I'm no longer going to be a priest. So are things still different?" I was beginning get a little nervous.

But she quickly responded, "Yes. Very much so."

"Then I have to ask." I paused, took a deep breath, "Will you marry me?"

She paused for what seemed a long time. Then said, "Yes Ignatius Costello I will marry you." She threw her arms around my neck and gave me a long kiss. I had never before been kissed that way by a woman. It was an incredible experience.

Then she broke away. "You know," she said. "We're both going to have a hard time containing ourselves at this rehearsal."

"I know. Actually probably impossible."

"So I have an idea." She was grinning mischievously. "Why don't we skip this rehearsal. Let's instead go to my apartment and have a celebratory glass of champagne."

"Why not? Sounds perfect."

And it was.

Chapter 48

✝

The next morning, I was walking on air while pretending not to be walking on air. It was an interesting challenge. However, I still had the problem of needing to inform my parents. And then, of course, my siblings and everybody else. But that had to wait until Father Clancy gave me the green light.

In the meantime, June and I had discussed what I would do once I left St. Ann's. The obvious solution to June was that I should move in with her. That prospect was rather mind-boggling to me when first proposed. But the more I thought about it, the more it made sense. Let's face it, where else would I go unless it was back to Philadelphia? I did not want to go live with my parents. I mean, a few days was one thing. But maybe for weeks while looking for a job? That was not an option.

Then, two weeks later, I was no longer a priest. Cleaning out my room and packing up all my paraphernalia was a somewhat saddening experience. I had been there for nearly ten years.

Finally, though, I moved in with June. It was quite an adjustment for me. After all those years living only with a bunch of men, I was now living with a woman, and not just any woman but June Noble, of whom I grew more and more fond as the days and weeks went by.

Our solution for telling my parents, at June's suggestion, was for the two of us to visit them and tell them we were going to get married.

So about a week after I moved in with June she and I headed down to Philadelphia in her Honda. I had phoned my parents and told them I had finally figured out my future and that June and I wanted to visit them.

"We've been wondering what you have been up to since you last were here. Sounds like you have made some pretty serious decisions," my father said.

"I have. And I want to fill you in. But not over the phone." I replied.

"And you want to bring your June with you." Mom said. They had their phone on speaker.

"Yes," I said. "We'd like to come down right away, if that's alright with you."

They agreed. So June and I left the next morning. It was about a three hour drive and we arrived a little before lunchtime. I had thought we might have a rather frosty greeting when we arrived but, surprisingly, Mom had prepared a light lunch for us.

"So," said Dad as we entered their home, "we finally get to meet Iggy's Dr. June Noble." He shook June's hand and actually was smiling, though I suspected he was hiding a certain sense of suspicion. "Welcome to our humble abode," he said.

"Thank you, Mr. Costello," she said. "I've heard so much about you and Mrs. Costello from Iggy. I'm glad we can finally meet."

I was floored. I had expected I wasn't sure what. But not this cordial a greeting.

"I have some lunch prepared," Mom said. "But I imagine you all would like to freshen up after such a long drive. I've put you in your regular bedroom Iggy and you, June, can have his sisters bedroom across the hall. Iggy can show you.

After thanking my parents June and I headed upstairs. "I can't believe this," I said to June once we got out of ear shot. "I was pretty sure they'd be really upset."

"They couldn't be nicer as far as I'm concerned," she said. "From what you've told me I suspect that ever since you phoned them they've been imagining what kind of change you might be making."

Sure enough Mom had put a towel and wash cloth on the base of my bed and another towel and wash cloth on one of the beds my sisters used to occupy. We would, of course be sharing the only bathroom.

When we came downstairs we found Mom had put some tuna fish sandwiches on the table in the living room along with a garden salad.

"What would you like to drink?" She asked as we sat down. "We have lemonade, coffee or plain old water."

"Lemonade would be wonderful," June replied.

"I'll have coffee please. Thanks Mom." I said.

"Same as June for me," Dad said.

There was a bit of a pause in conversation as Mom poured our drinks. Cream and sugar were on the table. As I was pouring cream into my coffee my father said, "I can imagine that you two must be on pins and needles wondering what we might have been thinking since you called. So let me set your minds at rest. We don't know for sure what it is you came here to tell us. But we think we can guess and we have agreed that whatever it is, Iggy, this is your future, not ours which is in the offing. And, of course, yours too." He said as he looked at June.

"Thanks Mom and Dad. I have to admit it's a relief to hear you say that." I took a sip of coffee. "OK. I'll come right to the point." I took a deep breath. "I have resigned from the priesthood and June and I are getting married."

I heard my mother gasp. "I was afraid that was the case," she said. "You're leaving the faith."

"I've told your mother that did not have to be the case." Dad interjected.

"And it's not," I said. "I want to make something very clear. Just so you don't get the wrong idea. June has been adamant that if she has in any way influenced me to leave my faith then she'll have nothing to do with it."

"It's true Mr. and Mrs. Costello." June said. "I would feel terrible if Iggy left his faith because of me. In fact I have to say a good part of the reason I fell in love with him was his steadfastness in his faith. He has faced an awful lot of issues during the past year that could cause anyone to question his faith. But that is one area where he has been steadfast."

Suddenly Cherry came bounding in. I had wondered where she had been. Her tail was wagging vigorously as she went over to June and looked up at her with her wide eyes.

"Oh my lord," June said. "You are so cute." She reached down and petted her. "I've heard about you," she said. "But I had no idea!"

None of us had bitten into our sandwiches. Cherry's sudden entrance gave us all reason to chuckle and smile and dig in.

My mother seemed to relax a bit. "I told Cherry she had to stay in her bed. But I guess she couldn't stand it anymore," she said.

We all laughed and whatever tension was left in the air seemed to dissipate.

We stayed with my parents overnight. It became clear that June's charm, intelligence and decency won them over. My father appeared to fall for her rather quickly. It took my mother a bit longer. But they gave in to the idea of our getting married and even said they would love to come to our wedding.

And they did. At St. Ann's. With Father Clancy officiating.

Epilogue

That was some five years ago. Now, as I write, I can report that June is three months pregnant with our second child, and while her professional name is Dr. Noble, her married name is Mrs. June Noble Costello. We are still living in her—now our—apartment.

Amazingly, I had quickly found a job at the YMCA working with people in need of social services. Over the years, I advanced at the Y and am now assistant director here in Riverdale.

That is where I am today, very happily married with one beautiful little daughter and another child on the way. And I have a wife whose beauty, deep intelligence, and insights constantly amaze and assure me that my ongoing quest for an understanding of my place, our place, and God's place in this universe of ours is perfectly okay.

I am truly blessed.

Afterword

Some time ago, a friend of mine told a joke during a break at one of our chorus rehearsals. It has stayed with me with the constant wondering on my part: *Yes, very funny! But what if? That priest would be in serious trouble. Wouldn't he?*

If you have read this far, then you probably can guess how the joke went.

There was a priest who couldn't find someone with whom he could play golf. Finally, he called Sister Mary. She turned out to be an excellent golfer. So good that at the first hole, their score was even. She sank her putt. He missed his and declared, "Damn, I missed." She said she couldn't play with him if he was going to swear. He assured her he wouldn't anymore. But at the next hole, the same situation occurred, and he yelled, "Damn, I missed again!"

You get the rest.

I spent a while thinking about this what-if question and finally decided to explore the possibilities. And here we are.

I was born and raised in New York City and attended Public School 81 in Riverdale in the Bronx. I went to the University of Pennsylvania Law School in Philadelphia, where Iggy's parents live. So the locales are basically authentic.

However, what went on in these locations is all my invention, as are the characters. Except for Cherry. I met Cherry in Ireland.

She was rescued as described and is a wonderfully delightful little dog. However, she still lives in Ireland.

When I started writing, I had no plot in mind and no idea how this story would evolve. I started with a description of what happened to the priest. His name came to me out of nowhere, as did all the characters who appeared as the story progressed. I was quite surprised as each new individual appeared. And I found myself becoming rather fond of Iggy, Jacob Rothschild, Father Clancy, and June Noble, just to mention a few.

I suppose now the question might be what has happened to Iggy and June as their lives have progressed? In light of current developments in religion and science, has Iggy's faith held strong?

Printed in the United States
By Bookmasters